Dear Readers,

On my book covers, Warner calls me "The Voice of America's Heartland." I am truly a product of the heartland. I was born in Texas, grew up in Oklahoma, and now live in Iowa. For fourteen years I worked as a newspaper reporter covering births, weddings, and deaths. Then I retired with my husband to travel by trailer from the Canadian border to the Yucatan Peninsula, solving crossword puzzles all the way.

All icing and no cake becomes boring after a while, so I began writing my first book in 1977. I was interested then, as I am now, in the men and women of the frontier and the people who faced hardships during the Great Depression. Three decades later, I still find writing great fun—manipulating characters into perilous or romantic situations, even killing them off if they get too ornery. And I'm pleased to say that I've infected my talented grandson with the writer's bug.

On this "golden" occasion of the publication of my fiftieth book, I want to thank all of you for reading my books. You have traveled with me and my characters from early frontier days, the years of the expansion of pioneers into the Midwest, across Route 66 to California and points in between. I have counted on your loyalty, and you have given it. No author could ask for more.

Sincerely,

Dorothy Garlock

RIVER RISING

"Garlock is the queen of American tales and *River Rising* is a perfect example of her superior writing talent."
— *Midwest Book Review*

"Stirring . . . strong suspense . . . top-quality reading."
— *Romantic Times BOOKclub Magazine*

"Once again, Garlock captivates . . . Her three-dimensional characters make this Depression-era town a living place that readers will want to visit and remember for years to come."   — *Historical Novels Review*

"Garlock does a terrific job . . . Fans will be delighted."
— *Booklist*

SONG OF THE ROAD

"Outstanding . . . Garlock introduces a charming group of . . . characters that will leave you laughing out loud and clutching your hand to your chest as they all come together on Route 66."   — *ARomanceReview.com*

"This romance is a treat, buoyed by strong characters and Garlock's old-fashioned, no-nonsense storytelling."
— *Publishers Weekly*

"Garlock's writing perfectly captures these plainspoken people overcoming the challenges of their hardscrabble lives."   — *BookPage*

"A wonderful romance . . . that readers will long remember."   — *Affaire de Coeur*

more . . .

HOPE'S HIGHWAY

"Delightful . . . This is a story that reminds us that dreams do come true."
—*Rendezvous*

"An entertaining cavalcade of characters . . . Garlock, known for her heartwarming Americana, does not disappoint here . . . a heart-throbbing romance."
—*Publishers Weekly*

"No one evokes the Depression like Garlock . . . A great, hopeful read." —*Romantic Times BOOKclub Magazine*

"An engaging Depression-era Americana tale. Dorothy Garlock knows her road rules as well as anyone."
—*Affaire de Coeur*

MOTHER ROAD

"Bestselling Garlock's endearing characters and vividly depicted milieu will enchant her legions of readers. Garlock's claim, 'I write to entertain my readers,' is fully validated with this suspenseful romance." —*Booklist*

"An engaging tale, spiced with Depression-era detail."
—*Publishers Weekly*

"*Mother Road* is a colorful personalization of a highway and the people who work and play along its byways. Garlock captures the work ethic and spirit of Americans during the Depression years with understanding. *Mother Road* is a novel of tribute to the common men and women of that era." —*Bookreporter.com*

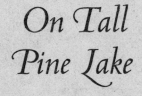

On Tall
Pine Lake

BOOKS BY DOROTHY GARLOCK

DOROTHY GARLOCK

On Tall Pine Lake

GRAND CENTRAL
PUBLISHING

NEW YORK   BOSTON

This book is a work of fiction. Names, characters, places, and incidents are the product of the author's imagination or are used fictitiously. Any resemblance to actual events, locales, or persons, living or dead, is coincidental.

Copyright © 2007 by Dorothy Garlock
Excerpt from *A Week from Sunday* copyright © 2007 by Dorothy Garlock
All rights reserved. Except as permitted under the U.S. Copyright Act of 1976, no part of this publication may be reproduced, distributed, or transmitted in any form or by any means, or stored in a database or retrieval system, without the prior written pemission of the publisher.

Grand Central Publishing
Hachette Book Group USA
237 Park Avenue
New York, NY 10017
Visit our Web site at www.HachetteBookGroupUSA.com.

Grand Central Publishing is a division of Hachette Book Group USA, Inc.

The Grand Central Publishing name and logo is a trademark of Hachette Book Group USA, Inc.

Printed in the United States of America

Originally published in hardcover by Hachette Book Group USA, Inc.
First Trade Paperback Edition: January 2007
First Mass Market Edition: October 2007
10 9 8 7 6 5 4 3 2 1

This book is for Adam, my grandson,
who loves books as much as I do.

MAGGIE CALLS

Where the lake shines gold in the setting sun,
Where the pines loom dark when the day is done,
Here I struggle and strain at the ties that bind me.
Will someone hear my call? Will someone find me?

Yesterday I laughed at my sister's fear.
But now harsh men have bound me here
Demanding I tell what I do not know.
Oh, sister, come for the light grows low.

Beg the man I know you secretly cherish
To search for me before I perish
I can't work loose. I cannot cope.
The night is black. I'm losing hope . . .

—F.S.I.

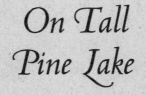

On Tall
Pine Lake

Prologue

NONA LOOKED DOWN AT THE PACKAGE Mr. Dryden had given her.

"I wasn't expecting a package."

"It was delivered by the postman about an hour ago," Mr. Dryden explained, running a hand through his thinning gray hair. During the six months that they had been neighbors, he had always been very cordial. "When I heard someone pounding on your door, I went out into the hallway. After I'd told him that you wouldn't be home for a couple of hours, he asked if I'd give you this package."

"Thank you, Mr. Dryden. We've been so busy getting ready to move that no one is ever home. I'm sorry you were bothered with this."

"I was glad to do it. I'm going to miss my good neighbors when you go."

The inside of Nona's apartment was dark. Mabel was out doing some last-minute shopping while Maggie visited friends one last time before they left. Walking among the boxes that held their meager belongings, Nona wondered

if she and Maggie would ever settle down in one place
and stay.

After flipping on a light, she gave the strange package
a closer examination. She tried to make out a return address, but the writing was smeared.

I haven't ordered anything. She opened the heavily
taped package only to discover another package inside
with a letter addressed to her taped to the top. Pulling off
the letter, she opened it, and to her amazement discovered
it was from her half brother, Harold. She quickly scanned
the contents of the letter then slowly read it again with a
puzzled look on her face.

Dear Nona,

    *I know that we have not kept in close contact
these past years and, for that, I am sorry. However, I
have a favor to ask. Please keep this package until
you hear from me. I beg of you . . . DO NOT OPEN
IT UNDER ANY CIRCUMSTANCES!*

    *Regardless of how you feel about me, I do care
deeply for you and Maggie. You are the only person
that I feel I can trust. I will explain everything soon.
For the sake of our father, I'm asking you to do this
for me. I promise that I will have your money and
Maggie's from our father's estate soon.*

                    Your brother,
                    Harold

*Now he's my brother. Other times he's called himself
our half brother.*

Nona stood in the quiet of her apartment and puzzled

over the strange letter. Simply hearing from Harold was an event; most times he wouldn't give her or Maggie the time of day. She was tempted to tear open the package and find out what was in it, but she resisted and buried it deep in the bottom of the suitcase.

It would come with her to Tall Pine Camp.

Mr. Dryden answered the knock on his door to find two men standing in the hall. Both were well dressed: button-down shirts, crisp pants, and shiny shoes. The older of the pair, bald with a thick black mustache, smiled thinly. His younger partner stayed silent at his side.

"Good afternoon, sir," the bald man began. "We're from the Postal Department and are tracing a package that was delivered to this address. I'm afraid the carrier forgot to have someone sign for it. You know how fussy the government can be about these little things." He laughed easily.

"You mean the package that came yesterday for Miss Conrad?"

"That's the one."

"She wasn't at home when the postman came, so he asked me to hold on to it until she returned. I never signed for it. I gave it to Miss Conrad as soon as she got home."

"At least she got it. That's what's important."

"It's a good thing that it came when it did," Mr. Dryden continued, "what with her taking the job of managing a camp at Tall Pine Lake. They left this morning."

"You don't say," the bald man said as he raised one eyebrow. "Tall Pine Lake? I've never heard of it."

"It's a beautiful place up in the Ozarks. You should visit sometime. There's fishing, hunting, and boating."

"How far is it from here?"

"I don't rightly know."

"Thank you, sir. You've been a big help. The United States Government appreciates it."

The two men got into their car, and the bald-headed man slapped the steering wheel with his palm. "What do you think? Pretty slick, huh? I told you that blood was thicker than water and that he'd send it to her."

"Sure looks that way," the younger man admitted. "We'll have to call Chicago and let them know what we've found out."

"I know just what the boss will say."

"What's that?"

The bald-headed man's chuckle was dry and without humor. "He'll say it's time to do a little huntin'."

Chapter 1

Home, Arkansas, 1980

EXCUSE ME." Nona had come out of the small grocery store carrying two heavy sacks of groceries and run head-on into a man coming into the business. She hadn't hit him hard, but she felt the red sting of embarrassment just the same. Glancing up quickly, she saw that he was definitely a city man. He didn't look like a person who belonged in Home, Arkansas.

His clothes were expensive, certainly too new to have been worn long, unlike those of most men in town, who wore faded work clothes that had seen many washings. His head was bald, but the black mustache on his upper lip was thick. Nona wondered why bald men were compelled to have hair on their faces. It was hard to tell if he was young or old. The coldness of his dark eyes unnerved her. Her mind absorbed these impressions in a few seconds. She hadn't realized that she'd been staring until he reached out and grabbed her by the arm.

"Apology accepted," he mumbled through uneven teeth. Even from those two words, Nona could hear an accent, but one that she couldn't place. With an expanding smile, the man added, "You're Mrs. Conrad, aren't you?"

"No," she answered, "I'm *Miss* Conrad."

"I was told you managed the camp at Tall Pine Lake. My friend and I are looking for a place to fish. Do you have a vacancy?"

"Not for a couple of weeks." The words came out of Nona's mouth before she'd given them any thought. Even though most of the cabins were currently empty, something unpleasant about the man prompted her to lie.

"That's too bad," he said.

His eyes began to roam across her body before settling on her breasts. "But then it might be worth waiting for." The thumb on the hand that held her arm began to move across her skin in a caressing motion. Suddenly angry, Nona tried to jerk her arm away, but the man's grip tightened.

"Let go." Her voice was loud and strong. She felt a quiver of fear and looked around to see if anyone was near. Her hopes leaped as she saw a deliveryman carrying a large box coming her way.

But before she could call to him, the strange man abruptly released her arm, stepped back, and opened the door for the deliveryman, who quickly disappeared inside the store. Nona feared that the stranger would grab her again, but instead he said gruffly, "I'll be seeing you, Miss Conrad." With that, he turned and walked away.

For a moment, she stood frozen in front of the store. *He knew my name!*

Shaking the thought loose, Nona hurried to her car. Bright sunlight bathed the small town, and the first hint of the July heat hung in the air. The leaves of the tall maple and oak trees fluttered in the light breeze.

As she moved down the sidewalk, Nona caught sight of her reflection in the large window of the hardware store. Mr. Finnegan's window was full of saws, hammers, nails, and even an antique cast-iron stove, looking out of season in the warming weather. Amid all the clutter, there was still enough space for her to clearly see herself, a slim woman with a mop of fiery red curly hair that floated around her face like a halo. It was what drew people's eyes to her. She wore slacks and a tucked-in shirt. Nona thought of herself as only passably pretty. Although small, she appeared taller because she carried herself proudly. She considered her large sky-blue eyes her best feature. They sparkled when she was angry or extremely happy. She had a light sprinkling of freckles across her nose. When she was younger, she had hated her red hair, but now she had to either accept it or dye it, and she didn't want the bother of that. She had grown used to being called "that redhead."

Nona finally reached her car, a ten-year-old Ford, dust-covered from its travels down the dirt roads. When she moved to open the driver's door, she was startled to find another hand there before hers. In that split second, her heart sank at the thought that the strange man had followed her. But when she looked up, she found the bright eyes of a tall cowboy in a battered Stetson and a faded plaid shirt.

"Ma'am." A smile lit the man's handsome, sun-browned face. "A pretty woman shouldn't be carrying such a load."

"That's all right. My husband will be here shortly," Nona said defensively.

"He's a lucky man," the friendly cowboy said as he opened the car door. "But until he gets here, let me help." Nona placed her bags on the seat and pushed them across to the other side. After she got into the car and slid under the wheel, the man shut the door behind her and stood at the open window.

"Thank you."

"My pleasure. Good day, ma'am." He smiled warmly as he put his fingers to his hat brim. His grin was contagious; Nona couldn't help but return the smile.

She started the car, put it in reverse, and began to back out. The loud blast of a horn caused her to slam her foot down on the brake. Glancing quickly over her shoulder, Nona saw the deliveryman frown at her before driving his truck past her and down the street. *Damn that bald-headed man! He's got me rattled*. When the road was clear behind her, she eased out and drove out of town.

Home, Arkansas, was a small town at the foot of the Ozark Mountains in the southwestern part of the state, the main supply hub for a twenty-square-mile area. Home had received its unlikely name more than a hundred years earlier when a travel-weary family from Ohio paused to spend the night along a clear stream. The man looked around, liked what he saw, and declared, "We're home."

The town now consisted of only two rows of business buildings lining a main street: the grocery store, hardware store, barbershop, pool hall, gun shop, and two cafes, Alice's Diner and the Grizzly Bear Tavern, where a man could get nearly anything that he wanted to drink. Nona had learned all of this when she and Maggie came to town to attend the Baptist church, a small clapboard building that sat on the edge of town. Church was the ideal place to catch up on the local gossip.

The Ozark Mountains loomed over a wild and unsettled terrain. The merchants in Home depended on hunters, fishermen, and campers for their livelihood, and the region drew them in droves. But this was not only a haven for hunters; hippies had also been settling here for the last ten years. The town was usually peaceful until sunset, when the roughnecks came to town and the bar was crowded to overflowing. Nona was becoming fond of Home and its wooded surroundings.

She drove east along a road that snaked through a heavily wooded area. The sound of the car's tires crunching over loose stone echoed off the looming pines that lined both sides of her route. She had traveled this road at least once a week since she and Maggie, her sister, had come to manage the camp, and had never been nervous about traveling it, but now, for some reason, she was uneasy as she drove away from town. Was it that the bald-headed man had held on to her arm so tightly? The encounter bothered her more than she was willing to admit. She would feel more comfortable when she made it to the turnoff to the camp. A little afraid but determined, Nona concentrated on her driving.

After a couple of miles, Nona became aware of a black car coming up quickly from behind her. In the rearview mirror, she could see a truck behind the car. It was probably old Mr. Wilson, who lived on the other side of the lake. He was almost eighty years old. Fearfully, Nona gripped the wheel. There was nothing along this lonely stretch until she came to the camp. She kept her eyes on the road and waited.

Checking the side mirror, she was surprised to see the car pull out to pass her! Tapping lightly on the brakes to keep from spinning out of control, Nona saw that the driver was the bald man who had grabbed her arm at the store. The black car passed her and barreled on down the road. The man in the passenger seat hadn't even glanced at her. The car rounded a bend and was soon out of sight. For the next several miles, Nona kept expecting to see the car blocking the road, the man out, a gun in his hand.

Nona rounded an easy curve in the road and came within sight of Tall Pine Camp. She could not remember it ever looking so inviting. The manager's house itself wasn't much; it was the largest of the buildings but was otherwise identical to the seven other cabins set back from Tall Pine Lake. All of the buildings were roomy and painted a crisp green. As she turned onto the lane leading to the cabins, Nona was proud of what she saw. With Maggie's help she had cleaned away the brush and clipped the hedges from around the cabins.

Approaching the three-room house she shared with her sister and Mabel Rogers, a longtime friend, Nona surveyed the campground. A battered old house trailer sat near the lake. Russell Story, the old man who lived in the trailer, had been hired by the owner to take care of the boats and the bait for the camp. He also cleaned, filleted, and packed the fish in ice for the camp guests. Mabel had won him over with her apple pie, and in return he kept them well supplied with fresh fish.

"Oh, for crying out loud!"

The words burst from Nona as she turned her Ford into the drive in front of her cabin. For the second time in the last three days, the man who was staying in cabin number two had parked his pickup in her drive, and she couldn't squeeze past it.

"Some people have a lot of nerve," she muttered angrily. She pressed her hand down on the horn and held it there. The horn's blaring bounced off the buildings and over the lake. Nona hoped it sounded as belligerent as she felt.

"Nona! Chill out!" Maggie shouted as she came down the steps of their cabin and knocked on the window of the passenger's side.

Nona let up on the horn, leaned over the seat, and rolled down the window.

"He isn't here," Maggie yelled over the knocks and ticks of the idling engine. "He took his dog and went off into the woods."

"Not here?" Stress lines formed between Nona's eyes, and the corners of her mouth turned down in a frown. "Well then, I'll just park behind him and see how he likes it."

Maggie stood by the car with her hands on her bony hips. At fourteen, she was a pencil-straight girl with light brown hair who had just begun to emerge from her child-ish awkwardness. While she and her sister were both slim, Maggie was already taller than Nona, who was twelve years her senior. Maggie's legs seemed endless, and her blue eyes shone large in her perky, freckled face. She wore blue jeans and a faded T-shirt. Not at all shy, she had an openness that was a large part of her charm. She made a frown of her own as she watched her sister park directly behind the truck, then get out of the Ford.

"Take a pill, Nona. Why are you so mad? You'd think this is the only parking place in the whole world."

"I'm not mad . . . just exasperated." She was still shaken from her encounter with the man at the store and on the road. "Ours is the manager's cabin, number one," she explained impatiently. "This is our drive. He has his own drive. It's simple. Why does he insist on parking on this side of his cabin?"

"Seems to me you're making a mountain out of a molehill," Maggie retorted with a shrug. She gathered up one of the bags of groceries and leaped up the steps like a young colt.

Nona edged through the front door that Maggie held open, dumped her large sack on the table, and sighed. A thin woman in slacks and a sleeveless shirt stood in front of the sink peeling potatoes. She turned and smiled at the two girls, her high cheekbones rosy with rouge, a ciga-rette hanging from her bright red lips.

Four years earlier, when Nona and Maggie moved into an apartment after the deaths of their parents, Mabel Rogers, a widow, had been their neighbor. A woman who had no family of her own, she had taken the two girls to her heart. Mabel had volunteered to care for Maggie while Nona was at work, a blessing to both the sisters. They loved her dearly. She had been "Aunt Mabel" to Maggie since they'd met. When Nona had taken the job of managing the camp, it seemed only natural that Mabel would come with them.

"Hi, Mabel," Nona said.

"Is something wrong, dear?" Mabel asked with concern. "Why were you honking the horn?"

"She's having a fit, Aunt Mabel."

"A what?" Mabel asked, wrinkling her brow.

"You know. Losing her cool."

"I am not!" Nona said nothing about what had happened in town and on the road to the camp. There was no point in worrying Mabel and Maggie. "There's the whole out-of-doors for him to park in, yet he insists on putting that pickup in our drive!"

"He's really very nice," Mabel said. "Handsome, too," she added, with a wink at Maggie. Pushing a strand of henna-colored hair behind her ears, she began unloading the sacks of groceries.

"This one is Mrs. Leasure's," Nona said. "I'll have Maggie take it down to her."

Once everything had been placed on the table, Maggie wailed, "Nona! You didn't get my *Seventeen* magazine!"

"I had to choose between a magazine and raisin bran. The bran won. Our grocery dollars will only stretch so far, you know. When I think of how fast our money is going, I get panicky."

"Did you call Little Rock again?" Mabel asked.

Nona was reluctant to place a long-distance call on the

camp telephone. "I tried to call while I was in town, but they said Harold was out to lunch."

"That's a heck of a note," Mabel mused as she carefully folded the empty sacks.

"I think it was a lie. He just didn't want to talk to me."

"Did you try to call the man who hired you?"

"No."

"We've been here for several weeks and haven't heard a word from the owner of the camp. Isn't that a bit strange?"

"I suppose so," Nona admitted. "I send everything we take in, plus the bills, to the accountant. Unless we get more bookings in a hurry, there'll be only the bills to send. To make matters worse, the pump on the well is acting up again. It'll cost a mint to have someone out here to fix it."

As she took a load of groceries over to the cupboard, Nona stumbled over a big dog stretched out on the kitchen floor. The mutt with the yellow coat looked up from where he lay, and then plopped his head back down onto the wooden floor. "Maggie! What's Sam Houston doing in here? I've told you time after time to leave him outside. He gets hair all over the place."

"Sam Houston doesn't like the dog next door."

"That's because he's a coward! It's time he decided if he's a dog or a pussycat," Nona declared.

"He's no coward."

Nona knew that Maggie regarded her complaints with the usual teenage tolerance for an adult's irritations, but she couldn't help insisting on what was right. The mass of red hair curled around Nona's face, and little tendrils of it clung to her cheeks and forehead. She blew the bangs away from her forehead and decided that rather than argue with Maggie, she would take Sam Houston and go outside.

"Come on, you mangy hound."

"You're gonna hurt Sam Houston's feelings, calling him that."

"I should call him a hairy, worthless, mangy hound."

Following Nona through the kitchen and out the back door, Sam Houston lumbered down the steps and eased himself into a cool spot of shade at the base of the porch. Nona sat down on the steps, rested her chin in her hand, and let her mind drift. She found herself back in Home, the strange man's hand on her arm. Inwardly, she shivered. Most of the men she had encountered since coming to the camp had been polite and rather bashful. This man had been quite different.

The loud blast from a car horn startled her, but then a secretive smile curled on her lips. The man in the next cabin was back and wanted to move his truck. *Not much fun is it, buster?* she thought. She went back into the kitchen and peeked out the window. A tall, well-muscled man in faded jeans and an old plaid work shirt was standing beside his truck, his hand firmly pressing on the truck's horn.

"Nona! Do something!" Maggie wailed.

"Not yet," Nona replied with a grin. "Let him stew for a while."

At a loud knock on the door, her smile widened. She stayed in the kitchen while Maggie opened the door.

Chapter 2

"TELL YOUR SISTER TO MOVE HER CAR. Better yet, call her to the door and I'll tell her myself." The deep masculine voice reached into the kitchen, where Nona stood at the sink and stared out the window into the thick woods surrounding the camp. The voice sounded angry.

"I'm busy right now. I'll be out in a minute," Nona called. A bright little devil with a pitchfork in his hand danced before her eyes, and her lips tilted at the corners. The man in cabin number two knew he had parked his pickup in her spot. It would do him good to wait a bit.

"She'd better move it now, unless she wants it run over by a moving van."

The booming words jerked the smile from Nona's face. *What in the world was he talking about?* She went quickly to the door, flung open the screen, and stepped outside.

"A moving van?"

"Yeah. A big truck that's used to haul furniture," he said as if explaining it to a toddler.

Nona folded her arms over her chest and stared at the man with a mixture of exasperation and confusion. Her blue eyes were analytical as they roved over his not-quite-handsome face and light brown hair. She'd only ever viewed him from afar; Mabel had checked him in when he arrived. He'd said his name was S. T. Wright. This was the first time she had seen him up close.

"Look here," she began, deciding that they needed to come to an understanding. "The cabin is furnished. You knew that when you rented it. If you want to bring in some of your own things, that's your business, but you'll have to store the furniture that we provided. We don't have the facilities to store it here."

"I've no intention of storing that stuff," he responded. "It wouldn't even make good firewood. Then again," he pondered, rubbing his hand along his stubbly chin, "maybe it would." Smile lines bracketed his wide mouth and his green eyes glinted as he assessed her.

"Burn it?" she gasped. "I'll call the owner and have you arrested!"

"You won't need to call very loud." The man grinned. "I'm not deaf."

Nona stiffened visibly. She opened her mouth to speak but couldn't force any words to come out. "Wha—," she finally managed.

"I'm the owner."

"You're the owner?" Shock flooded through Nona's body as she took in the full import of his words. *This was the owner? This was her boss for the summer?* Color came up her neck and flushed her face.

"The one and only."

"I'll need some proof of that. Mabel said your name was S. T. Wright. If you're the owner, why didn't you say so when you checked in?" Chin up, her body taut, Nona was mindful of the thudding in her chest and the pounding in her head. Mustering the remaining fragments of her self-possession, she locked her blue eyes to his green ones and refused to look away. The way that he looked at her, amused and confident, irritated her.

"I didn't lie. My name is Simon Thomas Wright, and I didn't know when I checked in if the owner had accepted my offer," he replied. He appeared to be amused by her proprietary attitude.

Suddenly, the screen door banged open behind Nona. Maggie and Mabel nudged their way past her to stand on the porch. Nona knew they had been listening to every word.

"Holy cow!" Maggie exclaimed. "You really bought this run-down place? You got ripped off."

"Hard to believe, I know." Simon spoke to Maggie, but his eyes watched the conflicting emotions play across Nona's face. "But yeah, I really did."

"What the heck for?" Maggie asked with the unabashed frankness of youth. "This place is a dump. And besides, it's way out in the middle of nowhere. Someone took you, but good, mister!"

"We'll see, won't we?" was his only answer. He spread his long, slim legs and hooked his hands in his hip pockets, evidently intending to offer no further explanation. He lifted a brow at Nona as if to ask if she had anything to add to Maggie's assessments.

Nona looked directly at Simon for ten full seconds.

She felt, suddenly, as if this man was not a stranger at all. There was something about him that nudged at her memory, teasing her. She tried to capture the elusive thought but couldn't. Embarrassed at having drifted away from the conversation, she tried to regain her poise.

"What's your dog's name?" Maggie asked, glancing at the big black dog at Simon's heels.

"Cochise."

"The Indian?"

"Yep. At first I was gonna call him Geronimo, but that was too long."

Maggie's eyes twinkled and she gave him one of her pixie grins. "I see what you mean. It would take a while to call, 'Here, Geronimo, here, Geronimo.'"

"So I called him after my other Indian hero, Cochise."

"Cool. Are you Indian?" Maggie asked, her eyes avoiding her sister's.

"Back a few generations."

Nona said to Maggie, "Don't ask so many questions. Get my car keys, honey," she said, trying to sound firm and in control.

Maggie was in and out of the house in record time. "Can I move the car?" she pleaded.

"If you're careful. But then you've got to take Mrs. Leasure her groceries," Nona murmured absently, her eyes lost in the man's intense gaze. She was convinced that she had met him before, but, for the life of her, she couldn't remember where. Her heart was thumping up a storm.

"She told me to call her LeAnn. Don't be so old-fashioned, Nona," Maggie answered.

Nona could see that Maggie was in one of her argumentative moods and decided that the best course of action was to ignore the question.

"I heard Maggie say you were having a fit. That I would like to see." Simon lifted a brow and grinned. "Did something happen while you were in town?"

"Nothing that concerns you, Mr. Wright."

"Anything that happens to one of the people who work for me is my concern."

"The only thing that should concern you is how I do my job."

Sensing the mounting tension in Nona's voice, Mabel chimed in. "She's been working her fingers to the bone cleaning the cabins, raking the yard, and washing curtains. I don't think the cabins had been thoroughly cleaned in at least a year or two."

"I don't have any complaints about her work," Simon said to Mabel. Nona was irritated by the way he was talking to Mabel while looking at her, his green eyes never leaving her face. "She's done more than her share. Speaking of which, she'll be getting help soon. I'm going to hire a handyman to help her."

"That's good to hear."

"By the way, how long has the woman in number six been here?"

"Mrs. Leasure? Two weeks. Her rent is paid up for two more. Her husband had something to attend to somewhere, but she expects him back any day."

"She's pregnant, isn't she?"

"Is that a crime?" Nona asked defensively.

"No. Only an observation," Simon stated calmly. "If

she's out here by herself, how does she get groceries or things she needs?"

"When we go to the store, she gives us a list and we bring back what she needs."

Maggie slid behind the wheel of the car and turned on the ignition. The motor sputtered, but refused to turn over. Frustrated, Maggie continued to push the key forward. A grinding sound came from the motor.

"For goodness' sake, Maggie," Nona said as she came down off the porch and approached the driver's-side window. "You'll run down the battery."

"I can't help it. The darn thing won't start."

Before she could respond, Nona felt a hand on her elbow that gently but firmly moved her aside. "Let me see what I can do."

"I didn't do anything wrong, did I?" Maggie asked as she got out of the car.

"I don't think so," Simon said with a wink. "These older cars can be stubborn sometimes."

"It's not so old," Nona said defensively. "It's probably newer than that old truck you're driving." She didn't like the way Simon had moved her aside, and she didn't like his know-it-all attitude. "It's only ten years old."

"I suppose you bought it from an old lady who let it sit in the garage for five of those years?" He grinned, stepping back to point at the dents in the fender and the door. Something about that grin set her teeth on edge.

With a wink, Simon got in the driver's seat. As soon as he turned the key, the motor sputtered once, then caught and purred like a contented kitten.

Damn you, car! Nona fumed. *It'll be a cold day in July before I wash you again!*

"Back in you go, kid," Simon said as he got out of the car and held the door open for Maggie. The younger girl grinned back up at him with a look that was nearly conspiratorial, as if the two of them had set out to embarrass Nona.

"Be careful," Nona called. "Back up carefully."

"Where will I park?"

"Park out front."

Before Maggie could move an inch, Simon contradicted Nona. "Don't do that. Go down and park in the drive of the last cabin."

"She can't drive that far," Nona said hurriedly. "She hasn't taken Drivers Ed yet."

"Then someone should give her a lesson or two before she goes to Drivers Ed." Simon smiled. He pulled open the passenger's-side door and got into the car.

Nona paced back and forth across the kitchen floor. Maggie and Simon had been gone for over thirty minutes. From time to time she glanced out the window for some sign of the Ford.

"Damn him," she said irritably.

"She'll be all right," Mabel reassured her. "Simon won't let her wreck the car."

"Why did *he* have to be the owner of the camp?" Nona said with another quick glance outside. "Something about him is familiar. I don't know what it is, but I have a feeling that I've seen him before."

"He's so handsome, I can't imagine you could have forgotten him."

Nona placed her hands on her hips and stared at the other woman. Giving the man a compliment offended her. "What are we going to do, Mabel? If he's bringing furniture, he isn't intending to leave soon. We won't be much more than cleaners, and I doubt he'll pay much for that."

"Don't borrow trouble, honey. We don't know what he'll want. Let's just wait and see which way the wind blows."

Their worries were interrupted by the sound of heavy footsteps crossing the porch. A giggle from Maggie was followed by the response of a deep voice. Nona groaned. Maggie was bringing *him* into the house! With her back to the door, Nona busied herself by putting the clean dishes back in the cupboard.

Maggie burst into the room, a smile plastered across her face, and plucked an apple out of a dish on the table. "Simon said I'm going to be a good driver. I just need a little more practice. He's going to let me drive his truck."

Nona turned to look hard at her sister. Without their parents, she and Mabel had done the best that they could to bring the young girl up right. Now, she was being encouraged to be irresponsible. The thin smile on Simon's lips irritated her.

"You did say you'd let me drive your truck, didn't you?" Maggie asked, turning to Simon.

"Yes, I did," he said, his gaze staying on Nona. For a moment, she thought that she saw concern flicker in his eyes. "But you need to get permission from your sister, or she'll send you to bed without any supper."

"That doesn't sound so bad," Maggie groused.

"Was to me. When I was a kid, that was my worst punishment. I loved to eat. I still do."

"Well, in that case," Mabel said, "come to supper. We're going to have fried fish, fresh okra, and I'm baking a peach pie."

Nona stifled a groan. What were these two doing? *He's invited to supper?*

"Why, thank you, Mrs. Rogers. I do believe I'll take you up on that offer. But first I need to go back to my cabin and clean up a bit."

"It'll be ready in a couple of hours," Mabel said.

As Simon was leaving, he looked over his shoulder and winked at Nona.

Damn you, Simon Wright! Don't think that I'll buy into your flirty ways. I have more than myself to consider. I've got to get settled before fall so Maggie can enroll in school.

It suddenly occurred to Nona that it might be a good idea for the three of them to leave the camp immediately. It would give her nearly six weeks to settle in a new location and find a job. She sighed heavily. She would talk it over with Maggie and Mabel; but, in the end, she would have to be the one to make the decision.

The rest of the afternoon was quiet. Maggie took Sam Houston with her when she went to take Mrs. Leasure her groceries. Nona watched them through the window. Sam Houston was trotting along behind as Maggie cajoled him to keep up. Mabel took her pie out of the oven and set it on top of the stove to cool. Her face was flushed from the heat and her hair clung to her cheeks.

"Whooeee! It's hot in here!" Mabel exclaimed.

"The stove has got plenty to do with that."

"I suppose so." Mabel chuckled.

"We're not going to have to use that kerosene stove all summer, are we?"

"No, we won't," Mabel said as she wiped her brow with the end of her apron. "Simon told me he'd order an electric stove to use when it really got warm."

"He's all talk!" Nona fumed. She hadn't been very polite to the man, even though he was her boss. There was something about him that made her nervous. "Why didn't he tell us he was the owner when he first arrived?"

"He must have had his reasons."

"You had no idea he was the owner?"

"No, I didn't. I thought he was on vacation."

Nona seethed. The way Simon had moved in without telling them his identity was devious. She felt that they had all been used. But what could they do? After thinking about it for a moment, she decided to confide her thoughts to Mabel.

"I'm afraid that we'll soon be unemployed. He doesn't need us now that he's going to be here. Why pay us when he can just do the work himself? We should probably leave here by the end of the week so I'll have time to find a job and an apartment near a school. Maggie's a good student, but she can't afford to miss even a few days."

"Before you make plans, you should talk to Simon."

"I'll talk to him all right. I'll walk right over, give him a week's notice, and collect the month and a half of wages he owes me. It won't be much, but with what I have in my savings, it'll see us through a couple of months."

As Mabel opened her mouth to interject, Maggie came bounding through the front door, Sam Houston, his tail wagging, at her heels. She came to the kitchen, danced around, and finally placed a kiss on Mabel's cheek.

"Don't you ever walk, Maggie?" Nona scolded. "You're getting to be as wild as a deer since we've been here."

"I'm excited about our dinner guest."

"I don't think he's anything to get excited about."

With her hands on her hips, Maggie frowned deeply at her older sister. "What's the matter with you? You've been in a funk since the moment you got back. What happened to ruin your day?"

For a moment, Nona was jerked back to her encounter with the strange man in front of the general store and his following her out of town.

"Nothing happened," she finally said.

"Something did. You need to chill out."

Changing the subject, Nona asked, "How was Mrs. Leasure?"

"She told me to tell you thank you for getting the milk and eggs. I feel sorry for her. She's down there all alone. I bet she's scared her husband won't come back."

"What makes you think that?"

"I don't know," Maggie said, shrugging her shoulders. "Some of the things she said, I suppose. She asked if we were going to be here all summer."

"Did she say anything about her husband?"

"Only that he was working with a crew taking out trees for a road-widening project and that he might have to go to Texas."

"That doesn't mean he won't be coming back."

"He wouldn't be much of a man if he went off and left his pregnant wife," Mabel exclaimed. "She told me that the baby is due the middle of September. Surely he doesn't intend to leave her here until then."

"But what if he does?" Maggie asked.

"It won't concern us. Mr. Wright can handle it," Nona said as she threw her arm across her sister's shoulders and hugged her.

Even though she could get on Nona's nerves from time to time, Maggie meant the world to her. All of her adult life, she had been taking care of herself and Maggie. Their half brother had not taken an interest in his sisters. She wondered what it would have been like to have a man to share the problems of bringing up a teenager.

Enough of that train of thought, she chided herself. She gathered the dishes to set the table. She paused and looked out the window at the smooth, tranquil lake that mirrored the tall pines that surrounded it. The hills rose in the distance, and Nona felt that she was falling in love with the rugged land. She remembered the thrill she had felt the first time she saw deer and elk. A man in town had told her that there were brown bears in the region, but she had yet to see one.

Nona sighed. She was not pleased with how she had handled things lately. It had been foolhardy to jump into a job, move Maggie and Mabel to this remote place, all without having ever met her employer. It wasn't all her fault. She had laid it out to Maggie and Mabel. Maggie was anxious to go, and Mabel had looked forward to a new adventure.

As she set plates around the table at the end of the kitchen, Nona's head began to pound. The stress of the day finally began to overwhelm her. The pain became so severe that she rubbed her temples with her fingertips. She glanced at Mabel, who was looking at her intently.

"Do you have a headache?"

"The beginning of one."

"Simon's not the devil, you know."

A throbbing pain lanced through Nona and she had to balance herself against the table. She was getting one of her dreaded migraine headaches.

"Go to bed, honey," Mabel said gently. "I'll explain your absence to Simon."

Before she could move, a deep masculine voice broke through the early evening air. "Something smells good!"

Speak of the devil.

Chapter 3

THE SOUND OF A RADIO WOKE NONA. She lay with her eyes closed and waited to see if the headache she had taken to bed was still with her. Thank goodness, in spite of the tossing and turning, her mind in turmoil over the news that the mysterious Mr. Wright was the owner of the camp, she had slept the headache away. The pain had been so strong when she went to bed that she had feared she was going to be sick. The last thing that she had heard was Mabel's voice explaining her absence from the dinner table to Simon Wright.

As she lay on her back, running her fingers through her hair, the sounds of the early day reached her; chirping birds competed with the clatter of iron against iron as Mabel prepared breakfast. It struck her again, for the hundredth time, that it had been foolhardy to bring Maggie and Mabel to this place in the wilds, so far from a town, so far from an indoor toilet. At first, Maggie had refused to use the privy and had instead used a slop jar, until she found out that she would have to carry it out and empty it every morning. After that, she went with Nona to the outhouse before going to bed. The outhouse was just one of the things to which they had all needed to adjust. Simon had told Mabel that he would modernize the cabins, put in a septic tank and indoor toilets. But, by then, they would be long gone.

They'd had to adjust to many things the last couple of years. The manufacturing plant where she had worked for five years as an assistant to the personnel manager had moved to Mexico, as had many other plants. She wasn't about to take Maggie down there. Jobs had been scarce in Little Rock, but she had done whatever was available to make ends meet and provide for her sister. She feared that she'd never find another job with a wage adequate to support the three of them, when out of the blue had come the offer to manage the camp. Without much hesitation, they had packed up and moved to this beautiful lake in southwestern Arkansas, near the town of Home.

They'd known that things would not be easy. When Mabel and her husband had first been married, they had run a fishing resort in Michigan. With this bit of experience, combined with all of their meager savings, they'd believed they could manage through the summer. Now Simon Wright had shown up and placed all of Nona's hopes in jeopardy.

She swung her legs over the edge of the bed and shielded her eyes from the bright sunlight that poured through the windows. As happy as she was to see that it would be a beautiful day, she still wasn't pleased with herself this morning. She'd made a fool of herself last night. The anger she'd felt when Mabel had asked Simon to dinner had shaken her. It was best that she'd gone to bed instead of sitting at the table glowering at the man. She could only imagine what she might have said if she had allowed her anger to go unchecked.

"Coffee smells good, Mabel," she said as she entered the kitchen.

"How do you feel? Headache gone away?"

"Yes, thank goodness. I was afraid I was going to get one of those full-blown migraines. What's for breakfast?" she asked and peered into the big iron skillet. Before Mabel could answer, Nona exclaimed, "Hotcakes again? What are you trying to do to me?"

"Fatten you up. You're as skinny as a starved alley cat. You need something to stick to your ribs when you're working so hard."

"I don't know about that." Nona set two mugs of coffee on the table and took a seat as Mabel served a plate of hotcakes. "How was dinner?"

"Fine." Mabel smiled. "Simon is a nice man."

"I'm sure." Nona frowned. "But I'm still puzzled as to why he didn't tell us he was the owner when he came here."

"Maybe he wanted to see how we ran the place before he told us he'd bought it. That'd make sense."

"There's really not much running to do. We clean the cabins when they're used, which is seldom. We fight the weeds and mosquitoes, although they aren't as bad as I expected. We run errands for people like Mrs. Leasure. What more does he want from us?"

"That's all that we do *now*," Mabel said, emphasizing the last word. "But Simon said something about turning a couple of the cabins into a dining hall and a recreation room."

"What?"

"He said we should try to get some larger bookings when the hunting season opens. He thought that home cooking and recreation would be an *enticement*."

"The hunting season is only two months away. I suppose he expects us to build these 'enticements'!"

"Don't be silly, dear. He'll hire professionals."

There was something about Mabel's tone of voice that unsettled Nona. The older woman acted as if her concerns were ridiculous or unnecessary. *Simon must have spent the whole evening sweet-talking her into seeing things his way!* "Who would be doing the cooking?"

"Why, me, of course. You know I can cook up a storm when I set my mind to it." Mabel's eyes had a vivid sparkle. "He said I would have all the modern conveniences, including a dishwasher."

"I won't let you do it," Nona argued. "You're in no condition to be slaving over a hot stove. Your blood pressure—"

"—is fine," Mabel said so reassuringly that Nona felt the battle nearly lost.

"Why didn't he discuss this with me?"

"He would have discussed it with you last night, but you went to bed."

"Then I'll tell him what I think about his harebrained idea the next time I see him!" The idea of telling that overbearing man what she thought of his ridiculous notions gave Nona a quick spurt of energy.

"Then you'd better hurry and decide what you want to say."

"What do you mean by that?"

"He'll be here any minute for breakfast."

A loud knock on the door brought Nona to her feet. She looked down at the older woman accusingly. "You invited him for breakfast?" she whispered, but Mabel remained silent as she sipped her coffee. "We didn't contract to feed him," Nona muttered before hurrying to her bedroom to make herself decent.

"I'm just trying to get in good with the boss," Mabel called. "I've said it before, and I'll say it again . . . there's nothing that gets to a man like good home cooking."

Hastily, Nona slipped on a pair of slacks and an old long-sleeved T-shirt. She couldn't believe that he was back again! Wasn't it enough that he'd ruined her evening? She could only imagine what Maggie thought of his idea; she was so moonstruck that she probably volunteered to put up the buildings herself! Nona came silently from the bedroom and paused in the doorway. All that she could see of Simon was his broad back as he sat on one of the kitchen chairs, looking as if he were in a restaurant expecting to be served.

"You're a jewel, Mrs. Rogers. How come you're still single?" His voice was deep, throaty, without a hint of accent to betray what part of the country he was from.

"Well, I do have to carry a club when I go to town," Mabel replied sassily. "And please, call me Mabel. My mother-in-law was Mrs. Rogers. She was a terror and didn't like me much."

Simon's answering laugh was warm and pleasant,

even if it grated on Nona's nerves. Before she could even announce herself, a deep "woof" came from the back porch. Mabel opened the door, allowing Sam Houston to lumber into the room. The big yellow dog made straight for the man at the table. The vision of the dog lunging at Simon and sinking his teeth into him played at the edges of Nona's thoughts, but the reality was disappointing. Sam Houston neither bit nor snapped at Simon, but instead laid his head on the man's thigh.

"Morning, Sam," Simon said as he scratched the dog's ears. "Now, aren't you the nice fellow? You keep it up, and Mabel might even give you a flapjack or two."

In answer, Sam Houston backed up a step, sank down onto the floor, and rested his jowls on his paws. Nona had to fight the urge to kick the mangy dog and instead poured herself a cup of coffee. Finally, her sense of good manners forced her to say, "Morning."

"Morning, Miss Conrad," Simon answered.

If he's waiting for me to say 'Call me Nona,' he'll wait till hell freezes over!

"Call her Nona," Mabel said brightly as she pushed the hotcakes forward. "Have these, dear. I'll make more."

"None for me, thanks," she grumbled. Her throat felt as if it had a rock in it.

"Oatmeal? Toast?" Mabel continued.

"Nothing right now. I'll eat later."

Simon suppressed a smile as he stared at the attractive young woman sitting across from him. With her curly red hair in a flyaway tangle that framed her high-cheekboned face, she was a beauty. But it was her mouth he couldn't seem to look away from. The upper lip was short, the lower one full and sensuous, though both were now pressed together stubbornly. With the glances she was giving him, he knew that the last thing he should do was tease her, but he couldn't help himself. She was too darn attractive to resist!

"Don't let me keep you from your breakfast, Nona. You really should eat something. Besides, you don't seem to have a weight problem . . . not yet, anyway."

Nona's palm hit the table and she glared at him.

"Arr—woof!" Sam Houston rose to a half crouch and the hair stood up on his back.

"Nona!" Mabel screeched in surprise.

Simon raised his brows and his lips pursed in a suppressed smile.

"You've a lot of nerve!" The look on his face only fanned her anger.

"It was the 'yet' that got to you, wasn't it? Let me guess, you're one of those women who constantly worry about getting a broad behind."

"That's none of your business," she sputtered. She couldn't believe the gall of the man! Even after his personal remark, he sat calmly at their table, drinking from his mug. "Why didn't you tell us you were the owner when you arrived?"

"Relax and drink your coffee." Simon lifted his cup.

Mabel was giving her the "what's got into you" look.

"I can clear up one thing easily," Simon said as he heavily laced his hotcakes with maple syrup. "I didn't tell you I was the owner because even though I had made an offer on this place, I only found out yesterday that it had been accepted. No use telling you before then."

"I suppose the moving van was just waiting up the road for you to give the word," Nona said skeptically.

"I leased the camp before I decided to buy it. My things were already on the way," Simon said matter-of-factly before tucking a huge wedge of pancakes into his mouth. With his mouth full, he asked, "Did you make this syrup, too, Mabel?"

When Nona opened her mouth to question him further, he hastily added, "Is there any more of this good coffee, Mabel?" Why was he being so evasive? Didn't they have a right to know what he had planned for them? But before she could demand an answer to her questions, he casually added, "By the way, you signed a contract to stay through the summer. I certainly hope you plan to fulfill it. You do plan on staying, don't you?"

"You want me to fulfill my contract?" Nona gripped the edge of the table and stared at Simon as he lifted another forkful of hotcakes to his mouth.

"She doesn't need a hearing aid, does she, Mabel?"

"Oh, land sakes!" Mabel's worried eyes went from one to the other. "Cut this out, both of you!"

"I heard what you said. I'm just not sure what to do about it." Nona sank down in her chair. "The place doesn't need two managers! Why do you want us here?"

"I've got plans for this place, plans that go way beyond what we have now. I've been talking to Mabel about remodeling the cabins. She's agreed to cook meals for our guests. I'm sure I can think of lots of useful things for you to do, too. You don't sing or dance by any chance, do you?"

Nona stared at him in stunned silence.

"Stop teasing her, Simon." Mabel's voice had an edge to it, nearly defensive. "She's in no mood for it. She's worked like a son of a gun since the day we came here."

"I know that. But I also need to know if she can carry on a serious conversation without flying off the handle."

"What are you guys talking about?" Maggie entered the kitchen wearing cutoff shorts that Nona thought to be at least three inches too short. Sam Houston greeted her with a whine, his tail wagging so hard it almost lifted his hind legs from the floor. Maggie nonchalantly swung her leg over the dog in order to hold him between her knees, and began to scratch his head.

"Maggie! I thought you had thrown away those old shorts," Nona admonished.

"I'm not showing anything." Maggie frowned.

"Hi, punkin'. Ready for breakfast?" Mabel was always ready to defuse an argument between her two favorite people.

"I guess so. What were you yelling about, Nona?"

"I wasn't yelling, and don't scratch that dog in the house. Hair flies all over."

"Does he catch a Frisbee?" Simon asked casually as he looked down at the dog. Sam Houston looked back up at him with an expression that Nona could imagine was a smile. Maybe it was because they were the only two males in the room.

"He might need a little bit of practice, but I bet he could."

"We won't be here long enough for that," Nona argued.

"You might be. Mabel likes the idea."

Nona's swirling mind was filled with equal parts confusion and apprehension. It was amazing how quickly both Mabel and Maggie had been won over by Simon's suggestion that they stay on. Was she the only one that thought his ideas impractical? Things were moving too fast to suit her.

"You'll teach him to catch a Frisbee?" Maggie asked.

"Why not? He's smart enough."

"Then you're not going to give us the ax?"

"Whatever gave you that idea? If I can get this thing on its feet, I'll even raise your sister's pay. What do you think about taking numbers five and six and turning them into a dining hall? We could put in a few pinball machines, a pool table, a TV, and a jukebox."

"Jukebox?" Maggie blurted.

"A jukebox," Simon repeated.

"Awesome!" Maggie's face broke into a beautiful smile. "Can I play it without having to put in money?"

"Sure you can, squirt."

"You'd better not include us in your plans," Nona warned the big man, who swung around to face her. For the briefest of moments, she was struck by how attractive he was.

"So you finally came to life. You're just not listening to what I'm telling you. Each of the cabins has two bedrooms. We'll rent them to couples and add bunks to the large rooms to make them into dormitories. Our guests will be mostly hunters and fishermen. They'll expect to rough it. All they'll want is a decent place to sleep and good food."

Nona looked into Simon's green eyes as they remained

steadily locked onto her own. *I've seen him before! I know I have!* It was on the tip of her tongue to ask him if they had ever met before, but instead she just continued staring as Simon tilted back in the kitchen chair.

Finally, she said, "I think you should have asked us what we thought of your plans before you assumed we'd be a part of them. Maggie starts high school in the fall. She can't do that from here. As a matter of fact, I'll need to start looking for a regular job in town right away."

Quickly, Simon stood. His face changed to what Nona thought was a scowl. When he spoke, his voice was firm. "You might as well make the best of it, Nona. This can be a pleasant arrangement, or it can be a battle every step of the way."

"What are you saying?" Nona asked.

"I'm telling you that you're staying here where I can keep an eye on you. Is that understood?" As shock settled over Nona, Simon walked to the door and opened it. "Thanks for the breakfast, Mabel," he said and shut the door behind him.

"He's crazy!" Nona exclaimed. "Did you hear what he said to me?"

"What a hunk," Maggie said dreamily.

Nona could only sit and fume.

Chapter 4

AFTER A RESTLESS MORNING spent mulling over the strange statement that Simon Wright had made about her not leaving the camp, Nona had come to the conclusion that he was trying to make sure she didn't leave without fulfilling her contract. For the life of her, she couldn't understand why he needed her and Mabel. Now that he was here, the place would practically run itself. He could hire a cook anywhere, and he had Mr. Story to take care of the guests. Besides, a cook and a cleaning woman would be cheaper.

Trying to put the problem out of her mind, she decided she would speak to Simon later about getting out of the contract and then begin the task of finding a school for Maggie. Why did this all have to be so complicated? When she'd signed the contract for this stopgap job, she hadn't thought ahead to the need to leave in the first part of August in order to get settled before the start of the school term. What if he didn't let her out of their agreement? If she remembered correctly, the contract lasted until the end of the fishing season. She had assumed that would be the end of August, but what if she was wrong? How long would they be stuck here?

During the next few days, the warm weather brought several carloads of fishermen. They kept Mr. Story fairly busy. Nona did not know where the old man had come from, or much else about him for that matter. He'd arrived shortly after they had. He didn't talk much about himself. From the little that Nona had gathered, he traveled to the Ozarks in the summer and then to the Rio Grande Valley in the winter. His passion was fishing.

Physically, he wasn't much to look at. A short man with long arms and a head of thinning gray hair, with stubble on his face that suggested he was not fond of shaving. Whenever he stopped by the house, Nona was reminded that he wasn't fond of bathing either. While not talkative about his own life, he was friendly and patient, especially with Maggie, who asked a thousand questions.

Nona stood on the porch, the warmth of the early afternoon sun shining down on her, and watched as a large truck, its back end loaded with furniture from the two cabins that were being remodeled, left for the Salvation Army store in Little Rock.

She had to admit that Simon had been a whirlwind once he started moving, and he was certainly moving full speed ahead with his plans to renovate the camp. His enthusiasm had rubbed off on Mabel and Maggie, and now they were wholeheartedly behind the project, each of them pitching in with ideas and suggestions. He was endearing himself to them more all the time with his smiles, compliments, and promises. He'd become the light of their lives. Nona was afraid that she would never be able to get them away from the camp.

Several days had passed since the "disastrous encounter," as Nona liked to refer to her confrontation with Simon. Since then, he had acted as if nothing had happened, coming to the cabin regularly for breakfast and dinner, all the while smiling and joking with Mabel and Maggie. *He eats like a starved alley cat,* Nona thought as she picked up a bucket of cleaning supplies and walked briskly down the drive to the cabin she was cleaning.

She hadn't forgotten the stern look on Simon's face when he told her she wasn't to leave the camp without his permission. It had upset her, although Mabel had poohpoohed the idea that he'd meant it. She'd insisted that he was only teasing, but Nona wasn't so sure. She was beginning to feel like a prisoner. Was he trying to control her or was it genuine concern? As much as these questions gnawed at her, the one that she couldn't stop asking was *Who is he?* He certainly didn't give out much information about himself. The thought still clung to her mind that she had seen him before.

While she cleaned, her brain worked furiously. She really should call Little Rock again and talk to the man who had hired her. Simon had told her he'd bought the property, but what did that amount to? Just because he was handsome, friendly, fun, and her sister and Mabel adored him didn't mean that he was on the up-and-up. She owed it to herself and to them to find out for sure. She also wanted to call Harold, her half brother, at the bank. He would be at the office at this time of day. She needed to tell him to send her and Maggie's share of the money he had received from sell-ing a piece of their father's property, as executor of his will. He had held on to the parcel of land for five years. She suspected that he had borrowed money against it and that had been the reason the property had not been sold before. Now she was determined to force him to honor their father's wishes and give them what was rightfully theirs. When they left the camp, they'd need the money.

After lunch, Maggie went down to the lake while Mabel went berry picking. The woods behind the camp held a variety of berries: wild raspberries, strawberries, and chokecherries. Mabel loved to forage among the bushes. With the others occupied, Nona decided it was a perfect time to slip into town and make a long-distance call. She put on a clean dress, ran a comb through her hair, and picked up her purse. At the door, she looked around the compound. Simon was not in sight. Not that it mattered if he was, she told herself firmly, and slid under the steering wheel of her Ford.

She turned the key in the ignition, but instead of hearing the motor come to life, she heard "rrrrrr." She tried it again, but the engine wouldn't catch. *What the devil is wrong?* She kept at it, her foot pumping the accelerator, until the strong smell of gasoline reached her.

"Dammit!"

In her desperate attempt to get the car started, she had flooded the engine. She'd have to wait awhile before she could try it again. Exasperated, she leaned resignedly against the door. Suddenly, and without warning, the door was flung open, forcing her to grab the wheel to keep from falling out.

"Going someplace?" Simon asked. From where she'd

slid, he was looking down at her with a full smile, the sun shining on his hair. He didn't offer a hand to help her as she pulled herself back into the seat.

"Yes, as if it's any business of yours," she said. She wanted to be angry with him, to tell him that he was rude, but when she looked at him, she feared that an unwelcome blush had crept into her cheeks.

"You flooded it," he observed.

"I know that!"

"Trying to sneak off, huh?"

"I have things to do. Am I a prisoner here?"

"I told you the other night that I didn't want you to leave here unless I was with you."

"You didn't say that. You said not to leave without your permission."

"Same thing."

With a groan, Nona pulled the car door shut and turned the key in the ignition, silently praying to herself that the engine was no longer flooded. In answer, she received the same "rrrrrr." Taking a deep breath, she tried it again. This time there was only a click. *Why is this happening?* Turning her head to glare at Simon, she found him standing beside the car with his hands inside his pockets, calmly waiting.

"Still flooded." He grinned.

"I suppose this just tickles you to death."

Pulling the car door open, he waited for Nona to exit. "You're not going anywhere in that car. All that grinding has run down the battery."

Nona forced herself to count to ten before speaking as calmly as she could. "Where's the nearest mechanic?"

"Home. Planning on going there?"

"Maybe. Maybe not." She was in a contrary mood. No matter what, she would not let this arrogant man tell her what to do. *The damn car always starts. What's happened to it?*

Nona got out of the car, lifted the hood, and peered at the motor. Maggie knew more about engines than she did, but she'd not admit it to this know-it-all. "Did you do something to my car?"

"Do you want a ride to town?" he asked, failing to answer her question.

Nona closed the hood with a bang. She swallowed hard, lifted her chin, and boldly met his gaze. "Yes, I would like a ride to town. I have some business, and I want to make an important call from a phone booth," she added and watched his eyes narrow dangerously.

"Who do you need to call?"

"None of your business."

Simon had opened his mouth to protest, but something behind her caught his attention. Nona turned to see Maggie running as usual.

"Where ya goin'?" she shouted before she reached the car.

"I'm taking your sister to make a phone call," Simon said matter-of-factly.

"Who are you calling?" Maggie asked as she came to a halt in front of them, her breath coming in fits from the exertion. "I hope it isn't that pukey Lester Graves. He makes me want to barf."

"Maggie! Watch your mouth."

"Well, he does. You're not going to get back together with him, are you?"

"I don't plan to, and we don't discuss personal matters in front of strangers." Nona knew that if her cheeks hadn't been flushed crimson before, they most assuredly were now.

"Simon's not a stranger," Maggie argued.

"Who's Lester?" Simon asked.

"He was trying to date Nona, but I never liked him. He was gross, with fish eyes that just sort of watched you funny," Maggie answered without once looking at her sister. "Can I ride along?"

"Not this time, squirt. I need to talk to Nona."

"Are you going on a date?" Maggie asked, her eyes suddenly very sharp. "Cool."

"Absolutely not!" Nona yelled.

"Why are you yelling? Are you mad?"

"Yes, I'm mad at this damn car."

"And me," Simon said as he reached into the Ford, took Nona's keys from the ignition, and twirled them around on his finger. With his bright smile, he looked to Nona like the cat that had caught the canary.

"What'd you do?" Maggie asked.

"I caught her trying to sneak off."

Nona held her hand out for the car keys, but Simon flashed yet another smile and put them in his pocket.

"Come on if you want to go to town." Taking Nona by the arm, he propelled her toward his truck, giving Maggie's shoulder a pat as he passed her. "Take care of things while we're gone, squirt. Is there anything you want from town?"

"I want a *Seventeen* magazine."

"I'll see what I can do." He opened the door of his truck and waited for Nona to get in. She hesitated.

"I don't know you, and I'm not sure I want to go off with you. I've never seen any proof that you're who you say you are."

"Way I see it, I'm the one taking the big chance. Who's to say that you aren't planning on getting me into the woods so you can have your way with me?" He laughed when he saw the anger in her eyes.

"I'd rather scratch your eyes out," Nona answered defiantly, her hands on her hips. Finally, she reluctantly stepped up into the truck, turned, and settled onto the seat.

"Don't worry. I like willing women." Simon slammed the door, walked around to the other side, and slid under the wheel. He started the truck and backed out. Maggie was still standing in the yard as they drove past. She waved and Simon tooted the horn. As they turned onto the main road, he took off his Stetson and placed it on the seat between them. His light brown hair flew back from his face. Nona watched his hands easily control the truck on the dirt road. Every once in a while, he glanced at her.

They had driven a mile down the road before Nona finally spoke accusingly. "You did something to my car so I couldn't go to town, didn't you?"

"Now, why would you think something like that? I'm a nice fellow."

"I don't know that. I don't know you at all," Nona said as she turned toward him. "I know that I've seen you somewhere before."

"A good-lookin' guy like me gets noticed." He smiled with a glint in his eye.

"I think it was when I visited the jail."

"I bet you're right," Simon said smoothly, the twitch in his lips irritating her. "I was locked up for kidnapping and rape."

"I can't believe the things that you joke about."

"I wasn't joking when I said I owned the camp."

"No, but you might have lied."

"Dammit!" he suddenly barked. "What do I have to say to prove myself to you? Are you always this damn distrustful?"

The sudden harshness of his words surprised Nona. Turning away from him, she glanced out the window at the tall pines that lined the road. She looked behind and saw nothing but an empty road. Silence enveloped them from all sides. Suddenly, she was reminded of the man that she had met at the store and who had then followed her back toward the camp. He had frightened her. For a moment, she wondered if she should tell Simon about what had happened, but she decided that he would just laugh and say it was her imagination. She wasn't going to give him any more of a reason to ridicule her.

"Why do you need to go to town to make a call?" Simon asked, breaking the silence.

"That's my business."

"Do you want to call the agent in Little Rock?"

"What for?"

"To find out if I'm lying to you about owning the camp."

For a couple of miles, they rode in silence. Finally, she turned back toward him. While he watched the road ahead, she looked at his profile and decided that she might have seen someone that looked like him in a movie. If she had seen him in person, she surely would have remembered him. It was hard to admit to herself, but he was an attractive man.

A car pulling a small trailer approached and then passed them going in the direction of the camp.

"It looks like you may have more fishermen. If you want to go back and fix my car, I can go to town by my-self and you can take care of them."

"No, sir! I'd have to be out of my mind to leave a pretty woman and spend the afternoon with smelly fish-ermen. Russ is more than capable of giving them what they need."

Neither of them uttered another word until they reached the outskirts of Home.

"You can drop me off at that phone booth on the cor-ner," Nona said and waved her hand in that direction.

"I have a few calls to make myself. I'll just go with you."

"I thought you might," she observed. "Are you afraid I'll take off down the street?"

"If you did, you'd have to walk all the way back to the camp."

"Not necessarily. There was a man in town the other day that wanted to get acquainted. If he's in town, he'll give me a ride." The thought of being alone with the bald-headed man fairly scared the daylights out of her, but she would use him to get a rise from Simon.

Simon's head jerked toward her, his smile gone and his gaze more intense than she'd ever seen before. "What man? What did he look like? What did he say? Did he know who you were?"

"My, my! That put some life into you." Nona smiled, happy that her ruse had worked. "The answers to your questions are 'a man,' 'handsome,' 'nothing,' and 'yes.' "

"Be serious. I want to know who he was and where he tried to pick you up."

"I didn't say he tried to pick me up. I said I talked to him."

"Good Lord. You don't have the sense God gave a goose. Don't you know any better than to talk to strange men when you are alone in a town like Home?"

"Well, what do you expect? A woman with a college degree to manage your run-down camp in the woods?"

"A little common sense wouldn't hurt," he shot back.

There was not much activity along the main street of Home; a couple of cars were parked in front of the cafe, and a lone man stood staring at the goods in the hardware store window. Simon stopped his truck in front of the telephone booth. Nona was still fumbling with the door handle when he pulled the door open. She wanted to hit him. Instead, she let him take her arm and help her out of the truck. At least his easy smile had returned.

"I'll meet you at the store," Nona explained. "I want to buy a few things."

"I'm in no hurry. I planned to devote the entire afternoon to you."

She blinked hard at him, snarled under her breath, and tossed her head. Red hair blew in the breeze, and she reached up and smoothed the unruly curls behind her ear.

"Don't be mad, honey," Simon said quickly. "Be glad that I came along with you to keep you company. Let's go make your call."

Nona hurried into the small booth and attempted to close the door, but Simon's foot blocked it.

"Do you mind?"

"Do you have the right change, sweetheart?"

"Yes," she said bluntly. "I'm not your sweetheart."

Ignoring Simon, Nona fed the coins into the money slot. The air in the booth was stale, and she knew that it would soon be swelteringly hot. She didn't care. She would endure it to keep Mr. Know-It-All from hearing her conversation. As she dialed the number, she peered out of the booth to see where he was and was relieved to see that he was over by the truck.

"Hello?" a woman's voice sounded over the other end of the line.

"Hello. This is Nona Conrad. May I speak with my brother, please?" Only silence met her request. Nona momentarily worried that the woman had hung up; but when she listened carefully, she could hear voices in the background. Suddenly, the woman's voice came back on the line.

"Miss Conrad! I'm sorry to say, but your brother left here almost three weeks ago."

"Three weeks? What are you talking about?"

"Haven't you read the paper lately?"

"Not really. My sister and I are vacationing for a few weeks," Nona lied slightly.

"Where are you?"

"We're at a camp in the southern . . ." Before she could say another word, a hand reached into the booth and severed the connection.

Chapter 5

Furious, Nona glared directly into Simon's eyes. Her heart thumped and her pulse raced. Her voice was sharp and angry.

"What in the world do you think you're doing?! You've got a lot of nerve!"

Simon grinned sheepishly. "I thought you'd finished."

"You know damn good and well I hadn't!" Nona fed money into the slot and dialed the number again and got a busy signal.

Simon stood next to the booth. The smug look on his face made her mad enough to spit!

After she had sat a few moments in the booth fuming, the operator came on. "Line's busy, miss."

"I'll try later."

Simon grabbed her by the arm. "Come on, honey." He grinned and tipped his hat at two women standing beside a car. "Let's get our groceries. We don't want to leave the kids too long by themselves."

Nona stomped off down the street ahead of Simon, passing a family sitting on a bench in front of the barbershop. Her face felt as red as a ripe tomato. "You're a horse's ass!" she hissed when he caught up with her. "Why did you cut me off? And what's the idea letting those people think we're a couple and have kids?"

"Don't you like the idea, honey?"

"Stop calling me that. I'm not your honey."

"Are you Lester's honey?" It surprised her that he had remembered Maggie telling him about Lester Graves. Rather than reply, she decided to ignore the question and continued down the street toward the store at a fast clip.

"Hold on." Simon hurried to catch up with her, his long legs eating up the distance between them. "What's got you so ticked off?"

"As if you didn't know!"

"Now, now. Let's not argue." Simon chuckled. "What do you need at the store?"

Nona's mind wasn't thinking about what she needed at the store; she was thinking about the words spoken by Harold's secretary. What she'd said had been mighty peculiar. *What had she meant when she'd asked about reading the newspaper? Had Harold had an accident? If it was something serious, surely she would have told me.* "A newspaper," she answered after a moment's hesitation. "I need to find a new job."

"You've got a job."

"Not for long. My contract says that I only have to stay until the end of fishing season. By the way," Nona said belligerently, "I may need to take a week off to go looking for permanent work. But don't worry, Mabel will take over my duties while I'm gone."

"Didn't you hear me when I said you're not leaving the camp unless I'm with you?"

"You can't hold me out there."

"Yes, I can."

It suddenly struck Nona that Simon was unbalanced, maybe even dangerous. Was he threatening her? Her eyes searched the street for a policeman or the county sheriff's office. She didn't see either. She decided she needed to speak with a policeman as soon as possible. A clerk in the grocery store would surely know where she could find one. Clamping her mouth shut so as to keep from saying something that would provoke Simon, Nona hurriedly walked down the street. At the grocery store, she opened the door and prepared to enter, but before she could, a voice called out to her. "Miss Conrad?"

Turning on her heel, Nona was surprised to see a tall, thin man with sparse gray hair standing beside a plain-looking middle-aged woman. From their appearance, they seemed to be down-and-out. The man's face and hands were work-worn; the woman wore a faded dress with several visible patches, and she had a worried look on her face. Nona had never seen them before, and the fact that they knew her name was surprising.

"Go on in, honey," Simon said with a gentle push. "I'll talk to them." The way that he grinned at her, combined with his use of a term of endearment, infuriated her.

She stepped through the door, letting the screen slam behind her.

The clerk was a pudgy little man with a white apron

tied around his ample middle. His jowls hung far below his chin, but the smile that he flashed was still friendly. "Good afternoon, ma'am. What can I do for you?"

"I need a few things," Nona said as she returned his smile. "But first, could you tell me where I can find the police station?"

"I'm afraid we don't have a police station. Home's not quite big enough, I suppose. If you want the law, you can call the sheriff and he'll come over from the county seat."

Nona opened her mouth to speak but said nothing. What was stopping her? What if she was wrong about Simon? "That's all right. It's not an emergency," she finally said. Forcing a smile, she took out the list that Mabel had been compiling and picked up a basket. Quickly she gathered the supplies and was checking out when Simon came into the store.

"About ready, honey?" he asked.

"If you call me that one more time . . . I'll . . ."

"You'll what? Kiss me on the way home?"

"You're the most irritating . . . ," she exclaimed, in a low voice so that the grocer wouldn't hear.

"Now, is that any way to talk? You should be nice to me, honey."

"Why should I be nice to you? I won't be here in another week. I'll call my lawyer in Little Rock and tell him to get me out of this contract. As soon as I find another job, I'm gone."

"Liar. You'll do no such thing." Simon's green eyes sparkled in amusement. He acted like this was all just a game, but Nona didn't feel like playing.

As the clerk was totaling up the bill, Simon interrupted by asking, "Do you sell cases of pop?"

"Sure do. Both six-packs and by the case. What kind do you want?"

"A case of mixed flavors and a case of Coke. Oh, and where can I buy a *Seventeen* magazine?"

"We have magazines at the back of the store."

Nona rolled her eyes and was about to complain that he was spoiling Maggie, but Simon cut her off. "Now, sugar," he said. "The kids need a treat once in a while. They're on vacation, too."

Try as she might to show no anger on the outside, Nona's insides were boiling. Forcing another smile, she asked the clerk, "What do I owe you for what I had in the basket?"

"Add it all together," Simon said.

"No. Absolutely not," Nona interjected. "I'll pay for my things."

"Now, love. Don't be contrary. I know you have a budget for groceries, but we're on vacation and can afford to splurge a little." The clerk merely shrugged his shoulders and went to answer the phone.

"What do you think you're doing?" Nona growled when the man was out of earshot.

"Just getting the squirt a treat."

Nona bit her tongue and waited for the clerk to reappear. The sooner they were out of the grocery store, the better. Simon had already embarrassed her enough for one day.

The man gave Simon the receipt from the cash register, and Simon handed him his credit card.

"Sorry about all that hullabaloo," Simon said with a wink at the grocer. He threw his arm around Nona's shoulders and pulled her hard against him. "She's a bit temperamental now that's she's over her morning sickness."

"Congratulations, ma'am," the man said with an uneasy smile. At first, all that Nona could do was stare ahead, openmouthed. When she'd regained a bit of composure, she dug an elbow into Simon's midsection so hard he grunted.

"Usually, she's as gentle as a lamb. This pregnancy's taken her by surprise."

With those words, Nona had heard enough. She turned and nearly ran for the door.

"Wait up, honey. The car's too far for you to walk in your condition. Stay here where it's nice and cool while I go get it. On second thought," he said as he hurried after Nona, "I'll walk with you in case you feel faint." When he neared the door, he called out over his shoulder to the grocer, "I'll be back with the car and load up."

Nona's back was as stiff as a board, her face red with anger. When Simon finally caught up with her, her blue eyes sparkled with rage.

"How dare you embarrass me like that! You have some nerve!" she hissed for his ears alone. "Maggie and I have been attending the Baptist church here. The people I've met know I'm not married! When they hear I'm pregnant, and I'm sure they will, what will they possibly think?"

"Nothing, probably. Women get pregnant every single day."

"Not unmarried women in a town this size." Simon

reached out and placed his hand on her elbow. At his touch, her skin crawled and she jerked loose. "Don't touch me, you lying shyster!"

"Why would you call me that? I've laid my cards on the table."

Nona refused to answer the question and instead swept her eyes from one side of the street to the other. If she could only find another way back to the camp that didn't involve riding with him!

"Let's go back to the car," Simon said.

"I'm going back to the phone booth," Nona countered confidently. "I want to try my call again."

"Nona, wait," he said sincerely. The joking tone of voice was gone. His gaze pierced her in its intensity, and she couldn't help but wait for his next words. "I'm sorry if I upset you with what I said. Sometimes I speak before I think. There are some things I want to talk to you about. Let's load up the groceries and head out of town."

As angry as she had been with him, his words, as well as the way he said them, dampened her anger. Nodding her head, she silently followed Simon back to the pickup.

They returned to the store and loaded the groceries. As they were pulling away from the store, they saw the older couple that Simon had talked to standing next to an old beat-up car. The old man waved and tipped his hat as they went by.

"Who were those people?" Nona asked.

"The Hogans. He's a carpenter. I hired him to help with the remodeling on the cabins. We'll have to let him and his wife stay in one."

"That's great. Maybe she can take over for me and we could leave."

"Oh, no! I'm too used to Mabel's cooking now."

They drove for many miles in silence. Nona could only stare out the window as trees whizzed by. When they were only a couple of miles from the camp, Simon slowed the truck and pulled to the side of the road, stopping beneath the shade of a large cottonwood tree. Nona's body tensed in anticipation of his pouncing on her, but he sat silently for a few moments before speaking softly.

"There's something that I need to tell you. Something that you should know."

"What?" His tone of voice was strange, nearly frightening.

"It's about Harold," he continued. "He's my cousin. His father was married to my mother's sister."

"What?" Nona exclaimed.

"I know this is strange, but listen. When we were kids, we were thrown together a lot. After Harold's mother died, his father married your mother and I lost track of him for a while. I'm sorry to say, I never really liked him much."

"I can understand," Nona agreed. "I've always felt the same way. Because his own mother had died, my mother tried extra hard to be good to Harold, but he seemed to resent her and then later me and Maggie."

"Harold has sticky fingers," Simon said flatly, with no apology or hesitation.

"That's a fine thing to say about your own cousin."

"It's true. He's been stealing things since he was a youngster. I don't think your father ever knew. Now money and jewelry are missing from the bank where he worked. Harold is also missing. It's believed that he made off with five hundred thousand dollars in cash and about that much in jewelry."

Shock crowded the anger from Nona's face and she stared at Simon openmouthed. A piercing pain filled her head and a tightness grabbed at the pit of her stomach. "Oh, no! I can't believe it! Harold wouldn't do that."

"It was in the newspaper two weeks ago. I'm sorry."

As surprised as she was, Nona could believe that there was some truth in what Simon had told her. The idea that Harold had sticky fingers wasn't a new one; several pieces of her mother's jewelry had been missing from her jewelry case after her death. No one else had had access to the box but Harold. She'd never leveled any accusations at him, but the suspicion had lingered. Now she was being told that the suspicion could be true.

After a long silence, she asked, "What does this have to do with me?"

"You and Maggie are Harold's next of kin, his family. If he's disappeared, it would be logical for people to think that you would know where he is."

"Well, I don't. The reason I called him had nothing to do with any of this business. It was about a piece of my father's property." Looking hard into Simon's face, Nona could see no trace of the joking character who had often embarrassed her. His face was deathly serious. "Why are you telling me this?"

"I don't want to see you or Maggie hurt."

"Who would want to hurt us?"

"I'm quite sure Harold was involved with some shady

characters who were in the business of fencing valuable jewelry. He may have originally stolen it for them, then changed his mind and decided to keep it all. They might decide to come after you or your sister and try to force you to tell them where Harold is hiding. They'll want the jewelry and the money before the insurance detectives, or the law, catch up with him."

Oh, my God! What if he sent me the money? I can't tell Simon. He'll think I'm an accessory to the crime. Damn that Harold for getting me involved in his mess!

Trying to come to grips with what she'd heard, Nona stared silently out the window of the truck. It was hard for her to take in all of this information at once. The idea that someone would try to force information about Harold out of Maggie sent her heart to thumping with fear. Her little sister meant the world to her. She'd cared for her for so long that she was like her own child.

"Maggie doesn't know anything," she blurted.

"How about you?"

"I don't know anything either," she lied, hoping that she sounded convincing. "Is that why you're here? You want me to tell you where Harold is?" Like a lightning bolt rippling across a stormy sky, a thought shot across Nona's brain: Was Simon one of the "unsavory characters" looking for the loot Harold had taken? "Let's get going. I want to get back to Maggie."

"Not yet," Simon answered calmly, his eyes searching Nona's face. "I can see the wheels turning in your head. You're afraid of me now. You think I'm trying to get information out of you."

"Are you?"

"I won't force you to tell me anything more than what you want to. All I want to do is look after you until this thing is settled. You, Maggie, and Mabel."

"But you still want to know, don't you?"

Simon looked away, staring out the windshield at the empty road. Tapping his fingers on the steering wheel, he turned the key in the ignition and started the truck. They drove the rest of the way to the camp in silence.

When they parked next to Nona's cabin, she made a move to get out of the truck but Simon stopped her with his hand on her arm. "I'm here to help you, Nona. I thought that the only way to keep you safe was to get you and Maggie up here to the camp, so I spoke to your former boss and told him about the job. When you called, you spoke to me."

"That was sneaky."

"Yeah, it was." He grinned. "But I got you here."

"You're really serious about this, aren't you?"

"Yes, I am," he said, the grin disappearing. "And you better be serious about it, too. I'll show you the article from the Little Rock newspaper so you'll know that I'm not lying."

Nona shook her head. "I still don't understand what your interest is in all of this. You don't even know us."

A sheepish smile once again teased at the corners of Simon's mouth. "Maybe not as well as I want to, but I've seen you plenty of times in the apartment building where you lived. I used to go there on business for my grandpa Wright. He owns the building. I even played with Maggie once, but you came storming down to the sidewalk like a mama bear protecting her cub."

"I knew I'd seen you before!" she exclaimed at the answer to the question that had been nagging at her from the moment she'd met him. "Did you know then that we were Harold's half sisters?"

"But, of course."

Chapter 6

ANGER FLARED ONCE AGAIN. "You're a manipulator. You knew I needed a job, and you used that to get me here!"

The pickup truck was parked in front of the cabins. Nona fumed at the way in which Simon had wiggled his way into their lives. Nothing was as it seemed.

"I knew you needed money after I talked to your former boss, who, by the way, is a friend of mine. Quite frankly, it was pure luck that I'd leased this camp. I thought it would be the best place for you and Maggie right now. Believe me, you're better off here than in Little Rock. From here on out, I'll look out for you."

The anger that had been bubbling in Nona's breast began to boil at the calm way he described guiding her life. The color drained from her face and her heartbeat quickened. "You did all of this without even asking me what I wanted!"

"I didn't have the time to try and convince you! You may find this hard to believe, but because of what Harold has done, you may have some very unpleasant people looking for you."

"I don't need your help. I've been taking care of myself and Maggie for a long time."

"Don't be stubborn about this. You can't handle this by yourself."

Nona lifted her chin and glared at him. She hated to admit that he might be right. If she had only herself to consider she could disappear someplace, but it would be hard to hide with a lively fourteen-year-old.

"I don't know if I should trust you. You haven't been truthful up to now."

"If we were in Little Rock, I could give you some references, but we're not in Little Rock, so you're just going to have to trust me. Besides, I'm not that bad," he said, straightening himself up in his seat and pushing back his unruly hair. "Don't I look like the hero type?"

"Absolutely not. If you like, I'll list the reasons. I think you're sneaky, manipulative, a charmer of old women and young girls, and you're even trying to win our dog away from us."

"Am I really that bad? I was just trying to put my best foot forward."

"You came here and lied. You didn't tell us who you really were," she added as if he hadn't spoken.

"Would it have made any difference?"

"Probably not." Nona fanned her face with an old newspaper that was lying on the seat. It did little to help in the sweltering heat of the truck's cab. "We'd better go inside."

Slowly, Simon moved his hand across the seat until

his fingers made contact with Nona's. The touch was tentative at first, but became firm as he swallowed her small hand in his. It surprised Nona that she did nothing to push him away. What was she feeling? She turned her head away and felt her cheeks flush hotly. Before she could say anything, something caught her eye in the distance.

"Look!" she shouted. "Maggie's in a boat on the lake! She doesn't have a life jacket! I told her not to go out there."

To her surprise, Simon flung open his door, jumped out, and started running toward the dock. Nona followed as quickly as she could, but Simon's powerful legs carried him ahead of her. Out on the lake, a small motorboat with two men in it had swung around and was headed toward the rowboat. Fear gripped her and she ran even faster.

Simon's boots pounded across the dock. He grabbed the rope that was tied to the rowboat and started pulling. "Maggie!" he shouted.

The voice of one of the men in the motorboat, a tall fellow with sandy-blond hair and a dirty white shirt, carried across the water to Nona. "Where ya goin', pretty girl? We just wanna talk to you."

"Get away from me!" Maggie yelled.

"Aw, come on, honey. Pretty girls shouldn't be by themselves."

"I said get away!" Maggie picked up the extra oar that was lying in the boat. She held it in both of her hands, but it was too big for her to manipulate. The man grabbed on to the side of the rowboat. He pulled it close, and it looked as if he was going to jump in.

"Get away from her!" Nona yelled.

Simon continued to pull on the rope, bringing the boat closer to the dock, but he could make little progress with the man hanging on to it.

"Maggie!" Nona shouted as she reached the dock and stopped next to Simon. Her breath was jagged after her run, but she began to pull off her shoes and prepared to dive into the water.

"Come on, sweet thing," the man continued. "We'll take you for a ride in our boat."

"Let go!" With all of the strength that she could muster, Maggie swung the oar at the man. The wood struck his hand as it held on to the boat.

"Ouch!" he yelled and fell back into his own boat, which rocked in the water. "You little bitch! You broke my hand!"

"I'll break your head if you don't get away from me, you psycho!" Maggie shouted.

With the rowboat now free of the man's grip, Simon made more progress and the boat slid through the water toward the dock. His muscles strained and his face was tight from the effort. The man piloting the motorboat saw that their prey was too far away to catch and swung the boat around and headed back out into the lake.

"Bitch!" the young man shouted over the growing distance.

When the rowboat was close enough, Simon reached a hand down to Maggie. "Get out of the boat," he said gruffly and then pulled her up onto the dock.

Nona, her face white with fright, grabbed the young girl and pulled her close in a tight hug. "I told you not to go out in a boat!"

"I was just sunbathing. The boat was tied to the dock, and Mr. Story thought it would be all right," Maggie explained.

Now, out in the middle of the lake, the two men in the motorboat had cut the engine and were sitting in the water watching them. One made a clumsy attempt to put a fishing line in the water, but Simon knew that they weren't fishermen. Nona scrutinized the men. Even though he was wearing a cap, she was sure that one of them was the man that she had bumped into at the store.

"Where's Russ?" Simon asked Maggie.

"I don't know," she answered nervously. The shock of what had happened had begun to wear off, leaving a frightened fourteen-year-old girl behind. "He was here a little bit ago. Oh, wait! Here he comes."

They turned to see the handyman coming down the path from the outhouse, pulling his old cap down over his head.

"Go to your cabin," Simon said sharply. "Both of you." He then walked over to meet Mr. Story. "Why did you let Maggie go out in the boat?" he said when he reached him. "I told you she wasn't to be on the lake when I wasn't here."

"I told her she could sit in the boat while I went to the can. To tell you the truth, Mr. Wright, I have loose bowels," the older man added in a low voice. "She's a good kid and usually does what I tell her. I told her to stay by the dock. I didn't think she'd go out onto the lake."

Simon turned and pointed out at the two men in the boat. "Do you know either of those men?"

"They ain't been around here before," he said as he peered out onto the lake. "I'd remember that shiny new boat and them pricey clothes. None of the regulars have boats like that."

"If you see them around here again, let me know."

"Will do, Boss."

Nona and Maggie left the dock and headed across the grass for their cabin. Nona couldn't believe that her sister had deliberately disobeyed her, but yelling at her now would only make it worse. Before they'd reached their cabin, Simon caught up with them and put his hand on Maggie's shoulder.

"Next time you want to go out in the boat, squirt, wait for me."

"You're too busy."

"I'll take time," he said, looking over his shoulder and out over the lake. The two men hadn't moved. "When do you want to go? Who knows . . . maybe we can talk Nona into joining us."

"I don't think so."

Nona walked on ahead of the others. Mabel stood on the small stoop drying a bowl with a towel. She smiled warmly at Nona, unaware of the drama at the dock.

"Did you get my vanilla? I've been waiting to make custard."

"It's in the truck."

"I'll get it," Simon said as he and Maggie reached them.

The two sisters trudged up the steps to the porch, Nona

leading the way for an unhappy Maggie. Her face was set in deep, stubborn lines. "Come on, Nona. I'm not a kid. I know what I can do."

"You are a kid."

"I'm fourteen, almost fifteen. A lot of girls go steady at my age."

"Do you have someone in mind?" Nona asked as she put her purse in the bureau drawer. How many times had they had this argument?

"No, I don't," Maggie answered tartly.

"I thought maybe you had your eye on Simon."

"He's way too old for me," the younger girl countered. "He'd be better for you. Besides, I think that new handyman is a dream. He's got the most heavenly blue eyes."

"He'll be too old for you, too, unless he's a high school boy."

"I guess that only leaves old Mr. Story. He doesn't think I'm a scatterbrain."

"I don't care what Mr. Story thinks. You are not to go out in that boat alone. Do you hear me?"

"Can't you stop yelling at me?" Maggie groaned, throwing her thin arms up into the air.

"I am not yelling," Nona disagreed sharply.

There was so much that she wanted to tell both Maggie and Mabel, but she didn't want to worry them. Even before the ordeal at the dock, she'd decided not to tell her little sister what she had learned about Harold and about the package she had received. It would only confuse and upset her.

Oh, Lord. I may be jumping the gun. Harold might

have sent me papers about Daddy's estate. But why would he tell me not to open the package?

Besides, she still hadn't sorted out all that Simon had told her. She couldn't understand why he would take such an interest in them. It surely couldn't be because her half brother was his cousin. As soon as she had a chance, she would open the package and talk to Mabel. Her old friend had an extra dose of common sense. Even though she'd been taken in by Simon's sweet talk, she'd listen with an open mind.

As she went to the sink to clean her hands, Nona admitted to herself that Simon was quite persuasive. And it was reassuring to have someone looking out for them, even if the man doing it was an arrogant son of a gun. It had been a long time since she'd had a shoulder to lean on. The pressure of taking care of her little family was a heavy load.

At the stove, Mabel lifted the lid on a pot and stirred the contents with a long-handled spoon. "While you were gone, I had a nice long visit with Mrs. Leasure. She's a pitiful little thing. I know she's worried about her husband."

"Have they been married long?" Nona asked.

"Several years, she said."

"Where are they from?"

"Someplace up in Missouri."

"What is she going to do if he doesn't come back? Does she have any relatives who would help?"

"She didn't mention any."

The screen door slammed with a bang, and heavy boot heels pounded across the floor. Simon appeared in the doorway, a large sack of flour thrown over one shoulder and a sack of sugar over the other.

"We're going to have to start buying more," he said to Mabel.

"What are you planning to do, Simon? Feed an army?"

"Just me and the new handyman for now." He grinned. "Oh, and I've hired a carpenter to help with the remodeling of the cabins. He and his wife can stay in cabin number eight."

"Do you expect us to feed them, too?" Nona asked.

"No, I don't."

"That's good. This place is starting to resemble Grand Central Station."

"I don't hear Mabel complaining." Simon winked and headed for the door. "Only you."

"Mabel never complains," Nona replied, ignoring his wink.

When Simon returned, he placed a large cardboard box in the center of the table and dug around inside. Finally, he pulled out a paper sack and handed it to Maggie.

"Here's your magazine, squirt."

"Awesome! Thank you!" Maggie exclaimed as she danced around the table and hugged Simon's arm. She glanced at her sister but didn't offer any thanks her way. "Did you get the pop, too?"

"There's two cases out in the truck."

"Cool!" Maggie shouted as she headed for the door and bounded down the steps to the truck. Sam Houston awakened from an afternoon nap on the porch and followed her.

"Did you tell her?" Simon asked.

"There hasn't been a chance," Nona said, slightly irritated at his tone. "Besides, I'm not telling her until I have to. I don't want her upset any more than she is."

"What in the world are you two talking about?" Mabel asked as she emptied the cardboard box of its canned peaches. "Don't tell me the two of you are planning on getting married and are afraid to tell Maggie?"

"Have you lost your mind?" The words exploded out of Nona's mouth.

"Now, honey." Simon winked. "We can tell Mabel."

"He's just teasing. Don't believe a thing he says."

"She's going to be stubborn about this." Simon continued to tease. He went over and put his hand on Mabel's shoulder. The two of them were beaming from ear to ear. For a brief moment, Nona felt a stab of disappointment. Her dearest friend was siding with this glib-tongued rogue who'd insinuated himself into their lives. She'd had Mabel's loyalty and friendship for more than ten years. Now, in just a few days, she seemed to have become Simon's bosom companion.

After everything had been put in its place, Simon grabbed Nona by the arm and moved her toward the door. "Now that all this is done, I thought you might like to meet your new handyman."

"All right."

Nona followed Simon out the door and across the yard to where a man was pulling new lumber from his truck and stacking it beside one of the cabins. He stopped, took off his work gloves, and wiped his sweaty brow with the back of his hand. When he saw them approaching, his eyes were on Nona.

"This is Jack Grant," Simon said as he introduced them. "Jack, this is Miss Conrad, the camp manager. She'll be telling you what she needs done."

"Hello again," Nona said, holding out her hand. When Jack took it, it disappeared into his large, rough paw. The man was certainly used to hard work.

"Howdy, ma'am." He smiled down at her. "Good to see you again. Nice to know you got back all right with your groceries."

"Did I thank you for your help that day? If not, I should have." Nona glanced up at Simon and saw a frown spreading across his face. As she held Jack Grant's grip, one thought filled her with happiness.

There was one thing he didn't know, and she'd be damned if she was going to explain how she knew the tall, handsome handyman.

Chapter 7

ACROSS THE LAKE, two men entered a dilapidated cabin in a run-down camp. One man sat on a cot, the other on a chair at the rickety table. Ten years earlier, the camp had been a summer retreat for members of a Methodist church group. Now eight cabins had rotted floors and cracked roofs. Only two of them were still usable.

"Damn, but we were lucky to find this place where we can see Tall Pine Camp." The young, sandy-haired man who had attempted to get in the boat with Maggie put a pair of binoculars to his eyes and looked out over the water. "Looks like the women are in the cabin while Wright talks to the old man."

Frank, the bald man with the thick black mustache, leaned back against the wall and rested his elbow on a decrepit table. "Damned bad luck Wright showed up when he did. We could've had that gal, got our information outta her, and been on our way by now."

"Aww hell! She's just a kid. She probably didn't know

nothin' anyway. Even if she did, she'd be too scared to tell us."

The older man laughed heartily and slapped himself on the knee. "If I didn't know better, I'd say you had a soft spot for the kid. Have you already forgotten she tried to break your hand with that oar?"

"Can't blame her for tryin' to protect herself."

As the two men watched the activity at the camp, the sun slowly lowered itself in the west. Scarlet streaks in the lazy clouds spread across the glassy surface of the lake, reflecting the heavens in the water. Still, the two men watched. "They've just got to know where Harold is," the older man mused. "Ain't he the kid's guardian or somethin'?"

"Nope. It's the older sister. If we can get the information we want, we won't have to kill her."

"Don't go soft on me now, Webb. It didn't bother you to shoot that bank guard in Chicago."

"Hell, no," Webb swore. "But that business was different. That fella was gonna shoot me, and I was just protectin' myself. This is just a kid. I ain't gonna kill no kid."

"Maybe it won't come to that." Frank Rice stood up and stretched. A petty crook out of Chicago, he was rumored to be part of the Chicago mafia; Frank did little to dispel the rumors. His whole life had been spent in the protection racket. Ruthless and violent when he needed to be, Rice had lost his conscience long ago.

"Hope not."

"At least we know what we're up against. The way I see it, it's Wright and the feds. From what I heard about

Wright, he works alone and is like a bulldog after a bone. Don't even know why the bastard does it. His granddad's loaded. If I had that money, it'd be nothin' but easy street."

"Maybe the old fart won't give him none." Webb picked up the folded Little Rock paper and looked at the story about Harold Conrad's disappearance with the money and jewelry. He'd read the article a dozen times and could swear he knew it by heart. Who would have thought it would come to this? When an associate who had jewelry to fence had contacted Webb, he'd thought it would be just another job. Then Harold Conrad didn't show up at the arranged meeting place, and everything changed.

Now that he was involved, the one thing that Webb regretted was that he'd been paired with Frank Rice. The man had the reputation of being ruthless. He feared that Frank would have no reservations about killing one of the girls in order to make the other one tell him what he wanted to know, and they'd be sought for murder.

Frank snatched a bottle of whiskey off the window ledge. He took a deep pull of the liquor and wiped his mouth with the back of his hand. "Ernie's gonna visit his wife tonight and find out what she knows. Seems like it's gettin' harder to hold him in line. He wants outta here."

"What about his wife?"

"What about her?" Frank growled.

"She's gonna have his kid, ain't she?"

"Yeah, but he ain't none too thrilled about it. She keeps naggin' at him to settle down and get a regular job. Problem is, ain't nothin' regular about Ernie."

"I can't see him settlin' down, but it ain't nobody's business but his. He shoulda thought about all that before he knocked her up."

"His problems don't have anything to do with what we have to do here. All he's got to do is his job. He better not skip out now. We need all the information we can get from over there. His old lady's talkin' to those women. We've gotta know what's bein' said."

"What do you make of that fella unloadin' lumber at the camp? Coulda been a deliveryman."

"We'll know after Ernie visits his wife."

"I suppose you're right," Webb said as he got up out of his chair and snatched his hat off the table. "Let's go to town. Ain't much we can do till Ernie gets back. Besides, I want a cold glass of beer."

"That shitty beer they serve tastes like horse piss. I want a bottle of booze."

"Might as well eat, too," Webb said as he headed for the door. "You can't cook for shit."

Simon and Jack sat on one side of the table while Nona and Maggie sat across from them. Mabel had outdone herself. She had prepared fried pork chops, fresh green beans, and new potatoes. As a pan of golden-brown corn bread was placed on the table, Simon let out a grunt of appreciation.

"You wouldn't be interested in getting married, would you, Mabel?"

"If you were twenty years older, I might give it a thought," the older woman answered with a grin and a wink. "As you are, I think you're a little young. I don't want another kid to raise."

"I'd be a lot easier than the two you have." Simon looked at Nona just as she rolled her eyes toward the ceiling.

"It's getting pretty thick in here," she said.

They enjoyed the meal too much to talk. The clinking of silverware was the only sound that could be heard in the cabin. Nona, with a worried frown on her face, glanced at her sister. Maggie had been unusually quiet and had done little more than move her food around on her plate.

"Aren't you hungry, Maggie?"

"I wouldn't be hungry either," Mabel said, "if I'd drunk four bottles of pop."

"Mabel! Do you have to blab everything?" Maggie grinned to soften her words.

Jack gave Mabel a deep smile as he reached for the plate of corn bread. "I must say that I haven't had a meal this good in a month of Sundays."

"I told you she was a good cook," Simon said, then forked green beans into his mouth. "Once the word gets out, people will be flocking to the camp just for Mabel's cooking."

"Once word gets out?" Nona frowned. "Are you planning on advertising?"

"Sure. We can be ready for deer season."

"Have you agreed to this, Mabel?"

"Now, now, you two. All of this talk is putting me on the spot," Mabel said uneasily. "I'm not yet sure what I'd like to do. I know I'd like to have the job, but I won't leave you and Maggie. You're my family."

"I know, Nona," Maggie said excitedly. "You could marry Simon and we could all stay here."

A flush of embarrassment spread across Nona's face. It was a feeling that she was, unfortunately, getting used to. "Maggie, you say the darnedest things. I don't have the slightest interest in marrying him."

"That's not very good for my ego." Simon frowned.

"You've got plenty of ego to spare."

"Who's up for custard?" Mabel asked as she got up from the table. All that Nona could do was stare at Simon, the grin on his face nearly sending her temper through the roof.

"She likes me," he said to Jack.

"I can tell." The man chuckled. "You seem to have a way with women."

"I don't know why Nona doesn't like him. I did right away." Maggie glanced at her sister's set face and knew that she was irritated. Heck, she'd been angry from the moment Simon arrived! "I'm just glad he was there on the dock today. I wasn't afraid at first, but when that fella grabbed hold of the boat, I got scared quick!"

"You did real good, squirt." Simon chuckled. "You swung that oar like you were going to hit a home run!"

"I don't even care if I broke his fingers. I wish I'd hit him upside the head!"

"Next time, kiddo."

"There won't be a next time," Nona said firmly. Frankly, what had happened on the dock didn't strike her as a laughing matter. She'd been nearly scared out of her wits. "Who were those guys? Did Russ know them?"

"No. He'd never seen them before."

"Let's hope we never see them again!"

Mabel brought back the custard and they all took a large helping, even Maggie, her sweet tooth not completely satisfied. Each bite was a treasure, and hearty congratulations were given to the cook.

"Are you from around here, Jack?" Nona asked after the table was cleared.

"Not exactly," he said, his voice a soft, smooth drawl. "My brother and I have a cattle ranch over in Oklahoma. But I've been here quite a few times hunting and fishing."

"If you have a ranch, why are you doing handyman work?"

"Well, that's a tricky one," he said as he rubbed his fingers across his stubbly chin. "See, I kept telling Simon to buy this camp, but he made me promise to help him with the repairs. When he finally bought it, I was stuck."

"So you already knew Simon when you helped me in town the other day?"

"Yes, ma'am. But I wasn't sure you were the same Miss Conrad who managed this place, although I should have guessed as much. Simon told me the manager was a beautiful red-haired lady. I sure didn't see anyone in Home with hair redder than yours."

"I suppose I should say thanks."

"I certainly meant it as a compliment."

"Your hair is beautiful," Simon added. His gaze was intense.

"I'm thinking of dyeing it black." Nona frowned.

"Now, why would you do something like that?" Simon frowned. "I like it just as it is."

"This hair is on my head, not yours. I'll do as I please."

"You're just being stubborn."

"That's just how she is," Maggie said through a mouthful of custard.

"Don't talk with your mouth full," Nona scolded.

"She's cute when she's embarrassed, isn't she, Jack?" Simon teased.

Nona got up from the table and reached for a clean plate. Everything that came out of that man's mouth annoyed her! He truly seemed to get pleasure out of irritating her. Trying to put him out of her mind, she said, "Dish up some supper for Mrs. Leasure, Mabel, and I'll take it down to her."

"Not without me or Jack you won't," Simon interjected, his protective side exhibiting itself. "I don't want any of you women to go out of the house after dark. If you have to use the privy, all three of you go together."

"This isn't the military," Nona chided.

"He's only trying to protect us," Mabel argued as she handed Nona a plate of food. After filling a bowl with custard and putting it in a basket, she covered everything with a cloth. "I know she has milk."

Gathering up the basket, Nona headed for the door without a word. She heard the scrape of Simon's chair behind her. His arm grabbed hers and brought her to a stop before she could go down the steps. He never said a word, his eyes searching the area around the cabins. When he saw nothing, they started down the path to LeAnn's. He held her elbow close to his side in a tight grip. She tried to pull away, but he refused to allow it.

"I can go by myself," she insisted.

"I thought you would have realized it after what happened to Maggie today. You shouldn't be prowling around by yourself."

Her mind flashed back to the sight of the men in the boat reaching out for her sister. A sickening feeling filled the pit of her stomach and her heart beat with fear. What if something were to happen to Maggie? Would she be able to endure it? Would it be her fault for not telling Simon about the package?

Moving through the darkness in silence, they'd nearly reached LeAnn's house when Simon stopped abruptly.

"What is it?" Nona asked breathlessly. Her eyes looked about her, but she couldn't see anything in the inky-black night. Simon's warnings had alarmed her, and she wondered what lurked out there, waiting to strike. When she looked up at him, she was surprised to see him staring back at her unworriedly.

"How long have you been taking care of your sister?"

"Practically her whole life. Our mother died when she was only three years old. I was still in school, so Daddy hired a woman to take care of Maggie, but it didn't work out very well. When Daddy died, she came with me."

"Are you her guardian?"

"Yes. I'm the only one she has left in this world who cares about her. I've done all I can to give her what she needs, but . . ." The words trailed off as Nona looked away. Why was she telling him this?

"But what?" he prodded.

"Daddy thought that he had left enough money to take care of us, but somehow it all disappeared."

"Harold," Simon said, the word not a question but a statement.

Nona couldn't bring herself to contradict him. He was too close to the truth. Unfortunately, she'd had no proof that Harold had lost their inheritance, but she'd seen enough of her half brother's devious ways to know he was capable of stealing from his own family.

"You've had it pretty rough, haven't you?" Simon's hands reached down and gently pulled her chin up until her eyes were looking directly into his. Even in the dim light, she swore she could see a glimmer in his gaze. Surprise filled her. This was an all-together different side of Simon Wright. The sly grin and flip manner were gone. Instead, his brows were drawn together as if in deep concentration. He and Harold were as different as night and day. She tried to look away but found that she couldn't.

"Why are we standing here?" she managed to ask.

"I don't rightfully know. I guess I just had the urge to look at your face. Once we get back to your place, you'll make yourself scarce. I wanted to be alone with you for a little while."

His quiet sincerity caught her unaware and she felt her face flush. As she stood there looking up at him, she could say nothing, her breath caught tightly in her chest.

"What's the matter?" His words floated closely over her face.

Like a spell being broken, words tumbled out of her mouth. "Nothing and everything. It's just that I don't understand all of this. I thought you were sorry you had hired me and that the sooner you got rid of me, the better you would like it."

"Is that what you think?"

"Well . . . ," she began, but he hushed her by placing a finger against her lips. Without understanding why, she didn't try to get away from him. For a moment, she wondered if, in that light touch, he could hear the pounding of her heart.

"What would you say if I told you I want very much to kiss you?"

"I'd say you were taking advantage of the situation."

A warm smile spread slowly across his face. "After some of the situations we've been in together, I'd say that it's about time I did."

He took the basket of food from her hand and set it on the ground.

Chapter 8

NONA FELT HER BREATH CATCH in her throat and her insides go warm with pleasure as she looked into Simon's quiet face. He leaned slowly toward her and she didn't back away. His lips settled gently on her mouth with sweet provocation. A lovely feeling unfolded in her midsection and traveled slowly throughout her body. When the kiss ended, Nona was disappointed; she wanted it to go on and on.

"I've wanted to do that for a long time," Simon's voice whispered from near her forehead. Nona leaned back and his green eyes caught and held her confused blue ones.

"You've only known me a week," she said breathlessly.

"One week, one year, ten years. What difference does it make?" He laughed softly. "I like kissing you as much as I thought I would. You like it, too, but you're too stubborn to admit it."

"Okay . . ."

"Okay, what?"

"So I like to be kissed once in a while, no big deal." She tried to sound nonchalant, but her voice was shakier than she would have liked.

"I'll keep that in mind."

Bending down, Simon picked up the basket and took Nona's elbow in his hand, but, before he could take a step, a dog growled. Cochise, Simon's black Labrador retriever, was looking off into the darkness between LeAnn's cabin and the one next to it. The dog's hair was standing up on his back as the guttural sound came from his throat.

"What is it, boy?" Simon set the basket down and put his hand on the dog's head. When the dog continued to growl, Simon stared into the darkness but could see nothing; the thin crescent moon offered little light. "Did you see a coon?" He spoke quietly to the animal. The dog fell silent and began to wag his tail.

"Was someone back there?" Nona asked.

"It could have been Russ."

"Why would he be back there?"

"Good question. Maybe it was Sam Houston."

"Maggie wouldn't have let him out."

"Whatever it was, it's gone now." As Cochise moved off into the tree line, Simon urged Nona toward the steps of LeAnn's cabin and up onto the stoop. He rapped on the door.

All was quiet from inside, the only noise coming from the cicadas singing in the woods. Nona had never been at the cabin when LeAnn didn't have the radio on. "Knock again."

Simon thumped hard on the door with his fist.

"Who is it?" a small voice called from inside the door.

"It's me, LeAnn," Nona called cheerfully. "Mabel sent you some supper."

The door opened a crack. A woman's face appeared, and then the door opened a little wider. LeAnn Leasure was a small woman, except for her rounded belly. Wheat-colored hair was pulled back tightly from a worried face. Her clothes were shabby, but clean. "I'm a little scared at night," she said meekly.

"Sorry if we frightened you." Simon held out the basket.

"Are you all right, LeAnn?" Nona asked when she saw the worried look on the woman's face.

"I'm fine," LeAnn answered as she took the basket and began to close the door. "Please give Mabel my thanks." Simon and Nona stood still on the stoop as they heard the click of the door's lock. They both wondered the same thing: Why hadn't she asked them in? LeAnn usually welcomed someone to talk to.

"Who did she think would be knocking on her door this time of the night?"

"I was wondering that myself." Simon scratched his chin. With his arm around Nona, they walked away from the cabin.

Nona looked back and saw that the light in the kitchen had been turned off. Why was that? Was she going to eat in the dark? Feeling uneasy, she allowed Simon to lead her back toward her cabin. "Do you think she's all right?" Nona's voice was full of concern. "She didn't act like her usual self."

"She said she's fine, honey." Simon's brows were

pulled together in a frown. Something wasn't quite right there.

They walked for a while in companionable silence, the night sky full of thousands of twinkling stars. A slight breeze played with the ends of Nona's hair.

"I want to talk to you about what happened today," Simon said as they approached her cabin, "but not out here in the open. Let's sit in the truck." He opened the door and helped her up into the passenger side. A warning bell rang in Nona's head.

After Simon slid behind the wheel, Nona warned him that if he expected her to neck with him, he was sorely mistaken.

"Why not?" He chuckled. "I've earned it."

"Are you never serious?"

"I'm serious about this," he said quietly, his joking demeanor gone without a trace. "The men in that boat would have taken Maggie and tried to get information about Harold from her."

"Are you sure?"

"Nothing in this world is for sure, but I'd be willing to bet they're looking for your half brother."

A feeling of disgust welled inside Nona. Harold had been nothing but trouble to her and Maggie. That her sister would be in danger because of something that Harold had done was sickening. "Maggie doesn't know anything about Harold. She hardly knows him."

"They don't know that."

"Maybe it would be best if Maggie and I went back to Little Rock."

"I don't think that's a good idea. You and Maggie

would be like two babes in the woods. You wouldn't have anyone there to look out for you. When those men caught up to you, and they would, you'd be at their mercy."

"The police would give us protection."

"Don't count on it. You're better off right here with me. These guys mean business. Harold probably ran out on a deal, and the mob wants more than the money and jewelry; they want revenge. They wouldn't hesitate to kill one of you to force the other to tell them what they wanted to know."

"You're just as much of a stranger to me as they are." Nona frowned.

"You may think so. But you're no stranger to me." At the intensity of his gaze, color tinged Nona's cheeks, but she returned his gaze steadily.

"What do you mean by that?"

"Just what I said, we're not strangers. I often saw you at the apartment building. I missed seeing you when you went to work at the plant." He grinned at the surprised look on her face. "I knew when you cut your hair short two years ago, just before Christmas, and I knew when Maggie was in the hospital with a kidney infection."

"This is unbelievable."

"Yeah, I know. I wanted to get acquainted with you then, but I'm here now."

"You couldn't stand against a hit man if he came after us."

"I wouldn't be alone. Jack Grant is a good man."

"Does he know about this?"

"Of course. I wouldn't have brought him out here without telling him."

"I still think Maggie and I should leave." *Should I tell him about the package? He may be just giving me a line.*

Simon threw an arm around her and pulled her close. "You're not going, so get that thought out of your pretty head. You're going to stay right here with me. When I first saw you at the apartment building, I found excuses to keep going back so I could see you again and again." He hugged her tightly to him. "You're right where I want you."

"And I don't have anything to say about it?"

"Not about this, you don't." He bent his head and kissed her softly on the lips. He rose back up and looked into her face, then gave her another quick kiss on the nose and said, "I mean it."

LeAnn closed the door, threw the bolt, and stood with her back to it. The room was poorly lit, but her eyes easily found her husband, Ernie, where he stood in the corner of the room.

Nearly as thin as his wife, Ernie Leasure was the kind of man who wouldn't draw a second glance, except for one thing. He had thinning brown hair and an ordinary face, but a pink scar crossed his left cheek. His shoulders sagged as he pointed a finger toward the door.

"What did they want?" he hissed.

"They brought me something for supper," LeAnn answered, her eyes never leaving the floor. She'd hoped that he would have been happy to see her after being away so long, but he'd done nothing but complain and accuse her of an assortment of things since he'd arrived.

"Well, what do you know?" Ernie chuckled. "Ya got in so good with them, they're feeding you now."

"They're just being kind to me, Ernie."

"They come here often?"

"Not really."

"Do you go there?"

"Sometimes I go down there to see if I have any mail or to ask them to get me something from the store when they go. They're nice people."

"Did they tell you how long they were gonna be here?" Ernie continued.

"Mabel was talking about the start of school the other day. Maybe that's it."

"When's that?"

"I don't know." LeAnn frowned. "But Maggie said something about them being here until fishing season was over. Honestly, I have no idea how long they'll stay."

"Hell. If they're stayin' until the end of the season, they could be here all year long!" Ernie stalked over to one of the kitchen cabinets and pulled out a whiskey bottle. He took a long drink as LeAnn, holding her protruding stomach, eased down into a chair.

"When are we leaving here, Ernie?" she asked hopefully.

"When I say so," he answered curtly. "Have you talked to the women about their brother like I told you to?"

"I mentioned it to Maggie, and she acted as if she didn't have a brother."

"Maybe she's been told to keep her mouth shut. That

makes me think they know something. I bet the older sister knows someone is after him."

"Why do you want to know where he is, Ernie?"

"That's none of your damn business!" he snapped. "You just do as you're told, then we can leave."

It had been a long time since Ernie had struck her, but LeAnn feared that he was now angry enough to do it. She frowned at the whiskey bottle; he was always worse when he'd been drinking. Finally, after she thought he might have calmed down, she dared to ask, "Where will we go from here?"

"I haven't decided yet. If you get the information I need, we'll have money to go where we want. All you need to do is find out if they're in touch with their brother. Just make up some kind of story about how you knew him once, or how a girlfriend of yours dated him. Hell, tell them you used to work in the same bank he did."

"Ernie, for God's sake!" LeAnn complained. "One look at me, and they'd know I've never worked in a bank in my life. They'd know I was lying!"

"Dammit! Just make somethin' up! Surely you're as smart as that kid. Talk yourself up to her and find out what I need to know!" Ernie snatched his hat off the table and slammed it on his head. "I'll be back tomorrow night. You'd better have some news for me."

As quickly as she could, LeAnn hoisted herself out of the chair. "You didn't give me any money. I can't keep taking food from Nona and Mabel and not pay them back."

"Then ask 'em for a job. You can clean their cabin or the outhouse." A wicked sneer came over his face as he stared down at her. "That's about all you're good for now. When I found you, you didn't have a pot to piss in and weren't touchy about taking welfare. Why'd you have to go and get so stuck up?"

"When we came here, you didn't tell me that we'd have to stay for weeks. You said you were going to work with a road crew. If you had done that, we would have had enough money to get a little place and be ready for the baby when it gets here," she argued, showing some spirit.

"Don't get your ass over the line, LeAnn," Ernie snarled. "I've got enough on my mind without having to listen to you bitch every time I come here." He fished in his pocket and pulled out some crumpled bills. "Here's twenty dollars. It's all I've got to my name, but there'll be more. The sooner you find out where Harold Conrad is, the sooner we can leave."

Storm clouds crossed LeAnn's face as it dawned on her that she was married to a man who cared nothing for her at all. "Are you doing something illegal?" she asked.

"Now, why would you say that?"

"Because I know you, Ernie. If you could get your hands on some easy money, it wouldn't make one bit of difference to you if it was legal or not, as long as you didn't get caught."

"You can bet your skinny little ass that what I'm doin' ain't no business of yours. But you can be damn sure of one thing . . . I won't go back to the pen. I've had all of that hellhole I can take."

"When you came home, you promised me you would never get mixed up in something crooked again," LeAnn said as a tear trickled its way down her cheek. "You promised me!"

"Yes, I did," Ernie said calmly. He took a step toward her and quickly raised his hand. LeAnn turned away and braced herself for the blow she was sure would follow. Instead, her husband patted her head as if she were a child. "Find out where Harold Conrad is, and we can be out of here before you can say 'scat.' We'll have money, and you can afford to have that kid in the hospital. If you don't do what I tell you, you'll have it right here in this cabin in the middle of nowhere. It's your choice. I'll be back tomorrow night. Leave the back door unlocked. That damn dog almost gave me away tonight."

"All right, Ernie."

At the door, he turned and looked back at his pregnant wife. "What about that Wright fella, the one that was here tonight? Is he always pokin' around?"

"Sort of. He owns the place. Mabel says he's remodeling the cabins."

Ernie nodded and cracked the back door. "Gotta go. Look out and see if it's clear."

LeAnn waddled over to the window and peeked out the curtain. "It's clear." When she turned to look at her husband, he was going out the door and into the dark night without even a good-bye. LeAnn sat down at the table, rested her head on her folded arms, and cried.

After all this time, Ernie hadn't changed a bit. She'd believed his many promises, although her head had told her not to trust him ever again. He had disappointed her so many times, but when she'd become pregnant, there'd been no choice but to stay with him. She couldn't go back to her parents' farm. They had all they could do to feed the three kids still at home. She fell asleep at the table, the cicadas' song breaking the silence of the night.

Ernie slipped out of the camp and walked the quarter of a mile down the lakeshore to where he had left a rowboat. He dreaded going back and telling Frank and Webb that he didn't have any news for them. Webb was all right, but Frank could be a wild man when he was mad. He shouldn't have told them LeAnn could get the information they needed. He should have slipped over into Oklahoma and made himself scarce.

For the life of him, he couldn't understand why she had become so bitchy! She'd managed just fine while he'd been in the pen. Besides, there was something else he really couldn't understand. She hadn't gotten pregnant the year they'd lived together, even though he'd screwed her morning, noon, and night. As soon as he got out of jail, bang, she's knocked up. *Hell, I'm not ready to settle down with a wife and kid!* There were too many other things to do and see. As soon as he got the money from Frank, he was going to hightail it out of Arkansas to a big city and do all the things he'd only dreamed about.

The thin moon cast its reflection from the treetops onto the water. Ernie hugged the shore until he got halfway around the lake. He sure as hell didn't want to tangle with that Wright fellow. He'd been warned that he could be full of hellfire when he got riled up. Everything had changed when they'd discovered Wright was involved. He was going to be a problem.

But problems could be eliminated.

* * *

Frank had been walking back and forth in front of the cabin for the last half hour. A cigarette dangled from between his fingers, an inch of ash having burned since he'd last taken a drag. Periodically, he would stop and strain for a sound that could be Ernie's approach. Time and time again, there had been nothing. Webb sat silently on the steps. "Where the hell is he?" Frank snarled.

"Beats me." Webb shrugged. "Why'd you hire that guy in the first place?"

"Because he said his old lady could find out what we needed to know. The bitch has been there for weeks now. She's gotta know somethin'. If she don't, he ain't gettin' one damn dime!"

"Seems to me he ain't much more than a blowhard out to get some easy money."

"I don't give a good goddamn what he is, as long as he finds that sneaky Conrad bastard! Another day or two is all I plan to wait. I'll shoot Wright if I have to, grab that redhead, and beat the shit outta her until she tells us where that lyin', cheatin' son of a bitch is!"

Webb shifted uncomfortably on the wooden planks. This side of Frank Rice was the dangerous one, the one that could get the both of them killed. "We need to be careful," he soothed. "We don't wanna do anything that'll bring the FBI down on us."

"They ain't interested in what happens out here in the sticks."

"Don't believe it. We go messin' around with those women, it could be us they come down on."

"Ain't no one gonna pay attention to a dead, faceless woman in the lake."

The calm way in which Frank spoke unnerved Webb. Killing was something that he was all too familiar with; it was part of the job. But the way Frank talked about it was wrong. To him, it seemed like a pleasure. "You'd go that far?" he asked.

"Hell, yes, I would! Don't forget, the big boys are depending' on us, and they don't like to be let down."

"They didn't say anything about killin' anyone."

"If you're too squeamish, just let me handle it."

Frank went back to his pacing as Webb thought about what Frank might do to that young girl over at the camp. A chill shivered its way up his spine. He shook his head in an attempt to get it out.

"You suppose that damn fool's run out on us?" Frank asked.

"I doubt it."

"Yeah, you're probably right. He's too big of a coward. He knows I'd hunt him down and beat the shit out of him. If there's one thing he doesn't like, it's pain. He got a good taste of it in prison."

"I'm goin' to bed," Webb said as he stood up and stretched. "If he doesn't come back tonight, he'll be here in the mornin'. Maybe he decided to stay and plow the old lady."

"A man would have to be hard up to sleep with that pregnant cow." Frank sneered as he followed the younger man into the cabin. "I ain't waitin' for that mule's ass. All I'll get is eaten up by mosquitoes."

Webb sat down on his bunk and pulled off his boots. "He'll be back. He wants the money."

Frank's shoes dropped onto the floor with a clunk. "I'm goin' to Home tomorrow mornin' and make a call. Who knows? Maybe someone else found Conrad and collected the percentage the boss was payin'."

Webb blew out the candle, lay on his back, and pulled the sheet up to his chin. A mosquito whizzed by so he pulled the sheet over his face. He turned onto his side and shut his eyes. The last thing he heard was the cicadas' song.

Chapter 9

SIMON STEPPED OUT THE BACK of his cabin and looked out over the lake. The sun was just coming up over the treetops, and its early morning rays stained the low-hanging clouds a deep orange. The lake was calm and tranquil. Not a sound was to be heard except for the birds in the trees welcoming a new day. He walked down to the dock, looked out over the water, and then came back to the small frame house where Mabel was cooking breakfast. The smell of bacon and coffee reached him as he stepped up onto the porch. She came to the door with her fingers pressed to her lips.

"The girls are still asleep," she whispered.

"That's good. They had a rough day yesterday." Simon pulled the squeaky door open slowly and went into the house. Mabel motioned for him to sit down at the table and brought him a mug of coffee. "Are you sure you don't want to get married, Mabel?"

"I'll have to wait for you to grow up." She grinned before turning back to the stove and flipping the pancakes on the grill. She placed a stack of three on a plate and took them to the table, setting them down in front of Simon. "Help yourself," she said softly, indicating the butter and syrup. "Is Jack coming over for breakfast?"

Simon grinned a toothy smile. "I couldn't keep him away with a team of mules. I expect he'll be here any minute."

"He's a good-looking fellow," Mabel mused with a twinkle in her eye.

"Now, remember," Simon warned with a sly glance, "I asked you to marry me first."

Mabel chuckled as she went back to the grill and poured more batter onto the hot metal. She turned a couple of pancakes that were still cooking and readied another plate. Deep inside, she smiled. No matter what Simon Wright might say, joking or otherwise, she knew that he had far more than a casual interest in Nona. *Maybe someday he'll propose to her . . . and mean it!*

A step on the porch brought Mabel quickly to the door, where she caught sight of Jack raising his knuckles to the door frame. He looked just as handsome as the night before. She gestured for him to be quiet and to come in. "The girls are still sleeping," she said as she motioned him to the table. "Have a seat, and I'll bring you a stack of pancakes."

Jack placed his Stetson on the hat rack by the door and sat down.

"Are there any left for me?" Nona's voice came from the doorway on the other side of the room. Her hair was a curly mess that hung around her face. The T-shirt that hung from her shoulders was old and faded. Her shorts were frayed at the hem, the color dimmed from too many washings. She had made no attempt to make herself presentable.

"You didn't need to get up," Mabel said as she brought a plate to Jack.

"I've slept enough. Besides, Maggie and I want to go to that little cove and go swimming this morning."

Simon's fork rattled against his plate. "I don't think so," he said as his eyes swept over her. "Not unless you want me or Jack to go with you."

"We can go by ourselves. Sorry to disappoint you."

"Can't say that disappointment is the right word for it." Jack grinned. "I'd say it's downright heartbreaking."

Mabel chuckled. "You're just as big a flirt as Simon!"

"But not as noisy and mouthy," Nona pointed out as she seated herself at the table, helped herself to the pancakes, and reached for the butter.

"Thanks a lot!" Simon groused.

"I've got more pancakes on the grill." Mabel had seen the muscle tighten in Simon's jaw when Nona spoke, and she knew he was gritting his teeth. She wanted to defuse an argument between the two if possible and was surprised that Simon hadn't retorted. Instead, he turned to Jack.

"Should have a pretty full day ahead of us. The electrician is coming out to wire the new building. The delivery truck should arrive with the paneling and flooring. Oh, and the plumber will be here tomorrow."

"What kind of a carpenter is this fella you hired?"

"His name's John Hogan. I had a visit with him last night. He's been working on a construction project down in Little Rock. He gave me the names of several people for references. His tools looked good. Old, but well taken care of. We'll know within a few hours if he knows his business. If not, we're not out anything."

"'Cept the time it'll take to find a replacement," Jack pointed out.

"I suppose so." Simon looked across the table at Nona. "When they arrive, you might want to go over and get acquainted with his wife. See if they need anything to help them get settled."

"Why? I'm not staying here."

Jack's fork paused in front of his mouth. "Where are you going?" he asked.

Nona's eyes passed over Simon before turning to settle on Jack. "I'm not sure just yet. I need to find another job and get Maggie enrolled in school before the September term begins."

All was silent in the kitchen as the four of them digested Nona's words. Nona's mind was in turmoil. While kissing Simon had been sweet with possibilities, the fact that men were looking for Harold scared her. That they would hurt her or Maggie was terrifying. Simon had sworn he could protect them, but *could he*? She couldn't be sure he was genuinely concerned with her and Maggie's welfare. If he was linked to the mob, he would say anything to make sure she stayed with him. It was too great a risk to take. The men in the boat had already made an attempt to get Maggie once; she couldn't wait around for them to do it again.

Nona got up from the table and carried her plate to the sink. "I think I'll go out and throw a few sticks for Sam

Houston." No one said a word as she walked out the back door.

She'd only gone a few yards, the early morning sun working to burn off the mist that hung over the lake, when she felt a hand grasp her elbow tightly. She knew who it was before she even turned.

"You're trying my patience." Simon glared angrily.

"And you're giving me a headache. Guess that makes us even."

"Not quite," he said as the familiar mischievous grin spread across his face.

Looking at his face, she swallowed the swearword that came to her lips. From around the corner of the cabin, Sam Houston trotted toward them with a large stick in his mouth. The dog stopped and Nona reached down to pat his head. She took hold of one end of the stick, but he refused to let go, then suddenly changed his mind and dropped it. Nona snatched it off the ground and tossed it toward the lake. The dog ran after it, his tail wagging furiously.

"There's one male that'll do what you say." Simon chuckled.

"That's because he's a good boy."

Sam Houston snatched up the stick and ran back to them. Much to Nona's chagrin, he dropped the stick at Simon's feet instead of hers. Simon winked at her as he picked it up and tossed it so hard that it carried out into the water. The dog dashed off after it but pulled up short after going just a few feet into the lake. He barked excitedly, his eyes locked on something in front of him.

"Sam Houston! Come!" Nona called.

The dog ignored her and kept barking at the water. Simon moved toward the shoreline and Nona followed.

"Wait, Nona," Simon said forcefully.

"What? Why?"

"Stay right where you are. Something's out there."

Nona looked past Simon and in the direction that Sam Houston was staring, but because of the mist she couldn't see anything. The dog continued to bark. "What are you talking about? I don't see anything."

"Stay right here! I mean it, Nona. Wait here!" Simon walked down to the water, pulled off his boots, and waded out to where Sam Houston stood. The dog was still barking. As he neared the animal, Simon began to make out an object floating in the water.

"What is it?" Nona called.

"Oh, my God!" The words shot out of Simon before he could check himself. There, floating facedown in the blue water, was the body of a man, judging from the clothes. The first thought that flashed through his mind was how he was going to get the body to shore without Nona seeing it. He composed himself quickly, grabbed hold of the man's belt, and turned to shout at Nona. "Go to the house and tell Jack to come here!"

"But what . . . ?"

"Don't stand there! Move!"

Mumbling under her breath, Nona walked back up the path to the cabin and stomped up onto the porch. Banging the door open, she stalked into the room. Jack was still sitting at the table talking to Mabel.

"Simon wants you down at the lakeshore, but I don't know why," she huffed to Jack.

"All right." Jack drained his coffee cup, put on his hat, and tipped the brim to Mabel, who beamed back up at him.

"All of a sudden he's in a bad mood, so you better hurry," Nona said.

"Okay, I'm gone. Thank you for the breakfast, Mrs. Rogers. It was delicious."

"You're very welcome, Jack. But call me Mabel."

Nona followed Jack out onto the porch and they both peered down toward the lake. Sam Houston was still barking as he ran along the shoreline. They could see Simon pulling something from the water.

"I can't tell from here what it is," Jack said.

They were halfway down the path to the lake when Simon shouted at her.

"Stay back, Nona! Don't come down here!"

Nona slowed as Jack hurried on to help Simon, but she never stopped. Apprehensive but curious, she approached the two men, who were peering at what seemed to be a water-soaked bundle of clothes. When she was near enough to glimpse the white face, she stopped.

Simon looked up at her, frowned, and said curtly, "Well, if you've got to see, come on."

Taking another step, Nona looked down at the man Simon had pulled out of the water. It was the most grue-some sight she had ever seen. His head and face had been bashed in. His eyes were gouged out. It looked like he'd been beaten to death. Her hand flew to her mouth, and she squelched the sudden urge to throw up.

"Who is he?" she asked breathlessly.

"I don't know," Simon said as he looked up and wiped

his brow with the back of his hand. "Here comes Russ. Maybe he'll know."

"What ya got there?" the fisherman asked as he approached. He stopped dead in his tracks, and when he saw the face of the dead man, his jaw dropped. "Oh, my Lord! It's that Leasure fella! He's the one who left his wife here. What happened? Did he fall out of a boat?"

"No," Simon hissed sharply. "Someone beat him to death."

"You sure?" Russ asked.

Simon grabbed the dead man's head and turned it so that Russ could see the back. "Look at this. Someone worked him over with a club before they threw him in the water."

"Jesus Christ!" the older man murmured.

Nona turned quickly from the body and put one hand to her stomach. The last thing that she wanted was to be sick in front of Simon, so she purposefully walked back to the cabin. Mabel stood on the porch.

"It's a man's body," Nona explained. "Mr. Story thinks it's LeAnn's husband."

A look of shock spread across Mabel's face. "Oh, no! Poor LeAnn! She's been waiting for him to come back. Is Russ certain it's Mr. Leasure?"

"He would have been here when they checked in. He says it's him." A sense of sadness for LeAnn's loss filled Nona. The woman had enough to worry about with her pregnancy. This could be too much for her. "How in the world are we going to tell LeAnn?"

"I'll do it," Mabel answered firmly. "But let's wait until they're sure."

Nona looked over her shoulder at the window to Maggie's room. The curtain was still pulled tight, but the young girl was certain to wake up soon with all the commotion. If she were to look out the window, she might see the dead body. The thought chilled Nona, but before she could move, Simon came quickly up the path, his face grave.

"Russ says it's Mrs. Leasure's husband," he said when he reached them. "There's no identification on him, but he swears it's the same man that was with LeAnn when they arrived. I suppose I should go over and tell her the bad news. Would one of you like to go with me?"

"I'll go," Mabel answered. "And it would be best if I went alone."

"You're a treasure," Simon said thankfully.

"I hate to have to tell the poor little thing, but it should come from someone she knows. Even though I didn't like the fact that he'd left her alone, he was all she had. I don't know what she'll do now."

"She can stay here until she decides what to do," Simon said solemnly. "Tell her I'll be by later."

"I will," Mabel answered and started down the road toward LeAnn's cabin.

For a moment, Nona stood looking at Simon, seeing him with new eyes. He could be controlled and calm when he needed to be. It surprised her that he also could be so compassionate.

"Is Maggie still asleep?" he asked.

"Yes."

"Keep her in the cabin until we move the body. Jack's gone to call the sheriff. Russ and John Hogan will help me put the body in one of the empty cabins. John is making a litter for us to carry it on."

"All right," she said weakly. Her stomach churned and her knees felt rubbery. She put her hand on one of the porch posts and steadied herself.

"Are you all right?" Simon asked. He placed his hand on her shoulder and gently pulled her to him, holding her tightly. Nona didn't resist and pressed her face to his chest.

"I'm okay."

"I didn't want you to see that."

"What happened to him? Why would someone kill LeAnn's husband?"

"I don't know, honey," Simon answered softly. "But someone wanted him dead. He could have been killed far from here and then dumped in the lake, but I doubt it. I think it happened nearby. He hadn't been in the water very long. The sheriff will sort it out."

"Simon . . . ," Nona began.

Before she could say more, the quiet moment was broken when Maggie spoke from the doorway. "Have the two of you kissed and made up? I sure hope so! I wish you liked each other."

"Maggie!" Nona pulled away from Simon, but his arm was still around her.

"Why was Sam Houston barking?" Maggie asked, trying to ease her sister's embarrassment. Then, "Where's Mabel? I saw her going towards LeAnn's place. Is she having her baby?"

Simon leaned down and whispered to Nona, "Do you want me to tell her?"

Nona nodded and he moved away from her.

"We found the body of a man in the lake this morning," he said bluntly. "We aren't certain, but we think it's Mrs. Leasure's husband."

"Oh, my gosh," Maggie muttered, her forehead creased with worry. But as quickly as that look had come, it was replaced by wide-eyed excitement. "Can I see the body?"

"No, you can't. It isn't something you ought to see."

Nona breathed a sigh of relief. She was glad that Simon had refused Maggie's request, but she was even happier that Maggie hadn't argued the point as she would certainly have done if Nona had raised it.

"Did Mabel go tell LeAnn?" Maggie asked.

"Yes," Simon answered. "It would be nice if you spent some time with LeAnn later. I'm sure she'd appreciate it."

"I will."

Nona looked up at Simon and had to admit the man increasingly surprised her. In spite of the grave situation, she smiled.

Maybe he wasn't so bad after all.

Chapter 10

As the late afternoon sun sank behind the treetops, LeAnn sat on the back steps and looked out over Tall Pine Lake. A pair of ducks landed with a soft splash on the glassy surface. A cool breeze blew from the south. After being told of Ernie's death, she had shed tears, but they'd soon stopped. She tried to grieve for him, to grieve for the loss of what they'd once had, but her love for him had died months earlier. She felt as if someone no more than a mere acquaintance had died. He'd broken so many promises that he'd taken away her respect, and, as her mother had once told her, without respect there was no love. Still, she was sorry that he had died in such a terrible way.

LeAnn had spoken with the sheriff for quite some time, but she hadn't been able to shed any light on who might have killed Ernie. She'd suspected that he'd been involved in shady activities and was now thankful that he'd never shared any details with her. The sheriff had looked at her questioningly, finding it hard to believe that a wife would know so little about her husband.

LeAnn felt the movement of her child and silently spoke to it. *It's just you and me now, baby. Someday I'll tell you about your daddy, tell you all the good things and leave out the bad.*

The first few months of their marriage had been happy ones. Ernie had taken a job working with a water-well digger. He'd been a good-looking young man, well thought of by the people of Collins. But as time passed, Ernie had changed. Before long he'd become involved with unsavory men and ended up in prison.

For the year he was gone, she'd moved back with her parents and helped with the work on the farm. It had been difficult, but she'd waited patiently for her husband to return to her. When Ernie finally had come back to Collins, he hadn't been the same man she'd married. He was hard and ruthless. When she became pregnant, he grew even more uncaring. Because he was an ex-convict, it was hard for him to get a job. Finally, they decided to move to Little Rock, where, for a short time, Ernie worked as a mechanic, a skill he'd learned while in prison.

The pregnancy had been a bone of contention from the very beginning. Ernie had been angry and had wanted her to visit a woman in the Little Rock area who knew how to get rid of a baby. She'd angrily refused, and he'd left her alone in a motel for over a week. It had been a time of fear and frustration. She didn't know what she would do or where she would go if Ernie didn't come back. When he'd finally returned, his mood had changed dramatically. He was full of plans that he claimed would put them on easy street. He never confided the details of his plans, and LeAnn had been afraid to ask. Now that he was dead, she'd never know.

Thinking back over the events of the day, she would never forget how relieved she'd felt after telling Mr. Wright she hadn't known what to do about burying Ernie. It had been hard to confide her concerns to him, but he'd given her a reassuring smile and had told her not to worry, that he would take care of it. His kindness, as well as that of Mabel and Nona, had nearly overwhelmed her. She'd cried tears of gratitude, along with her tears of loss. Someday she would pay them back, all of them. Maybe it had been fate that had brought her here. Maybe the only thing that Ernie had ever done right was to bring her to this cabin and leave her. She would ask Mr. Wright if she might be able to stay at the camp and work for her room and board.

Now that Ernie was gone, things would be forever different. Poor Ernie! He'd wanted so much but hadn't wanted to work to achieve it. All he'd wanted was for people to look up to him, even if they were the wrong kind of people. That he should have met the fate he had was sad but not unexpected. Still, she winced every time she imagined the pain he'd endured.

As she looked out over the peaceful camp, LeAnn caught sight of Maggie playing with her dog down near the shore. The breeze stirred the pines above her. Their scent wafted down to the porch and she inhaled deeply. Looking toward the future, she was surprised that she felt no fear for either herself or her baby. Somehow they would get along.

*   *   *

Jack Grant stood and wiped the perspiration from his brow. He and John Hogan, the carpenter Simon had hired, had been working on the new dining room and kitchen facilities since early morning. Simon had gone with the sheriff to take Ernie's body to town, and now, as lunchtime approached, he still hadn't returned. Even though Jack had been working, he'd managed to stay close to the cabin where Nona, Mabel, and Maggie lived. LeAnn was with the women when they called him for lunch.

When he walked into the cabin, Jack's eyes were immediately drawn to LeAnn. It was the first time he'd seen her up close, and he was surprised by how young she was. Even though her pregnancy had thickened her waist, she was still slender. A wealth of thick wheat-colored hair cascaded down and framed her oval face. She kept her soft brown eyes on her plate and ate very little in spite of Mabel's coaxing.

"You're eating for two, LeAnn. Have some more potatoes and gravy."

"Save room for the berry pie," Maggie added.

"Don't talk with your mouth full, Maggie," Nona said gently.

"I knew that was coming." The young girl groaned.

Jack looked up from his plate, his eyes moving from one sister to the other. Nona was certainly a beauty; her curly red hair would have grabbed any man's attention. While Maggie was younger and didn't have that remarkable hair color, Jack could see that she would break a heart or two during her lifetime. One thing was for certain: The two of them sure argued like sisters.

"Just stop your moaning, Maggie. Our mother would never have permitted such bad table manners. She had dignity, something you need to learn."

"Did she have red hair like yours?" Jack asked.

"Not quite as red as mine, but it was beautiful," Nona told him. "Our father loved her red hair. He used to sit and watch her comb it. He was glad that I'd inherited it from her."

"And I got this hair," Maggie said as she pulled a strand from her head and held it out for everyone to see. "It's the same color as Daddy's."

"What color hair does your brother have?" Jack asked.

Mabel and Nona fell silent as Maggie answered, "Brown like mine."

Nona looked up at Jack with new eyes. Was he one of the men looking for Harold? How did he know she had a brother? Surely Simon wouldn't have him staying with them if there was a doubt about his intentions. But what if they were in it together? What if they were trying to lull her into a false sense of security? Maggie was innocent and would talk until the cows came home. *Oh, Lord, how did I get into such a mess?*

Simon didn't return until the middle of the afternoon. When he arrived, he went directly to Nona's cabin. Mabel met him at the door.

"Come on in, Simon. I saved dinner for you."

"You're a treasure, Mabel. I'm as starved as a grizzly bear coming out of hibernation. I didn't have time to eat in town." He hung his hat on the deer-antler hat rack inside the door. "Mind if I wash up?"

"Of course not," she said as she moved the skillet over the fire and added a little milk to the gravy. Simon turned on the water spigot. He rubbed his hands furiously before toweling them dry.

"Has LeAnn been here today?"

"Yes, she was here most of the morning. As long as we don't know what happened to her husband, we thought it would be best if she stayed with us. We even went to the outhouse together." Mabel chuckled.

"Bet it was pretty crowded in there." Simon grinned. "Where is she now?"

"Jack's with her."

Footsteps echoed across the porch and Nona came in. She took a long look at Simon. "Did everything get taken care of with the sheriff?"

"Pretty much. How's LeAnn holding up?"

"As well as one could expect from a woman whose husband was murdered."

"I don't think they got along very well," Mabel added as she lifted the skillet and poured the gravy into a bowl. "She seldom said anything about him."

"She'll have a rough time alone," Simon said.

"I asked her once if her husband had been happy about the baby," Mabel said. "She shook her head and said that he'd rather they weren't having one now. She even hinted that he wanted her to get rid of it."

"What a cruel, insensitive man," Nona declared. "Maybe she's better off without him, but you're right, she'll have a rough time. I can tell she's worried about what she's going to do."

"Does she have family she can go to?" Simon asked.

"From what she told me, they're dirt poor and have three more kids at home to feed. I doubt she'll go back there unless she absolutely has to." Mabel set a pan of corn bread on the table. "It'd be hard for a woman with a baby to make a living for herself."

"I know something about that," Nona explained. "It was hard enough for me, and Maggie was older. But then I've always had Mabel to help."

Mabel placed her hand on Nona's shoulder. "You're my family."

"Didn't your brother help out?" Simon asked.

"He wasn't a part of our lives. I didn't even hear from him until after Daddy died. He came to the house to tell me that it would be several months, maybe even a year, before the will could be probated and we would get any money."

"Why was that?"

"He said it was complicated, that there were legal things we wouldn't understand. Most of Daddy's money was tied up in stocks and real estate. Harold said it would take time to get it out."

"Didn't you have a lawyer to represent you and Maggie?"

"I didn't think we needed one. Harold's our brother."

"But Harold is the type of man who . . . ," Simon began but clammed up as Maggie bounced through the door with Sam Houston at her heels.

"Simon! You're back!" The young girl straddled a chair at the table and grinned brightly. "Does the sheriff know who killed LeAnn's husband? Where'd you take the body? Will there be a funeral? Do I have to go?"

"Whoa there, squirt. One question at a time," Simon cautioned. "If the sheriff knows who killed the man, he didn't tell me. We took the body to the funeral parlor. I don't know if there will be a funeral. It's up to Mrs. Leasure and your sister whether or not you go."

"Out of courtesy to LeAnn we should all go," Nona said. "That is if there's a service, and if LeAnn wants us there."

"There's going to be a lot of togetherness around here from now on until they catch whoever murdered Leasure," Simon said.

A knock sounded on the back door.

"Mr. Wright?" Russ's voice called from the porch.

Mabel walked over to the door and opened it. Russ stood with his hat in his hand and smiled warmly at the older woman. "Hello, Mr. Story. Come on in," Mabel said.

"She saved some berry pie for you," Maggie called.

Russ stepped into the kitchen and nodded to each of them. "Well, what do you know? I've sure got a fondness for berry pie."

"Then have a seat."

Mabel set a slice on the table in front of the old fisherman.

"Thank you kindly, ma'am. That looks delicious. I ain't had no berry pie since I lost my wife years ago." He sat down at the table and took a large bite. His eyes lit up as he said, "Just as delicious as it looks."

"You sweet-talker, you!"

After a couple more bites, Russ turned to Simon and said, "I'm sorry to interrupt your dinner, but there's a couple of guys down at the dock who want to rent a cabin."

"Did they come over by boat?" Simon said with a furrowed brow. Nona knew that he was wondering if they were the same men that had frightened Maggie the day before.

"Nah. They got a pretty good-lookin' car." Russ took the last bite of pie, then, after resting his fork on the edge of the plate, grinned at Mabel. "That was more than delicious. That was a slice of heaven itself."

"If Russ is any indication," Simon said, "you're going to be a big hit with the hunters this winter. If I don't watch it, I just might lose you to a big oilman. I hear there's a dozen or more who come here to hunt."

"Well now, wouldn't that be grand." Mabel beamed. "I'd marry him for his money, buy that run-down place across the lake, and then drive you out of business."

"But I'll have Nona," Simon said, laughing, "and that red hair will draw hunters like flies to a honey pot."

"You're taking a lot for granted," Nona fumed.

Without a word, Simon got up from the table, snatched up his hat, and headed to the door, followed by Russ. As he pulled it open, he stared at Nona. "You won't talk to me that way after we're married." He winked at Maggie and closed the door quickly behind him before she could answer.

Nona sat at the table, her face flushed with embarrassment. *That man has more nerve!* Her irritation grew when Maggie started snickering.

"I don't know why you fight it." She chuckled. "Just marry him."

"This is exactly why I keep a close eye on you," Nona scolded. She turned in her seat to face her sister. "Young lady, you're getting too smart for your britches!"

Maggie's face crumpled. Her eyes searched her sister's face for a sign that her harsh words were a joke, but Nona's frown grew deeper. "I didn't mean it like that," Maggie said meekly.

"And another thing," Nona continued. "Don't go trying to arrange things for me. I'm perfectly capable of deciding who I will marry without any help from you!"

Without another word, Maggie shot up from her chair and ran out the door, slamming it behind her. Her anger subsiding, Nona found herself shocked at what she'd said. One look at Mabel, and she knew that her old friend felt the same.

"Go after her," Mabel prodded.

Nona went out the door and stood on the porch. She didn't see a sign of her sister. *Why did I snap at her like that?* She had taken her frustration with Simon out on Maggie.

A splash of color down near the lake caught her eye. Looking closer, she could see Maggie out on the dock, trying to untie a small boat that bobbed on the water. Sam Houston barked loudly behind her. Fear gripped Nona's heart and she jumped down off the porch and ran toward the lake.

"Maggie!" she shouted.

The young girl turned at the sound of the shout, but instead of stopping she hurried even faster to untie the rope. Nona scanned the area for Russ, or Simon, wanting to yell at them to stop Maggie from getting in the boat.

Nona ran. After what seemed forever, she reached the wet planks. Maggie had stopped at the end of the dock and sat down, hugging her knees to her chest. As Nona called to her again, Nona's feet slipped out from under her and the world turned upside down.

For a moment, she felt weightless, but then a searing pain filled her as the back of her head slammed into the dock. Her vision swam and stars jumped in the afternoon sky. She tried to get back on her feet despite the pain.

Without warning, the ground dropped out from under her. There wasn't any time to wonder what happened before the cold water of the lake surrounded her.

Normally, she would have just swum to the surface, but the throbbing pain in the back of her head disoriented her. Even worse, her mouth was full of water. Her arms flailed, but she couldn't grab hold of anything. Panic seized her. She couldn't breathe; nor could she see what she was doing. Her lungs felt as if they would explode. She was pulled down into the blackness and knew with certainty she was going to drown.

Chapter 11

Oooaahh!" Water coughed its way out of Nona's lungs. Someone was pounding on her back. She turned on her side and lake water gushed out of her mouth. Coughs racked her as her vision slowly began to clear. The pain that filled her was a happy reminder that she wasn't dead.

"Cough it up, honey. You'll be all right." A man's voice seeped into her mind.

Darkness came and went. The coughing slowly began to subside.

"Feeling better?"

"Will she really be okay?" Another voice—Maggie's, she thought.

"She'll be fine."

"Simon?" Nona mumbled. She rolled onto her back and blinked her eyes rapidly. Simon was kneeling on the dock beside her, his shirt soaked to the skin. His face was creased with worry. Maggie stood behind him, her face wet with tears.

"Whatever am I going to do with you?" he whispered softly.

"What happened?"

"Maggie says you were running on the wet planks, fell, banged your head, and tumbled into the water. She tried to reach you, but you'd slipped too far under. Luckily, I was close enough to hear her yelling. If I didn't know better, I'd swear you were doing your best to drive me out of my mind."

Nona's head was pounding. She reached back to tenderly touch the knot growing at the base of her skull. She tried to rise up, but dizzily fell back onto the dock.

"Whoa, there," Simon warned. "Let me handle that."

He picked Nona up off the dock as if she were nothing more than a doll. He pulled her close and cradled her against his chest. She coughed up more water as Simon carried her off the dock.

"Why are you carrying me?" she asked.

"How else are you going to get to the cabin?"

"I can walk."

"I don't think so. Just be still and enjoy the ride," he whispered.

"Is she hurt bad?" Maggie asked as she trotted along beside them.

"She'll be all right. Run ahead and open the door." Maggie sprinted ahead and jumped onto the porch. She'd pulled the screen door open when Mabel appeared in the doorway.

"Lord have mercy! What happened?"

"I'm all right," Nona said weakly.

"All right? My foot! You fell in the lake," Simon ex-

plained as he walked through the door and headed
straight for Nona's room. Mabel followed behind. He
continued, "She's going to have a lump on the back of her
head the size of an egg. We'll need to get some ice for it."

"I'll get some," Maggie said and hurried away.

Inside the bedroom, the mid-afternoon sun poured
through a crack in the curtains. Simon gently placed
Nona on the bed and took off her shoes. Her chilled body
was shaking.

"Go help Maggie," Mabel ordered. "I'll take off her
wet clothes." Mabel soon had Nona stripped and wrapped
in a blanket. The warmth of the cover was welcome.

"Ohhh . . . ," Nona groaned as she snuggled into the
blanket. She lifted her hand to once again reach for the
knot on the back of her head, but before she could touch
it, Simon snatched her hand and held it tightly in his own.

"Don't," he said firmly. She wasn't sure if she was
delirious, but she could feel Simon's hands trembling as
he wrapped her in another blanket. "Do you feel sick to
your stomach?"

"I don't think so."

"How about your vision? Is it blurred?"

"A little," she admitted. "I feel sleepy."

Mabel came into the room with a chunk of ice
wrapped in a towel. She handed it to Simon and then
stood next to Maggie at the foot of the bed. Even with her
splitting headache, Nona could see worry etched in their
faces.

"Tell me if this hurts," Simon said as he slid the ice
pack behind Nona's head and touched it against the knot.

She flinched hard, her face twisted in discomfort. "I'll take that as a yes."

"It's not that bad. I don't need a doctor."

"I'll be the judge of that. You may have a concussion," he said gravely. "What do you think, Mabel? Do we need to take her to town?"

"As long as she can focus her eyes and move her head without getting sick to her stomach, I don't think she has a concussion. But we'll need to watch her. We need to keep her awake for a while."

"If she doesn't snap out of it within an hour, I'll take her to the doctor whether she wants to go or not."

"You're the most 'take-charge' man I've ever met," Nona said weakly.

"And don't you ever forget it." Simon leaned in close, his mouth only inches from Nona's ear. She could feel his hot breath against her skin, and her own breathing became ragged. "You scared the life out of me, you sweet girl. I've gone to a lot of trouble to get you right where I want you. I'll do whatever it takes to keep you with me."

She wanted to reach out, touch his face, and tell him that she'd never felt safer than she did at that moment. Instead, the darkness closed around her and she closed her eyes.

"Here now. Don't go to sleep yet. I'll do something to make you mad, or I'll kiss you," he whispered for her ears alone. "But I prefer the latter."

Nona slept restlessly through the night. When she looked in the mirror the next morning, she thought she looked like something Sam Houston had dragged in from the woods. Her face was pale, except for the dark bruise on the side of her head. Her hair was plastered to her head in tight curls. The bump on the back of her head was still tender.

Glory! What a sight!

Walking on not-quite-steady legs, she went to the kitchen, where Simon and Mabel were having breakfast. Suddenly weak, she grasped hold of the knobs on the high-backed chair for support. Simon jumped up from the table, took her elbow, and eased her down into the chair.

"You're as white as a ghost!" he exclaimed. "What are you doing up? How did you sleep?"

"Not well. I tossed and turned."

"You poor little lamb." Mabel set a cup of coffee and a piece of toast in front of Nona.

"I'm not hungry, Mabel."

"Eat anyway," Simon ordered. "Where are Maggie and LeAnn?"

"Maggie was down by the lake with Russ," Mabel answered. "LeAnn went with Jack to her cabin to get some clothes."

Just then, the door flew open and Maggie rushed in breathlessly. For a moment, she hung her head low, her hands on her knees, trying to gather herself to talk; she'd obviously been running. Nona braced herself for news of trouble, but the young girl finally composed herself and said, "Mr. Story wants Simon. A couple of fellas are asking about renting a cabin. High-roller types, Mr. Story said. They had questions he couldn't answer."

"Thanks, squirt."

Simon got up from the table, picked up his hat, and

headed to the door. "I want the three of you to stay together. Jack and LeAnn will be back soon. So will I."

Maggie sat down across from Nona.

"Do you want to eat? One hotcake or two?"

After Mabel had given her a plate of food, the young girl didn't do much more than pick at it. Occasionally, she'd glance up at her sister, but if Nona made eye contact, she'd quickly look away.

Nona understood how Maggie was feeling. She had appeared to be frantic on the dock and had hovered over Nona's bed like a mother hen for most of the night. There hadn't been a chance for them to talk about their argument, about the harsh words that had been spoken, and Nona worried that Maggie blamed herself for what had happened. Guilt gnawed at her; the knot on the back of her head was no one's fault but her own.

"I believe I'll go and fold some laundry," Mabel said as a way of excusing herself from the room. After her footfalls had disappeared, the kitchen was silent except for the occasional clink of silverware.

"I'm glad you're better," Maggie nearly whispered into her plate.

"I just needed some rest."

"Nona, I . . . ," she began, but a lump caught in her throat. When she finally looked up, her eyes were moist and her brow furrowed. "I was so afraid that you were gonna drown . . ."

"Me, too, Maggie. Thankfully, Simon was there to help."

"But what if he hadn't been there? I couldn't reach you."

"Don't worry about that. He was . . ."

Before Nona could say another word, Maggie bolted out of her chair, rounded the table, and fell to the floor beside her sister. Her arms snaked around Nona's waist and held on tight. Tears began to slide down her face. "I'm sorry, Nona!" she cried. "I'm sorry I made you run!"

Her hands stroked Maggie's hair, and she felt like the biggest fool on earth! She'd overreacted to her sister's teasing and had lashed out at her. Sometimes she forgot that Maggie was still only fourteen years old.

"Shhh," she said softly. "It wasn't your fault that I slipped."

"If I hadn't run off, you wouldn't have gotten hurt!"

"If I hadn't opened my big mouth and said those hurtful things, you wouldn't have had to run off in the first place." With her hand, Nona lifted Maggie's face until their eyes met. She smiled down gently. "I slipped on the wet dock because I'm clumsy, not because of you."

"I was scared," Maggie said.

"I was, too. If anything were to happen to you, it'd just kill me. You're all the family I've got, you and Mabel, and a life without you wouldn't be a life worth living."

"I'm still sorry."

"Not as sorry as I am," Nona said, a tear of her own falling. She reached down and hugged her sister as tightly as she could.

It was over an hour before Simon's boots made loud thumps on the wooden porch to announce his return. Maggie had returned to her normal joking self, and she, along with Nona and Mabel, had been laughing and talking when the screen door opened and Simon entered the room.

"So how did it go?" Mabel asked.

"A couple of guys from Little Rock trying to find a place to do a little fishing. I told them that with the renovations it would be several weeks before we accepted guests again." With a wry smile, he added, "I neglected to tell them that we'd just fished a dead body out of the lake. Didn't think that would be good for business."

"Good thinking." Mabel chuckled.

"Do you think they were looking for Harold?" Nona asked. After everything that had happened, all who came to the camp were under suspicion. Were they responsible for Ernie's death? Were they with the men in the boat who'd tried to get Maggie?

"Harold?" Maggie asked in surprise.

"I don't think so." Simon ignored Maggie's question. "But that doesn't mean I don't want the three of you to be extra careful. That especially means you, kiddo," he said to Maggie.

"Why me?"

"Because I said so."

"What does this have to do with Harold?"

Simon looked at Nona for approval to continue. They'd tried to keep things from Maggie, not wanting to worry her, but now she deserved to know the truth. Nona nodded.

"Your half brother took money from a bank," Simon said, putting a hand on Maggie's shoulder and giving it a light squeeze. "He hid the cash, and these men think you and your sister might know where Harold or the money is."

"Did he rob the bank?"

"Not with a gun."

"He took the money from the bank where he worked," Nona explained.

"That sounds like Harold, the creep," Maggie said matter-of-factly. The three adults in the room were surprised at the girl's statement. "Don't look so surprised," Maggie continued. "It didn't take much to figure out Harold is so crooked he'll have to be screwed into the ground when he dies. I'll be surprised if we get any of the money Daddy left us."

"You never said anything about this," Nona exclaimed.

"I never needed to. We had other things on our minds."

"My little sister is growing up."

After they'd chatted awhile longer, Maggie got up from the table and went back to the room she shared with Nona. Simon took a seat at the table and motioned for Mabel to join them. "Sit down. I think it's time we cleared the air around here a little."

Nona took a long look at Simon. His features had taken on a no-nonsense appearance. His face had an inherent strength. His green eyes searched hers questioningly. It made her conscious of her unruly hair, her bruises, wrinkled blouse, shiny nose, and colorless mouth. She looped a strand of hair behind her ear and folded her hands on the table.

"Feel all right?" Simon asked her.

"I'm fine."

"That's good." He paused before continuing, "There's something that I haven't told you ladies yet. I didn't tell you that it was my grandpa Wright who owned the bank where Harold was working. It was his vault that held the bank money and jewelry that had been placed there for safekeeping by a depositor."

"Oh, no!" Mabel exclaimed.

"Why didn't you tell me this when you told me Harold was your cousin?" Nona asked angrily. Everywhere she turned there were surprises!

"Because I was hoping I wouldn't have to tell you."

"But wait," Mabel said. "If your mother and Harold's mother were sisters, don't you have the same grandfather?"

"No. My grandpa Wright was my father's father."

"It's all so confusing. I should have known it was too good to be true when my ex-boss told me about this job. You had no right to manipulate us the way you did!" Nona scolded.

"You're right, I didn't," Simon admitted. "But let me ask you a question. If you had known my connections with Harold and my grandfather's bank, would you have accepted this job?"

"That's beside the point."

"No, it's not. It's exactly my point. I did what I had to do to get you here."

"I can't believe you! I don't believe Harold thought Maggie and I would be put in any danger."

"Then you don't know him half as well as you think you do."

Chapter 12

FRUSTRATED, FRANK POUNDED on the steering wheel with both fists as the car bounced down the road. His bald head glistened with sweat and his face grew redder by the second. Life in the sticks was getting to Frank, and his frustration had begun to boil over.

"I think we should stay out of sight for a while," Webb said.

"I'm tellin' you, we're gonna do somethin' and we're gonna do it soon." After another blow against the wheel, he added, "Let's grab the kid the first chance we get; she's gotta know something. She'll have to use the can sometime, and when she does . . ."

"I won't be part of a kidnappin'."

"How the hell else are we gonna find out what they know?"

"Beats the hell out of me," Webb groused. "We've been out here too friggin' long. Besides, I can't think worth a damn when my stomach's growlin'. I gotta eat somethin' soon."

"Damn, you're a pain in the ass!" Frank sneered. "They're lucky we ain't in Chicago. I'd just kick in the door, snatch that brat, and make her talk. When we were done with her, we'd sell her on the street or dump her in the lake."

Webb looked out the window at the passing landscape to keep Frank from seeing the look of revulsion on his face. Frank was a member of a mafia that had no fear of the law. They'd bought and forced their way into high places. Out here, it was different. Get on the wrong side of the men in these parts, and they'd come after you vigilante style. They'd been known to throw a rope over a tree and hang a man. If he wanted to keep his bones inside his skin and his head on his shoulders, he had to be careful.

It was nearly noon when they drove into town. Usually, there were few people around; most were home for lunch this time of day. Today was different. Groups of excited men and women gathered, talking loudly and gesturing wildly.

"What the hell's goin' on?" Frank asked.

"Beats me."

Frank brought the car to a stop in front of the bank and hollered at an older man in overalls. The old man hobbled over and spat a wad of tobacco out onto the sidewalk. He put his arm on the truck's cab and smiled, showing his stained, uneven teeth.

"What's goin' on?" Webb asked.

"Found a fella floatin' out in Tall Pine Lake. Sheriff said that he'd been beat somethin' fierce. Don't nobody know who it was, but that hadn't stopped people from guessin'.'' The old man spat again. "Town like this needs somethin' to jaw about."

"Thanks," Frank said and drove on.

"Reckon it was Ernie? After all, he didn't show up last night."

"If it was, that'll take care of him."

They stopped in front of the diner with a faded sign naming it "Alice's" hanging above the door. Inside, Webb and Frank sat on the two remaining bar stools at the scarred counter and looked at the hand-printed menu on the blackboard hanging on the wall. Frank ordered a cup of coffee, while Webb ordered two hamburgers and a bowl of chili.

"I don't see how you can eat that shit," Frank growled.

After the waitress had brought their orders, Webb dug heartily into his. He didn't give a damn what Frank thought. He hadn't eaten anything except pork and beans, salami sandwiches, and potato chips for a week.

The waitress brought Webb a dish of crackers, and when he looked up to thank her, he took a good look. She was certainly overweight. She reminded him of a sack of potatoes with a string tied in the middle. Her eyes lingered on him.

Webb smiled easily. She was obviously embarrassed that he had caught her looking at him. She lowered herself down, putting one pudgy arm on the countertop. "Did you hear about the man they found out in Tall Pine Lake?"

"Not a word," Frank butted in. "Who was it?"

"I'm not really sure, but the sheriff was in here earlier and he mentioned that the fella's wife was staying out at the camp. I guess they'd been staying there for a couple of weeks."

"Poor guy likely fell outta a boat," Webb said before putting a big spoonful of chili in his mouth.

"That isn't what the sheriff was saying," the waitress explained. Webb smiled to himself; just let her keep talking. "He said the man was beat up pretty bad before he was dumped in the lake."

"I'd bet your one-horse sheriff wouldn't know his own ass from a hole in the ground," Frank said drolly before taking a gulp of his coffee.

"Does this sort of thing happen often?" Webb asked.

The waitress turned her glare from Frank and looked Webb straight in the eyes. He knew that she found him attractive when compared to what Home had to offer, and he could use that to his advantage.

"Oh, the lakes around here get one or two a year. Some people don't have any brains at all when they get out on the water. How about you two? Are you here to fish?"

"I'm all thumbs when it comes to rods and reels." Webb laughed. "No, we're just here long enough to see the sights."

"That's too bad." The waitress frowned. "But if you're around, there's a dance every Saturday night over at the Grizzly Bear."

"You don't say," Webb said, trying to make himself sound excited. "If we're still in town, I'll try to stop by."

Frank dropped his empty cup onto the counter. "Get our check, girl."

The waitress wrinkled her nose at Frank like he was

last week's garbage. "Yes, sir, Your Majesty. Right away."
She winked at Webb and left the counter.

"Little bitch," Frank growled.

When the waitress returned with the bill, Webb picked
up his hat. With a nod and a wink at the waitress, he said,
"Thanks, honey."

"You're welcome," the woman answered with a sigh.

The two men walked to the door and exited to the
street. "You sure as hell gave her a thrill," Frank said. "I
doubt anyone in this town's ever called that cow
'honey.'"

"My mama always said you catch more flies with
honey than vinegar." They stood on the sidewalk in the
afternoon sun, neither man moving toward their car on
the other side of the street. Finally, Webb spoke. "You
think that body they found in the lake was Ernie?"

"I ain't gonna assume anything," Frank argued. "But
we gotta find out, one way or the other. If it is him, we
gotta know if it was an accident or if someone killed
him."

"Who do you think did it?" Webb looked at Frank with
suspicion.

"That's something we gotta find out. If Wright did it,
that means Ernie might've told him about us. We're
gonna have to be careful, or we're gonna end up floatin'
in the lake ourselves. We're gonna ask around. People in
this town like to talk, just like that fat cow back in there."
Frank jerked his thumb back toward the diner. "You go
down to the bar, order a drink or two, and start listenin' to
what you can pick up. Somebody'll talk."

"What are you gonna do?"

"I gotta make a call. Chicago'll wanna know what's happenin'." He took off his hat and wiped his brow. His shoulders slumped as he said, "They ain't gonna like this one bit."

An hour later, Frank returned to the car in a black mood. He'd talked to the head man, who hadn't been at all pleased with what Frank had told him. They were becoming impatient to get their hands on Harold and the money. He hadn't been concerned over Ernie's death.

"Just as well," the man had said, "you would've had to off him anyway."

Frank hopped into the car, drove to the other side of town, and stopped in front of the Grizzly Bear Tavern. Webb stood out front talking to a middle-aged man who looked, even at three o'clock in the afternoon, as if he'd had too much to drink. Webb nodded to the man before walking over and getting in the car.

"Find out anything?" Frank asked before speeding out of town.

"That fella was sayin' the deputy told him they didn't have a clue who'd killed the man. 'Bout the only thing they did know was that he hadn't just fallen out of the boat and drowned. Whoever it was beat the shit out of him."

"Huh," Frank grunted.

The hot summer wind flew through the open window and struck Webb in the face. For the briefest of moments, he longed for the wide-open spaces and simple life of west Texas and the hometown he'd left behind. *How in the hell have I ended up here?*

Frank turned the wheel recklessly, sending the car

whipping around the blind turns, its wheels sliding on the loose rock. Webb asked, "What'd the big man have to say on the phone?"

"They act like we ain't got no more worth than Leasure," Frank seethed. "If it was you or me floatin' in that lake, they wouldn't give a shit as long as the other one found the money."

"What did you expect?"

Ignoring the question, Frank kept complaining. "We could just walk over there and take what we want if it weren't for that son-of-a-bitchin' Wright. He's the problem."

"He ain't but one man."

"Yeah . . . but he's got a hell of a lot of connections."

"Then what do you plan to do?"

Frank was silent for a moment, his hands gripping the steering wheel so tightly that his knuckles became white. "We're gonna do what I told you about."

"We're gonna snatch the kid?" Webb's eyes narrowed as he turned to look at Frank's profile.

"You got a better idea?" the older man growled.

The thought of grabbing the girl sickened Webb. He'd been told to come to this backwater place to find the missing money and jewelry, not to take part in kidnapping some kid. Still, they weren't any closer to finding the money. "I guess not," he muttered.

"We'll snatch her and make her talk. If she don't tell us what we wanna know, her prissy sister will. We don't even need to take her far, just out in the woods. Hell, if she don't talk, we'll leave her overnight. By mornin' she'll be so scared that she'll be singin' like a canary. Then we'll get the hell outta here."

"All right, but I ain't gonna stand by and let you hurt her."

"Goddammit, Webb! Get some balls!" Frank barked. "We've only got a few more days here. If we don't have somethin' to report soon, they're gonna pull us out. Ain't but one thing happens when the boss ain't happy."

"Yeah," Webb groused. "We end up in Lake Michigan."

"Exactly. You remember that next time you're feelin' squeamish!"

Jack stood next to the door while LeAnn wrapped a light shawl around her shoulders. He'd offered to walk her back to her cabin to retrieve a few things. "Don't worry," Jack said to Simon. "I'll check the place before she goes in."

"Don't let her out of your sight," Simon said. "There's a murderer around here someplace."

"We'll be careful."

LeAnn turned to Mabel and said, "I'll bring back the things I have that will spoil." Her face was already fiery red with embarrassment at the thought of being alone in the dark with Jack. She wasn't afraid he would hurt her, but she didn't know what she would say to him.

"Go along with Jack, dear. He'll see to it you get there and back." Mabel understood LeAnn's shyness.

After promising to return quickly, the two of them went outside. The moon, not quite full, shone brightly in the mostly cloudless sky above. A soft, warm wind blew across the lake from the north and rustled the leaves.

They walked slowly down the hard-packed road to LeAnn's cabin.

"Thank you for coming with me," LeAnn said softly, her eyes downcast as she picked her way carefully in the night light.

"My pleasure."

They moved along in silence, the distant hoot of an owl the only sound. After a couple of minutes, her cabin came into view. Its dark silhouette looked ominous. LeAnn swallowed her fear and walked up the steps to the porch. "You don't need to come in. I'll put what I need in a pillowcase and be right out."

"I'll come inside, if it's all the same." Even in the near-darkness, LeAnn could see his warm smile and instantly felt safer. It had been a long time since a man had cared about her welfare.

Jack followed LeAnn into the cabin and stood with his back to the door, his eyes surveying the room. The place was neat and clean. A fruit jar full of wildflowers sat on a table. A beat-up chair was next to the window that faced the lake. He didn't see many personal possessions as he watched her fold up several garments and put them in a pillow slip. After adding some toiletries, she clutched the pillow slip to her chest.

"I'm ready."

"Do you have everything you need?"

"Oh, wait!" she exclaimed and gathered up the few items she wanted to take back to Mabel. "Thank you for reminding me."

Jack walked to the back door and checked to make sure the lock was secure. He returned to the front of the cabin, took the pillow slip from LeAnn's hand, and ushered her out the front door. After locking the cabin behind him, he led her back down the road toward the other cabins. Glancing at her as she walked beside him, her head even with his shoulders, he took note of her sandy hair.

"You're not very big."

"You mean not very tall compared to you," she corrected.

He grinned down at her as she smiled shyly back. Before she could say anything more, he asked a question that took the air out of her lungs. "How far along are you?"

She felt her face redden, and, though he couldn't see it in the darkness, she turned away from him. She hadn't thought he'd ask about her *pregnancy*!

"Have I embarrassed you?" he asked softly. He stopped on the path and turned to face her. "If I did, I'm sorry. I've lived on a ranch all my life. On a ranch, birth is an everyday occurrence."

"I understand." LeAnn nodded and started walking. The awkwardness of his words faded quickly, and she was surprised by how at ease she felt with him. Secure beside him, she answered his question. "I'm in my seventh month."

"Will this be your first child?"

"Yes." She felt his hand cup her elbow. Confidently, he guided her around a rough spot in the road. She liked his touch. "Tell me about the place where you live."

"I live on a thousand-acre ranch near Sharpton, on the north side of the Red River in Oklahoma. It runs along the south edge of the land. My parents left the ranch to me and my brother with the stipulation that we take care of our two maiden aunts for as long as they live." Jack laughed heartily before adding, "It's no chore at all. They're a couple of live wires."

"Is your brother married?"

"Not yet. But he's going with a girl, and I'm sure they'll marry."

"Isn't a ranch life busy?" LeAnn asked. "I'd think there would be so much to do that it would be hard to find the time to come to a camp in Arkansas."

"This is the slow time of the year. Besides, I've worked off and on for Simon for years. It's good money. Cash is always scarce on a ranch. Now," he said with a grin, "enough about me. Tell me where you lived before coming here."

"It was a tiny town in southern Missouri called Collins." She shuddered to herself and took a deep breath before saying, "It's not much more than a wide spot in the road."

"That'd suit me just fine. I don't care to live in a city."

"Then Collins would be perfect for you."

"How long were you married?" Jack asked. When LeAnn paused, he sighed before adding, "I'm sorry for asking so many questions, but I'd like to get to know you better. I hope I didn't upset you."

"It's fine. It's just hard to believe I'm a widow."

"I'm sorry for your loss."

"We weren't married long. Two and a half years, but Ernie was gone for one of those years."

"Gone?" Jack asked.

"This is hard for me to say," LeAnn said softly, "but

you will probably find out anyway. I'm sure it will come out now that he's dead. Ernie was in prison for that year."

Up ahead, Nona's cabin came into view, a bright light shining through the windows. Jack was silent, and it unsettled LeAnn that he hadn't replied to what she'd said. She pulled her arm free of his hand and stopped. Jack stopped and turned to face her.

"Aren't you going to ask me what he went to prison for? Don't you want to know if I had any part in it?"

"I'd bet my life you had no part in what sent your husband to prison." Even though it was hard for her to see his face, she could feel his blue eyes on her face.

"I didn't have any part in it," she said stoutly. "Some of the people in Collins didn't believe me."

"Then they were damn fools."

They reached Nona's cabin and stepped up onto the porch. "Thank you for the company," LeAnn said.

"I enjoyed it more than you know." Jack knocked on the door and opened it. "Good night, LeAnn."

"Good night, Mr. Grant."

LeAnn stepped inside and closed the door behind her. Jack stood on the porch until he heard her talking to Nona, then walked down the drive to the cabin where he bunked. Something about LeAnn pulled at him. Her eyes were filled with a deep sadness, but there were intelligence and maturity there as well. Was it the sadness for the husband she'd just lost or did it go beyond that? Beneath her fragile exterior lay strength and determination. He didn't know how he knew this, but he did.

As a rule, he wasn't shy with women. But when he was with LeAnn, his tongue clung to the roof of his mouth. He credited his reaction to the fact that he hadn't been around a pretty girl for several months.

Inside Nona's cabin, LeAnn's mind was in similar turmoil. Guilt racked her heart. Her husband hadn't been dead a day. What kind of a woman was she to have enjoyed the company of another man? She excused herself by thinking that when he'd returned from prison Ernie had not been the man she had married. The baby had meant nothing to him.

Ernie had died only yesterday, but her love for him had died a long time before.

Chapter 13

MABEL AND NONA stood in the kitchen drying dishes as the day's last remaining light faded. Simon and Jack had gone back to their cabins. Sam Houston paced in front of the back door, whining.

"Just hold your horses, Sam," Mabel scolded. "You can go out with the rest of us in a minute or two. We'll have to make a trip to the outhouse before we go to bed. You'll get your chance."

"I'll wake up Maggie," Nona said as she hung the dishtowel on the rack behind the stove. "I don't know what's the matter with that girl. Since we've been here, all she does is sleep. Back in our old apartment, I had to shoo her to bed every night."

"Things are different here. She's constantly on the go. She follows Simon around and takes three steps to his one in order to keep up with his long legs. Maggie is becoming a country girl. I've never seen her so happy."

"That's what I'm afraid of," Nona sighed.

"What do you mean?"

"We'll be leaving here soon. She needs to go to school. I don't want to break her heart by doing what's best for her."

"We'll cross that bridge when we come to it."

Nona entered the room that she shared with her sister. Maggie was huddled under a blanket, sound asleep. Nona walked over and lightly shook the girl's shoulder. "Honey. We're going to the outhouse. You'd better come with us."

Maggie made no response. After several shakes, each one harder than the one before, she finally opened her eyes and groaned. Nona repeated her words, but Maggie mumbled, "I don't have to go."

"You should still come with us. You might have to go later."

"I don't have to go," Maggie insisted. "I went before dark."

"What?" Nona exclaimed. "I didn't know that. With everything that's happened, Simon told us not to go to the outhouse alone. You know better than that."

"I didn't see anybody around. Besides, I had Sam Houston with me."

"That doesn't make any difference. Simon said not to go out there alone. Why didn't you mind him? You're the one who thinks the man walks on water."

"He does . . . almost." Maggie chuckled. With that, the girl turned her head, squeezed her pillow, and closed her eyes.

"If you don't go now," Nona said crossly, irritated by her sister's refusal to get up, "you won't be able to go until morning. Don't think of waking me up in the middle of the night."

Maggie grunted and turned her face to the wall. "I won't."

Maggie woke from a lazy dream and sat up in her bed. Faint light came from a part in the curtains, and she blinked her eyes quickly. All around her, the house was quiet. Nona slept soundly on the bed next to Maggie, her mouth slightly open. Sam Houston was stretched out on the floor between the two sisters, one paw thrust up in the air. It was still so early that the morning birds hadn't begun to sing.

A painful pressure in her stomach had awakened Maggie. Her bladder was full. Last night, she had been so tired she'd ignored Nona's urging to go to the outhouse, and she was now paying for it. All she wanted to do was roll up in her blankets and go back to sleep, but she knew if she didn't go pee, she'd do nothing but toss and turn uncomfortably.

As she swung her feet out of the covers and put them on the floor, she thought for a moment about waking Nona. Her sister had said they shouldn't go to the outhouse alone. *She'd blow her top if she knew how many times I've gone by myself!* It would only take a couple of minutes to get there and back. No one would be the wiser.

Maggie stood up, grabbed a light shawl from the bedside table, and wrapped it around her shoulders. As she left the room, the floorboards beneath her feet creaked loudly. Nona moaned and shifted in her bed. Standing stock-still, Maggie turned and held her breath. Seconds passed as she waited for Nona to wake. But she kept on sleeping. Maggie sighed to herself. Heck! Nona had nearly drowned just the day before! She needed all the rest she could get.

Kneeling down next to Sam Houston, Maggie whispered, "Come on, boy. Let's go outside."

In answer, the big dog yawned, stretched, and closed his eyes.

"Fine, then," Maggie complained. "Keep on sleeping, you lazy hound."

The day was just beginning to show itself. The eastern sky was streaked with light; no breeze stirred the leaves, and a slight chill was in the air. Maggie huddled her arms to her body and shivered; no doubt about it, fall was almost around the corner.

The outhouse sat fifty feet from the back of the cabin and about the same distance from the nearest tree line. It wasn't sturdy; its frame sagged at the top, and it needed a new coat of paint, but they'd made do. Still, it was kind of isolated. Maggie scanned the tall elms and oaks for any movement, but didn't see anyone about. Even the squirrels were still sleeping in their nests. All was calm and silent.

The grass between the cabin and the outhouse was wet. The morning dew clung to Maggie's light shoes as she hurried across. She went inside, closed the outhouse door behind her, and sat down on the cold, hard seat. It was nearly pitch-dark and it certainly didn't smell like a rose garden, but she instantly felt better. In a minute or two, she'd be back in her warm bed.

Just as she'd started to imagine what Mabel was going

to make for breakfast, the crack of a stick from outside the outhouse startled her. *What the heck was that?* A sliver of fear slid its way into her stomach as she strained to hear more. A minute passed and then another; no other sound reached her ears. Slowly, Maggie began to relax. *It was probably a rabbit or a squirrel.* All of the warnings she'd been hearing from Simon and Nona had made her jumpy.

Maggie stood, straightened her nightdress, and opened the door. Without warning, a hand grabbed her wrist like a vise and yanked her the rest of the way out of the small building. The force was so great that she fell onto the wet grass. With a flash of panic, Maggie tried to scream, but a hand clamped tightly over her mouth.

"Watch the damn cabin," a man's voice commanded.

"Hurry up," another said.

"Don't make a sound, or you'll be sorry," he sneered.

"Get away . . ," Maggie thought frantically. The man dropped a knee into the middle of her back, pinning her to the ground. A cloth was pressed tightly over her nose and mouth. The only thing greater than the burning pain in her chest was her fear.

"Don't hurt her," the other man said.

"You worry about the cabin. We're only gettin' one chance at this."

"Be careful. She's no good to us dead."

"She ain't gonna die . . . not yet," the man snarled.

Desperate now, Maggie clawed at the hand covering her mouth. Nona, Mabel, and Simon were only feet away, but she couldn't call out to them. Why hadn't she listened? Why hadn't she gone with Nona the night before?

Before she could regret anything else, Maggie's world went black.

Nona woke slowly and ran her hands through her snarled red hair. The knot on the back of her head was still tender. She yawned, stretched, and got out of bed. She noticed that Maggie's bed was empty and shrugged her shoulders. The kid had gone to bed so early the night before, she should have been up at the crack of dawn! The fragrance of breakfast had begun to waft through the cabin as Nona put on a shawl and left the room.

"Something smells delicious," she said to Mabel as the older woman stood at the stove, flipping pancakes.

"They were such a hit yesterday that I decided to do them again. Wash and sit yourself down before Simon and Jack get here. These pancakes will disappear fast enough then." Mabel smiled broadly.

"I suppose you're right," Nona answered as she put maple syrup on a stack. "Did Maggie eat before she left?"

"I haven't seen her," Mabel said. "Isn't she still in your room?"

"No. Her bed is empty." Before Nona could use her fork, something made her put it down. A nagging feeling tugged at her. She got up from the table and walked over to the cabin's front windows. She scanned the yard for any sign of her sister or Sam Houston. She checked the rear windows, but there was still no sign of Maggie. Still, something caught her eye; the door to the outhouse was closed. Could she be inside? "Mabel, how long have you been awake?"

"Nearly an hour. I got up, started breakfast, and let Sam Houston out."

"And you didn't see her?"

"No, I didn't," Mabel said with concern in her voice. She set down her spatula and nervously wiped her hands on her apron. "What's wrong, Nona?"

"Could she have gone to the outhouse and you didn't notice?"

"I suppose so, but . . ."

Nona didn't wait to hear more. She dashed out the back door of the cabin, down the steps of the porch, and across the grass to the outhouse. The ground was wet and cold on her bare feet. *Where is that girl?* Anxiety turned to anger. She thought that finding LeAnn's husband floating in the lake would have scared Maggie sufficiently for her to take Simon's warnings seriously. That her sister had not made her livid. Nona whipped open the door to find the outhouse empty. Irritation was instantly replaced by alarm.

Turning around in a circle, Nona scanned the lakeshore and the edge of the forest for her sister. When she'd gone to bed, Maggie had been sleeping peacefully in the bed next to hers. Now she was nowhere to be seen. Where could she be?

A door slammed behind her, and Nona turned to see Simon coming down the steps of his cabin and heading toward her own. Without another thought, she began to run toward him.

"Simon!" she shouted. He stopped in his tracks. When she reached him, she grabbed his arm.

"What's wrong?" he asked anxiously. "What's happened?"

"It's Maggie!" Nona said breathlessly. "I can't find her. She wasn't in our room when I woke up, and Mabel hasn't seen her either."

"Calm down, Nona," Simon said firmly. His deep green eyes scanned her face. "You know Maggie. She and Sam Houston are probably down by the lake. Let's not jump to conclusions until we've looked around."

"I told her not to go out alone," Nona complained, her stomach churning with fear and anxiety.

"Where's Mabel?"

"In the kitchen cooking breakfast."

"Go back and wait with her. I'll get Jack and Russ. We'll look around. She'll turn up. Just go." Simon turned, hurried up the steps to Jack's cabin, and pounded on the door.

Nona ran back to where Mabel was waiting on the porch. "Did you find her?" Mabel asked nervously.

"No," Nona answered and grabbed Mabel's hand, tears beginning to run down her cheeks, fear eating a hole in her heart. "Simon and Jack will look for her on the grounds and by the lake. He wants us to wait here."

"Surely she didn't go out in a boat."

"I hope not. I thought she was sufficiently scared the last time."

Slowly, the darkness at the edges of Maggie's vision began to fade. A pounding in her head made her sick to her stomach as she blinked herself awake. The first things she saw were the tall pines and thick bushes around her.

Little sunlight made it to the ground. She tried to move, but couldn't.

Then she remembered what had happened. *Two men attacked me as I left the outhouse!* Something held her tight. She looked down to see she was sitting on the ground, her back to a tree. She was tied with a thick rope, her arms at her sides. Rough bark scraped at her bare arms and against the back of her head. When she shouted, no sound came out except for a muffled cry; a gag was tightly bound in her mouth.

She heard a rustling in the underbrush and turned her head from side to side. The sound grew louder and louder, building in equal proportion to her fear.

Two men came into view. Fear filled Maggie's thoughts when she recognized them as the men on the lake who'd tried to get her into their boat. The bald man stared at her with a mean look on his whiskered face.

" 'Bout time you woke up, little bitch," he snarled.

"Let's get this over with," the younger man said. He was handsome, in a rugged sort of way, with sandy-blond hair that hung over his ears. His green eyes locked with Maggie's, but he spoke to the other man. "Ask her and be done with it."

"Keep your shirt on." Frank moved closer to Maggie, his face only a couple of inches from her own. The smell of alcohol was on his breath. "We're gonna have us an understandin', bitch. I'm gonna take that handkerchief outta your mouth, and you ain't gonna let out a peep. If you do, you'll get hurt. Understand?"

Maggie nodded quickly.

"Now, wasn't that easy?" Forcefully, the man yanked

the gag out of Maggie's mouth, and the handkerchief, still tied in a knot, fell below her chin. She'd never been more scared in her entire life, but she didn't cry out.

"What do you want?" she asked fearfully.

"You just tell us where that good-for-nothin' brother of yours is," he growled, "and we'll be happier than pigs in shit."

"My brother?" Maggie was shocked. Simon had been right; this was all about what Harold had stolen from the bank.

"He's got what's ours. Where is he?"

"I don't know. I haven't seen him in years."

"Don't give me that shit." The man stepped closer to her. Purple veins stood out on his neck and forehead. "I bet my ass he gave you the money, and you and that sister of yours are hidin' it somewhere."

"No!" Maggie shouted.

"Where the hell's the money?"

"I don't know!"

"Maybe seein' your sister's body floatin' in the lake'll shake your memory!"

For the first time since she'd been attacked, an emotion other than fear coursed through Maggie's veins. Anger. Even though they could kill her with no more effort than swatting a fly, the thought of their hurting Nona was too much for her. Hot tears poured down her face and stung her eyes. Straining against the ropes, she shouted, "If you touch her, I'll kill you!"

As fast as a rattlesnake, the man's hand shot out and slapped Maggie hard across the mouth. Dazed by the force of the blow, she cringed in fear of another. Coppery blood filled her mouth. A strange, scraping noise made her look. The man was pulling a large knife from a sheath. He held it in front of her, and the faint light reflected off its steel.

"If there's any killin' to be done," the man spat, "I'll be the one doin' it!"

Chapter 14

B Y THE MIDDLE OF THE AFTERNOON, Nona was sick with fear. Simon, with Russ at the motor, had taken a boat across the lake to check out the abandoned campground on the western shore. They'd scouted around but found no sign that Maggie had been there. They'd also searched up and down the lakeshore. Now, along with John Hogan, they were walking through the woods on the other side of the main road. Jack prowled the road in front of the cabins.

After frantically searching the campground with Jack, Nona and Mabel dropped exhaustedly into their chairs, their shoulders slumped and their hearts heavy. Nona refused to let her mind dwell on the possibility that she would never see her sister again. Maggie was such a darling girl, trusting to a fault. It would be easy for someone to lure her or overpower her. Had the men in the boat taken her? Was it one of them who'd murdered LeAnn's husband? If it was information about Harold they wanted, Maggie could tell them nothing.

"I shouldn't have brought her here," Nona muttered.

"Better here, where we have Simon, than the city," Mabel countered. "You were doing what you thought was best for that girl. Nobody would disagree with that. Maggie is happy here."

"What are we going to do?"

"We're going to keep looking until we find her," the older woman assured her. "Simon will find her and bring her back to us."

"But what if he doesn't?"

"Don't think about that. He will," Mabel repeated.

Nona wished she could share her friend's optimism. Maggie was more like her daughter than her sister. With everything that had happened—the death of her parents, an uncaring brother—Maggie had been solely her responsibility, and she had done the best she could. She had wanted Maggie to have a normal life. Even when it meant giving up some of her own dreams, she'd done it without a moment's hesitation. Maggie was her sunshine, and the thought of losing her forever brought tears to Nona's eyes and an emptiness to her heart.

"Oh, my God! Why didn't I take her away from here when I first heard about Harold?"

"You can't blame yourself for this." Mabel rose from her chair and put an arm around Nona. "Maggie could be lost in the woods. She could have gotten turned around and not known where she was. Simon could be back with her any minute."

"She wouldn't have done that," Nona argued. The tears began to flow more freely, falling from her cheeks and soaking her blouse. When she could bring herself to speak again, her voice was little more than a whisper. "I can't lose her! I can't."

"You won't, sweetie," Mabel said soothingly.

Loud footsteps sounded on the porch and then Simon opened the door. Jack and LeAnn were behind him. Nona jumped to her feet, grabbed his forearms, and searched his face. He shook his head lightly and frowned. "We haven't found a trace of her, Nona."

"Oh, God," Nona sobbed. She collapsed into Simon's arms. He pulled her tightly to his chest as her body heaved and fell. No one could offer a word of solace.

Maggie stared at the knife in the man's hand. Her heart raced and her mouth was dry with fear. She had no doubt that he was serious; he meant to hurt her if she didn't tell him what he wanted to know. The only problem was, she didn't have the slightest idea where Harold was!

"Now, how's it gonna be, girlie?" the man continued. He squatted down beside Maggie and grabbed her by the chin, holding her head in place. Pressing the tip of the knife against her cheek, he said, "You talk, or I'm gonna have to cut that pretty face of yours."

Maggie was so frightened that she couldn't breathe, couldn't move, or even close her eyes. Instead, she stared ahead, fearful of the knife blade. Tears poured down her cheeks.

"That's enough, Frank." The other man moved closer.

"No, it ain't near enough."

"That's enough!" The voice was more forceful. Webb grabbed his companion by the shoulder and turned him away from Maggie. With the knife gone from her cheek,

the air rushed back into her lungs and she began to sob.
She sagged against the ropes that held her. The enormity
of what was happening to her overwhelmed her.

"She knows. Damn her!" Frank growled. He and Webb
ignored the crying girl and stepped away from the tree.
"This is the only chance we're gonna get."

"She ain't gonna tell you shit with that knife in her
face," Webb countered. "She's just a kid."

"And that's why we gotta scare the hell outta her! She
sees the blade and thinks we're gonna slice her up, she'll
spill her guts." Frank peered back over his shoulder. "If
she sees some of her blood on this blade, she'll sing like
a goddamn canary."

"I told you not to hurt her."

"You sound like a broken record, Webb." Frank
sneered. "All right, Mr. Wiseass, you have a go at her. But
let's get one thing straight right now," he said as he lifted
the knife so that it was between both their faces. "If you
don't get results, we're doin' things my way."

Webb's guts tied themselves in knots at Frank's words.
The Chicago mob man was the sort of guy the bosses
loved; he got results no matter what it took. But it was
that same violent side that unnerved Webb. He'd do
everything he could to keep him from killing the kid.

Webb took a hard look at their captive. Her head hung
down, her body limp against the ropes, and her long
brown hair hid her face. Her body rose and fell as she
sobbed. The nightdress that she'd been wearing when
they'd snatched her was streaked with dirt from her being
thrown to the ground outside the outhouse. *She can't be
more than fourteen*, he thought as he lifted her head up

and stared into her eyes. Tears, mucus, and saliva covered her face. Taking his handkerchief from his back pocket, he wiped her face. She stared at him with swollen eyes filled with fear.

"Your name's Margaret, right?" he asked.

The girl's face flinched at the mention of the name, but she didn't acknowledge what Webb had said. Her eyes looked to either side of his head, searching for Frank and his knife.

"Look at me, girl. I've got a sister about your age. I don't want to see you hurt." Webb continued, "So I'd start answerin' if I were you."

Her gaze settled on Webb's face and her sobbing abated. "Maggie," she whispered. "My name's Maggie."

"See how easy that was." Webb smiled. "By the way, you really hurt my hand with that boat oar."

The fear instantly returned to Maggie's face. "I'm sorry," she said quickly.

Webb smiled. "There ain't no reason to be sorry! Hell, if some fella tried to grab me out of a boat, I'd clobber him with whatever I could get my hands on, too. You were protectin' yourself. I understand that."

"I was scared."

"Just like you are now, I'd reckon." Webb nodded. "But I gotta be honest with you, Maggie. You got good reason to be scared. More scared than you ever been in your whole life. See, Frank over there ain't the type a fella that can live with not gettin' what he wants. Makes him crazy! Makes him do things that normal folk don't do. You follow me?"

Maggie nodded her head slowly.

"That's good. Now," Webb started, leaning closely to Maggie, the easy smile still plastered on his face, "he asked you a question and I'm gonna ask you the same thing, except I ain't gonna stick a knife in your face. When I ask it, you're gonna answer."

"But, I—," Maggie began before Webb cut her off.

"Hush, girl. Think before you say somethin' you might regret." Webb paused for a moment, then asked, "Where is Harold? Did he give you or your sister anything to hide?"

"I already told you," Maggie cried, her eyes wet with tears. "I don't know! We aren't close to Harold! He cheated us over Daddy's will, so Nona and I don't talk to him much! We haven't talked to him in a long time! I don't know anything about him. I swear!"

"Didn't your mama teach you not to lie," Webb scolded.

"I'm not lying! I'm not!"

"Yes you are, Maggie. We know your sister went to town and called your brother's office just a couple of days ago. She's called him a buncha times the last couple a months. We got somebody watchin' that end just like we're watchin' this one."

"I didn't know," Maggie exclaimed.

The look on the girl's face made Webb unsure. Over the last couple of years, he'd forced dozens of people to tell him things they didn't want to tell, and on each and every one of their faces, he'd seen the moment where they'd been caught in their own lies. It was never much; a twitch, a guilty look in their eye, something to give them away. But Maggie's face betrayed none of those things.

"Harold is family," he pressed. "Ain't much in this world a fella can count on, but family is the sort a thing you can downright depend on. Now, Harold's a bright guy, but he ain't bright enough to do all of this by himself. He'd need help. Way I reckon it, that's where you and Nona come in."

Maggie's eyes grew wide at the mention of her sister's name.

"Surprised that I know your sister's name? Don't be. I know all sorts of things about your family. For instance, I know you and Nona have been poorer than dirt the last couple a years. I bet that when Harold came up with his plan to steal the money, the two of you jumped at the chance. You came down here, to the camp, with the money Harold sent you to hide. Once things quiet down, you get a cut and are on easy street."

"Nona would never be part of something like that! We're not like Harold! He's a snake and has been trying to keep us from the money our daddy left us."

"Where's the money?" Webb repeated.

"I don't know!" Maggie wailed.

"I don't believe you," Webb lied. If Maggie had known, she'd have talked by now. They had grabbed the wrong sister!

"Goddammit, Webb!" Frank snarled. "I'll make the bitch talk!" He came toward Maggie quickly, the knife still clutched tightly in one hand. He raised his other hand and Maggie clenched her eyes shut, bracing herself for another blow, but it never came.

"Wait!" Webb said, stepping in front of Frank. Frank stopped, a wild look in his eyes. He was a predator who was used to getting his prey. "Hurtin' her now ain't gonna get us anywhere."

"The hell it won't!" the older man roared. "Her and that sister of hers know exactly where the money is! Harold ain't gonna protect you now, little bitch. I promise you that!"

"Not yet!" Webb said firmly. If he was wrong, if Maggie really did know where the money was, Frank would probably kill her before they got what they wanted, and then he'd go after the other sister. What Maggie needed was time. "I got a better idea."

"It sure as hell better be better than the last one!"

Webb turned his back on the other man and faced Maggie again. The girl looked at him pleadingly, but he had no compassion to give. He wanted the same thing Frank did; he just wasn't willing to go as far to get it.

"What she needs is time to think about it. She needs to spend the night tied to this tree, all by her lonesome, with no food or water, and then we'll see if she's willing to talk in the mornin'."

"Hell, that ain't half-bad!" Frank exclaimed. He moved closer to the tree, and the girl shivered. "Course, there ain't no guarantee there'll be anything left of her come daylight. There's wolves in these woods, girlie."

"Wolves?" Maggie choked.

"Packs of 'em," Frank continued, his eyes gleaming with a sinister glee. "Big and mean with fangs and claws near as long as this knife." He held up the blade to help illustrate his point. "You spend the night cryin' out, they'll find you. Won't take but a couple a minutes for a wolf to rip the flesh off your bones. We won't find nothin' but a skeleton come mornin'."

Maggie's eyes grew wide, and her heart began to beat faster. She was already miserable tied to the tree. A night alone in the woods would be unbearable, especially if there were wild animals. She glanced up at the trees above her, trying to see the sun. When she finally located it, she couldn't tell if it was still rising or setting. She might only have a couple of hours until nightfall. They couldn't be serious about leaving her in the woods overnight.

"Last chance," Webb offered.

"I don't know anything about any money!" Maggie cried as she strained against the ropes. They cut into the bare skin of her arms, leaving painful red burns, but she paid them no heed. The fear of being left overnight in the woods was greater.

"Then you'll rot," Frank barked and yanked the handkerchief up from her neck and forced it back into her mouth. Once he was sure it was tight, he stepped back and smirked. "That might keep you quiet enough so the wolves won't hear you screamin', but I wouldn't take no bets on it."

"Think long and hard about what you're gonna tell us in the mornin'," Webb said. The two men stepped around the tree and were lost to sight. Their footsteps slowly grew fainter before they were lost to Maggie's ears. She was alone!

"Uhhhhh," Maggie moaned into the gag as she

strained against the rope, but nothing changed. She was tied fast. Her mind raced.

Now that she was completely alone, every sound in the woods was magnified. Every snap of a twig, or rustle of a leaf, was a sign that someone or something was approaching. She was struck by the thought that she would never see Nona again, and it was nearly more than she could bear. Why hadn't she listened to Nona and Simon? She was going to die because she'd been stubborn with the people she loved!

Alone, Maggie sobbed into the gag.

LeAnn sat beside Jack as they watched the sky darken and stars appear, one by one. From Nona's porch, the view across the lake would have been beautiful and serene at any other time. Now the open expanse served to remind LeAnn of the unknown and the frightening. Someone out there had killed Ernie. Someone out there had taken Maggie from them.

"Will the sheriff be any help or will he think she's just run off?" LeAnn wondered. After they had exhausted their search of the camp, Simon had called the sheriff and gone into town to ask for volunteers. Now, as darkness approached, he still hadn't returned.

"The more people who're looking for her, the better."

"But what if they can't find her? What if they've taken her out of the state or . . ." LeAnn's words stuck in her throat and she left the thought unspoken. It was too painful to even imagine Maggie meeting the same fate as her late husband.

"Hush now," Jack said soothingly. "There isn't any

point in worrying ourselves sick just yet. The sheriff will have men combing the woods come morning. They're bound to turn up something."

"You're right," LeAnn agreed. She turned to look at Jack's profile and smiled. Even in the scant light she could see his rugged features, but that wasn't what she found endearing about the man. On the inside, Jack was caring and protective. While the others had searched for Maggie, he'd stayed close to the cabin and watched over all of them. She'd never met a man like him.

Chapter 15

THROUGH A BREAK IN THE TREES, Maggie could see the dark orange sun as it lowered itself toward the horizon. Lazy clouds drifted across the sky and birds chirped in the trees. The shadows grew longer with each passing minute. Then it was dusk. Soon it would be dark.

She had no idea what time it was; it seemed like hours since the men had left her and walked away into the woods, but she wasn't sure. The fear that had paralyzed her when they were near had receded a little when they left, but as the few remaining hours of light began to dwindle, the fear returned stronger than ever. While the daytime in the woods had been gloomy, she'd still been able to see for a short distance. She'd seen only a pair of squirrels, and they'd ignored her. Once the sun was gone, it would be pitch-dark. If what the older man had said was true, if there were wolves in the woods, she'd never see them until they were upon her.

Simon, Nona, I'm sorry I didn't listen to you.

She felt the rumbling of her stomach. It had been a full

day since the last time she'd eaten, and her stomach was protesting. *How can I think about being hungry? I may die before the night is over.* She was thirsty. Her throat and lips were dry. The gag sopped all the moisture from her mouth.

Maggie expected the men to return. They couldn't possibly plan on her spending the night tied to the tree! They were trying to scare her, trying to force her to tell them what they wanted to hear, and they would come back and cut her loose. What they intended to do with her then was still a mystery, but it had to be better than her current predicament! She'd strained her ears waiting for some sign, a male voice or the snap of a branch, to signal their return, but so far there'd been only silence. What if they left her here? What if the wolves came? She shivered and tried to put the thought out of her mind.

She hadn't learned anything new from the men who'd abducted her. She already knew her half brother, Harold, was a no-good thief! He not only robbed her and Nona of the money their father had left them, but he'd also stolen from these mean men! It was silly for anyone to think that she and Nona could be involved with Harold. But someone had believed it; that was why she was tied to a tree. If she only knew where the snake was, she'd have gladly told them. That way, she'd be free and Harold would get his! The problem was that they *didn't* believe her. Surely they wouldn't kill her!

Suddenly, a thought flashed across Maggie's mind. Were these the men who'd killed LeAnn's husband?! Even though Simon hadn't let her see the body, she'd heard that it had been badly beaten. If these were the men who'd done that, then they'd have no problem doing the same to her. The realization made Maggie sick to her stomach.

Simon! Please come! Simon!

Straining against the ropes with all the strength she could muster, Maggie tried to wiggle free, but no matter how hard she pushed, she couldn't budge. She'd rubbed up and down against the tree so much that her arms were a mass of scrapes and burns. She was too weak to do anything. Sagging against the ropes, she began to cry.

Through her tear-blurred eyes, she could see the sun's last moments before it dipped below the tree line. She held her breath and gave a silent prayer that somehow it would stay light, but the sun disappeared and the woods quickly grew noticeably darker.

She was hungry, thirsty, scared, and increasingly cold. Questions raced through her head. How was she supposed to go to the toilet? She would have to go against the tree, her pee staining her nightgown and her legs. What was Nona doing? She was probably worried half to death.

"Somebody help me." Her jaws worked, but the words didn't come out.

Nona sat on the porch step and stared off into the night. Her hands were fidgety and her mind heavy with worry. Inside the cabin, Mabel, LeAnn, and Jack sat around the table talking in hushed tones, their voices heard but their words not understood. She'd had supper with all of them but had left after the table had been cleared. Tonight, she needed some time alone.

Simon still hadn't returned from his visit to the sheriff.

He'd been gone for several hours. At sunset, Nona wanted to go to town and find out what was keeping him, but Jack had talked her out of it. They all needed to stay together, he'd argued, and she'd known he was right.

After the initial worry of her sister's disappearance had gone, Nona had been angry with Maggie for disobeying her. In the end, her loving care hadn't been enough. Maggie was gone.

As she worried and waited, a vehicle's headlights turned from the main road and approached the camp. After a few moments, she could see that it was Simon's truck bouncing along the dirt road. She was at the bottom of the steps when he brought the truck to a stop next to his cabin and shut off the engine. A feeling of disappointment filled her when she saw he was alone.

"What did the sheriff say?" she asked quickly.

"Let's go sit down, Nona," Simon said gently as he led her back up the steps and sat down next to her. "How are you doing? Did you eat any supper? You need to keep up your strength."

"Don't try to coddle me!" Nona protested. "What did you find out?"

"Not much, I'm afraid. Sheriff Carter's a nice man but not very experienced. He's mighty concerned about Maggie's disappearance and finding LeAnn's husband in the lake. This is a pretty quiet place, and he'd like to keep it that way."

"He doesn't have any idea what could have happened?"

"His suspicions are a lot like mine." Simon sighed. He put his rough hand on Nona's and gave it a light squeeze.

"I don't believe Maggie wandered off and got lost in the woods. I think she was kidnapped by the men looking for Harold. They may call and say they are holding Maggie for information about him."

Nona had tried to steel herself for his words, but they still shook her. She'd been trying to disbelieve, to hope. But she knew in her heart that Simon was right. Tears began to well in her eyes. "What do we do now?"

"The sheriff will be out in the morning with a bunch of volunteers. He hopes there'll be something that we all missed. He's also going to have his deputy talk to some of the folks who live deep in the woods. They're what remains of a commune of flower children who came here in the sixties and seventies."

"That's good." Nona nodded. "Maybe someone saw her. Maybe they saw who took her."

"Don't get your hopes up." Simon frowned. "Sheriff Carter says that people in these parts are pretty private folk. They keep to themselves and aren't too likely to talk, but the sheriff's men are going to ask them anyway."

"I pray we'll find her," Nona managed as her tears began to flow. "I just want . . . ," she began but couldn't finish as Simon pulled her close to him. She buried her face in his neck as sobs shook her. All of the anguish that she'd managed to hold in since Maggie had vanished poured out of her as Simon held her tightly. She felt like a child in his arms. He was no longer the man who joked at her expense or enraged her with his inappropriate comments. Now he was a comfort.

"We'll find her," he whispered.

"You don't know that," she sobbed. "Don't give me false hope!"

"I made a promise to you, don't you remember?" he said soothingly as he ran one hand through her curly red hair. "I told you that I'd protect you, Maggie, and Mabel, and I intend to. We'll leave no stone unturned. I promise."

The door to the cabin creaked open and Mabel came out onto the porch. She stood silently in the dark, her arms folded across her chest, gazing at the two of them. Her face was creased with worry. Simon nodded to her, then lifted Nona's chin up off his chest. Even in the darkening gloom, he could see the wetness on her cheeks.

"You need to get your rest," he said. "Tomorrow's going to be a busy day. Let Mabel take you in and put you to bed. I'll be in to check on you before long."

"We have to find her," Nona mumbled.

"We will, sweetheart." Simon nodded. "We will."

Without another word, Nona got up. The older woman put a steadying hand on her elbow and they both went into the house, leaving Simon alone on the porch.

The night air was growing cooler. A slight breeze began to stir, and the treetops rustled in the darkness. Worry filled Simon's gut. He tried to stay confident in front of Nona, but he was certain that the men looking for Harold had taken Maggie. It could be the work of the same bastards who'd killed LeAnn's husband. *Are we going to receive a ransom note? Is Maggie still alive?*

"I'll find you, squirt." He whispered his promise to Maggie into the night.

*   *   *

Maggie awoke with a start, blinking her eyes quickly. Around her, the world turned from black to hazy green; the early morning sunlight hardly sifted through the tree cover. For the briefest of moments, she was unsure of where she was, but the pain in her arms and shoulders quickly reminded her.

The night had been one horror after another. In the pitch-black darkness, menace seemed everywhere. Every snapping branch, every call of some unseen animal, every passing hour had been worse than the one before. She'd held her breath and tried not to cry, fearful that someone or something would hear and know where she was. She'd waited for the pack of wolves the man had spoken about to come, but they hadn't. Somehow she'd managed to fall asleep. Now her joints ached from being tied to the tree for so long, and her stomach growled loudly from hunger. She didn't know if she'd ever been so cold. As the light of the new day began to shine, she allowed herself to cry.

Suddenly, something before her caused her breath to catch in her throat and her heart to skip a beat. Before her tear-filled eyes, a figure parted the bushes in front of her, paused for a moment in a crouch, and then began to move quickly toward her.

"Mmmmm!" Maggie yelled into the handkerchief, her eyes large with fright.

As the figure got closer, she began to see it more clearly. She was surprised that it was a young boy, probably not much older than herself, with long hair and a thin frame. Even in the scant light, she could see that his clothes were well worn. His head darted from side to side as his gaze swept the woods around him. When he reached her, he clamped one hand over her mouth and looked her straight in the eyes.

"Don't make a sound," he whispered, and pulled the handkerchief loose from her mouth but clamped his hand back down on her aching lips. Reaching behind him, he pulled something from his back pocket. Maggie's eyes strained to see what it was, and the boy obliged by holding the knife up in front of his face. Maggie nearly wet herself with fear.

"Mmmmm!" She tried to yell again and strained with all of her might against the ropes but couldn't move them an inch. Somehow she'd managed to survive a night alone in the woods only to be attacked by a wild boy! To her further surprise, the boy seemed more worried than angry at her protests.

"Be quiet," he hissed through clenched teeth. "I can't cut the ropes if you're squirmin' like a worm."

Before Maggie could utter another sound, the boy sliced through the ropes that had bound her to the tree. Released from their hold, she tried to stand, but her weak legs collapsed and she sank to the ground.

"Who are . . . ," she began in a whisper, before the boy yanked her to her feet and pulled her along behind him as he moved back into the bushes from where he'd come. Branches whipped by in the near-darkness, scratching along her face and arms. With her legs so weak, she struggled to stay upright as they ran, stumbling on tree roots and rocks. The boy never slowed, pulling her hard by the arm. Finally, after what seemed like forever, he stopped still as a deer and crouched to the ground next to a large elm. Yanking her down beside him, he put a finger to his lips to hush her.

Maggie strained her ears for any sound. At first she heard nothing more than the normal woods sounds of wind and birdcalls, but, faint at first then growing louder, the sound of voices reached her. Whoever it was, they were coming right for them!

". . . all I'm saying is that nothin' better have happened to her." Maggie's breath caught and her heart jumped out of rhythm as she recognized the voice of the younger man who'd kidnapped her and tied her to the tree!

"Ain't nothin' happened," the older man said. "I checked on the little bitch not more than two hours ago. She ain't dead. Just sleepin' like an angel whose wings are in need of clippin'."

"I told you, I won't be part of hurtin' her."

"And I told you that little bitch is gonna tell us what we want to know," the older man snarled. "We tried it your way and didn't get shit. A night outside will have loosened her tongue. I'm gonna make her talk."

"Maybe she don't know nothin'."

"I'm startin' to think you ain't cut out for this line a work. That dumb son of a bitch Harold sent his sisters the money or told them where he put it. Why the hell else would two city women come all the way out here to the sticks? She'll talk whether she wants to or not."

The sound of the voices grew louder and louder before finally beginning to fade. At their closest, they must have been only a few yards away. They were headed for the tree where she'd been tied. When they discovered her gone, they'd come looking for her with a vengeance.

Without warning, the boy tugged Maggie back to her feet and was once again off into the underbrush. It was all that she could do to keep up with him. Questions began to run through her head. *Who is he? Where is he taking me?*

After scampering up a soft incline, the boy halted. Before them lay a fallen tree trunk that spanned a dried-up creek bed. Bright green moss covered its sides. Maggie peeked over the edge and saw a bed of rocks twelve feet below. Scanning the area, she could see that getting to the other side would be difficult.

The boy let go of her hand and pointed toward the other side. As quickly as a deer, he darted out onto the fallen tree, his arms spread out to either side, and nimbly made it across the space. Once on the other side, he turned and waved for Maggie to follow him.

Maggie was frozen in place. If she attempted to cross on the tree and follow the boy, she could fall to the rocks below. Still, if she stayed and tried to make her own way, the men who'd taken her from the camp would certainly find her. By now they'd have discovered that she was missing and would be looking for her. She couldn't possibly hope to escape them without help. With as much courage as she could muster, she stepped out onto the tree trunk.

For the first couple of feet, she tried not to look down. One foot in front of the other, she inched across the space. She spread her arms out as the boy had done and found that it helped her sense of balance.

More confident with each step, she looked up to see that she was only a couple of steps from the other side. Making eye contact with the boy, she smiled easily at him and hurried to join him. However, with her gaze lifted from the tree trunk, she failed to see a large patch of green moss. As soon as her foot touched it, she slipped and teetered on the log. Panic gripped her. A scream welled in her throat, but before she could voice it, a hand locked onto her wrist to steady her. Confused, Maggie looked up.

"Help me!" she pleaded.

"What do you think I'm trying to do?" the boy answered. "Stay still and get your balance. I can't pull you up if you go over!"

Safely off the log, Maggie fell on her hands and knees. She was winded, but before she could relax, the boy yanked her to her feet and started to move away.

"Wait!" Maggie said. "Who are you?"

"We don't have time for this," the boy answered impatiently.

"But I don't know your name!"

"It's Dusty," he answered. "Now keep quiet!"

Chapter 16

GODDAMMIT!" Frank spat angrily. He and Webb had entered the small clearing expecting to find Maggie tied to the tree. Instead, they'd found a tangle of ropes at the base of the tree . . . and no girl.

"What the hell?" Webb bent to the ground.

"I knew I shouldn't have left it up to you to tie her up!" Frank cursed his partner. "You did a piss-poor job!" he accused.

"Shut up!" Webb shouted. "I'm getting sick and tired of you blaming me for everything that goes wrong." Picking up the rope, Webb found the place where it had been cut. "Look at this." Webb held up the cut rope.

"Son of a bitch," Frank roared. "Do you think Wright found her?"

"Could be," Webb answered, but he didn't think so. They were a good five miles into the woods. The day before this, they had scouted the location and brought in their bedrolls and some food. If someone had come through, they would have heard him.

"When I checked on her a couple of hours ago she was sleeping like a baby," Frank snarled at Webb.

"Well, between then and now, someone's cut her loose. This rope was cut by a sharp knife. Someone knew what he was doing. She certainly didn't get away by herself." Webb squatted on his heels beside the tree. "She ain't nothin' but a scared kid."

Frank picked up the end of the rope. "I don't give a shit how scared she is; when I catch that little bitch, I'm going to beat her ass."

For the next several hours, the two men searched in an ever-widening circle around the tree. At noon, the temperature under the canopy of trees was stifling hot. They met back at the tree where they had tied Maggie, sweat soaking through their dirty clothing.

"There's one thing we can do." Frank wiped his brow with a handkerchief.

"What's that?"

"She, and whoever cut her free, will go right back to the camp."

"Unless she goes to the sheriff instead," Webb muttered. "If she does that, the whole area will be crawling with wannabe heroes looking for us. We'll have to get the hell out of here."

"We'd better go back to Tall Pine Camp and see if she's there."

The men returned to where they had left their bedrolls and supplies. Frank hung his binoculars around his neck and rolled up his bedding, leaving Webb to carry the rest.

"When I catch her, I'll teach her a lesson she'll never forget."

*   *   *

Maggie was determined the boy would not get out of her sight as he moved quickly through the dense underbrush. She had no idea where they were or where they were going. It took all her strength to keep up with him. She ached all over and her stomach growled. Hot, thirsty, and hungry as she was, the thought of being left behind kept her going forward.

Ahead of her, Dusty suddenly stopped. "We're here," he said.

"Where?" Maggie asked.

Rather than answer, Dusty held back tangled bushes and nodded for her to go ahead. Still unsure of what she was to do, Maggie stepped through the opening.

Before them, in a small clearing, was a weathered frame house set up on blocks. Two bentwood rockers sat on the porch. A tub full of yellow and gold flowers flanked the steps. Dusty whistled and two large shaggy dogs shot out from under the porch and ran to him, their tails wagging a welcome.

"Is this where you live?" Maggie asked.

"Yes." The boy grinned.

Before Maggie could say another word, a voice called from the house in a deep baritone. "Dusty? Is that you?" A man walked across the porch and down the steps toward them. He was tall and thin, and his long black hair was streaked with gray and tied at the nape of his neck. He was wearing jeans, boots, and a T-shirt with a peace sign on it.

"Hi, Pop!"

"Who's that with you, son?"

As Dusty's father neared, the enormity of where she was and what she was doing came sharply into Maggie's focus. The fear she had been fighting as they'd run through the woods came back fivefold. She was hungry and tired. Her cheeks flushed with embarrassment when she realized she was still wearing her torn and dirty nightgown. By the time the man reached her, Maggie was hugging herself tightly with her arms.

"This is my father, Avery Hathaway."

"Maggie. My name is Maggie Conrad. I was kidnapped from Tall Pine Camp," she blurted over the barking of the dogs.

"I found her in the woods. Tied to a tree," Dusty explained.

"Tied to a tree? Holy Moses!"

"A couple of men were camped not too far away, so I waited until they were asleep before cutting her loose."

Avery Hathaway's sharp eyes settled on Maggie. They were kind eyes, not cruel like those of the man called Frank. Tears of relief filled her eyes.

"Do you have a telephone?" Maggie asked hopefully.

"No, I'm sorry, we don't have one," Dusty's father said.

"My sister and I are staying at Tall Pine Camp. I need to get back there. She'll be worried sick."

"You need some clothes and a meal. Dusty, do something with those dogs."

"Sir, I'm afraid the men will come looking for me," Maggie said.

"We'll handle it if they come," he reassured her.

"You won't let them take me, will you?"

"No, not if we can help it." The man turned and called to his wife, who had come out onto the porch. "Denise, come here, please. We have company."

The woman who approached wore a long colorful skirt. Her straw-colored hair was tied in two bunches and hung down over her breasts. She and Dusty shared the same hair color and blue eyes. Her husband reached out and pulled her to his side.

"Dusty found this young lady in the woods. She needs something to eat and something to cover her nightgown."

"This is Maggie, Mom," Dusty said.

"Hello," Maggie said shyly, holding her folded arms protectively over her chest. She looked at the smiling face of Dusty's mother and, for the first time since her abduction, felt the burden of fear start to leave her.

"Come with me, Maggie. I'll find something for you to put on. Then you can eat and rest." She gently put her arm around Maggie's shoulders, her blue eyes filled with concern.

"She was tied to a tree all night," Dusty continued. "She's worn out."

"Poor child. Avery, you and Dusty look around. We don't want whoever did this coming here."

Avery nodded. "Dusty, get the rifles."

Maggie went with Dusty's mother into the house. The large, comfortable room was cluttered with books and pottery. Colorful braided rugs covered the floor, and a couch with a collection of pillows sat against one wall. The easel that stood by the window held a half-finished painting. Pots of flowers were arrayed along the windowsill. A tall plant in the corner of the room almost reached the ceiling.

"I've been busy with my painting this morning, so things are a bit messy," Denise commented.

"I'm thankful to be here." Maggie's lips trembled. "I was so scared in the woods. The really mean one was going to cut me with a knife, but the other one wouldn't let him. I was afraid they were going to do more . . . you know, but they didn't." Tears rolled down Maggie's face.

"There, there, honey. You'll be all right now." The woman put her arms around Maggie and pulled her close.

Nona watched from the porch of her cabin as the sheriff and his men trudged down the lane toward her. They'd spent the morning and early afternoon hours combing through the woods and along the lakeshore for any sign of Maggie. As they came closer, Nona could see their faces were grim. They had found nothing. Her heart sank. She turned away and entered the cabin.

Inside, all was quiet. Mabel had gone with LeAnn to her cabin. Even Sam Houston was occupied in a rambunctious dream, his legs kicking in his sleep. Nona was alone. The thought of her sister being alone, or at the hands of unscrupulous men, filled her with dread. She allowed her shoulders to slump and buried her face in her hands.

Buck up, Nona. You won't do Maggie any good if you fall apart.

She took a handkerchief from her pocket and headed out the back door and down the path to the lake, refusing to let herself wallow in pity.

"Nona!"

She turned to see Simon hurrying to catch up with her. His face was red and sweaty. She was grateful, so grateful that he was here with her. How could she ever have thought he was cold and unfeeling? When he reached her, his gaze was piercing as he scrutinized her face.

"Did the sheriff and his men find anything?" she asked hopefully.

"It might be nothing, but the sheriff talked to an old fellow who lives about a mile up the road. The man's name is Galloway, and he's been in these parts as long as anyone can remember. He said he saw a couple of men entering the woods south of his place a couple of days ago."

"Did he recognize them?"

"No." Simon shook his head. "He said they were too far away for him to get a good look, but they didn't seem to be the type to be camping in the woods. He watched them until they disappeared. The way they were going, he figured they were headed for Tall Pine Camp."

"When did he see them? Was it the morning Maggie disappeared?"

"According to Galloway, it was a couple of days earlier." Seeing Nona's disappointment, he quickly added, "But that doesn't mean it wasn't them. The guys Galloway saw could be the two who were in the boat. I'm going to the boathouse and ask Russ if he's seen any strangers. He's about worn himself out tramping the woods. Come with me." Simon held out his hand.

Nona walked beside him toward the lake. Even though her mood was stormy, the day was another beautiful one.

The mist had burned off the lake. A trio of ducks splashed down on the mirrored surface of the water, sending ripples in their wake. A gentle breeze stirred Nona's fiery hair.

When they reached the boathouse, Russ was working on an outboard motor. Parts were spread out on the dock around him. He looked up as they approached. His hands were black and a large streak of grease was smeared across his forehead.

"Afternoon," he called out. "Figured it was time to fix this old hunk of junk. Damn thing sputters and chokes no matter what I do to it. It's about to drive me crazy."

"Seen anything, Russ?" Simon asked.

"No, not a thing." Russ had a look of concern on his face. "Maggie's a good kid. Anything new?"

"We might have something to work with." Simon filled Russ in on what the sheriff had learned from Galloway and mentioned the possibility that it could be connected to the men who'd accosted Maggie on the lake.

"Can't say I've seen anything out of the ordinary." Russ frowned. "The lake has been pretty quiet lately. It's too early for duck hunters, and the fishing's been poor this summer."

"The sheriff also told me there were a few families of hippies living up in the woods, but as far as he knew, they had never bothered anyone. Keep your eyes open. If you see anything, anything at all, tell me."

"I will." Russ nodded. Turning to Nona, he added, "Don't you worry, Miss Conrad. Maggie will be home, safe and sound, before you know it. I'm certain of it."

"Thank you, Russ." She didn't know Mr. Story very

well, but he seemed an earnest and hardworking man. Maggie had obviously wormed herself into his affection. "I hope you're right."

"I know I am," the older man said confidently.

As Simon and Nona walked back toward the cabins, Russ shouted up to them. "Please tell Miss Mabel how much I liked that pie!"

Chapter 17

MAGGIE AWOKE. A feeling of panic sent her heart racing in her chest as she struggled to remember where she was. Then she recalled rushing through the woods with Dusty, meeting his parents, and lying down on his mother's bed. She was covered with a thin blanket. She had no idea how long she'd slept.

On one side of the room stood a battered bureau, and on the other side was a curtained window. An oval braided rug lay on the floor. The room was spartan, but clean and cozy. Through the open window, she could see the woods beyond.

A skirt and top lay across the back of a chair next to the bed. Dusty's mother must have put them there. It felt good to strip off the grimy nightgown and put on the T-shirt and skirt. The T-shirt with the words "Make Love Not War" hung loosely from her narrow shoulders and the waist of the skirt was too large, but she tucked the shirt into the waistband, folded the band over, and pinned it with a safety pin that was already there.

Pulling the bedroom door open a crack, she surveyed the rest of the house. Dusty was sitting at the table with his parents in the center of their living space. In a small kitchen area set off to the back was a wood-burning stove. A hand pump sat beside a tin-lined sink. A black-and-white-spotted dog lay curled into a tight ball underneath the table. The Hathaways were eating supper. Maggie's stomach rumbled.

The family was unlike any that Maggie had ever met. She had heard about hippies, but hadn't thought they would be as nice as these people were.

"Maggie, come join us," Dusty's mother called. Then to her son, "Please get Maggie a chair." When she was seated, Mrs. Hathaway brought her a plate and utensils. The delicious smells made Maggie's mouth water. A large bowl of potatoes, one with turnip greens, another of fried okra, and squares of corn bread were passed to her.

"Maggie might want a glass of milk, Denise," Avery said.

"It's goat's milk, Maggie."

"I've never had goat's milk."

"You might like it." Dusty nodded at her.

"I'm hungry enough to try anything" was all Maggie could manage before she attacked the food on the plate. She'd never been so starved in her life! "This is delicious!" she exclaimed between bites.

Dusty chimed in. "My mom's a darn good cook."

"Hush, boy, and let the girl eat." Avery smiled.

When Maggie's appetite was finally appeased, she recounted her harrowing ordeal. She told the Hathaways about being abducted from the camp, waking up tied to the tree, and her and Dusty's flight through the woods.

"Why did the men take you?" Avery asked.

"They're looking for my half brother. They claimed he owed them money. I don't know where he is, so I couldn't tell them anything. Dusty came along just in time. They said they'd hurt me if I didn't tell them by morning."

"Some people are just plain crazy," Denise said with a shake of her head. "I thought we'd be safer living here. Now I'm not so sure."

"I want to go back to my sister," Maggie said. "She's frantic by now."

"Dusty and I will take you back in the morning." Avery glanced at his son.

"Do you have a car? Can't we go now?" she asked anxiously.

Avery shook his head. "No car. We'll have to walk to the camp."

"Do we have to go back through the woods?" Maggie moaned.

"We know a shortcut. It won't be too bad."

"But what if we run into those men?" Maggie persisted. "They'll still be looking for me."

"At first light I'll take a look around and be sure they're out of the area," Avery assured her.

"But what if they see you? I'd be sick if you got hurt because of me!"

"They won't see me. I've lived in these woods a long time."

Maggie quickly stole a glance at Dusty. He smiled

broadly. He was confident his father could make good his claim.

"I have an idea," Maggie offered. "Why doesn't Dusty get the sheriff? He could lead him back to the house and then to where those men tied me up. We could catch them!"

"By the time the sheriff got here, they'd be long gone."

"Don't worry, honey," Denise said soothingly. "Avery and Dusty will do whatever it takes to get you back to your sister."

"All right." Maggie nodded. She felt she was in good hands.

"Now then." Denise stood up from the table. "Who wants molasses cookies?"

"We should just kill one of 'em."

"What did you say?" Webb looked up from his plate and stared across the table at Frank. The older man didn't return the look, instead continuing to shovel forkfuls of beans into his mouth.

"I said that we should kill one of 'em. It'd make a hell of a lot more sense than traipsin' around in the woods lookin' for 'em. The boss wants results, I say we give him results."

After finding that Maggie had escaped from the tree, they'd gone back to Tall Pine Camp to survey the area through binoculars. It had been hard going; the sheriff's men were poking around in the woods and stopping every car to ask questions. Hours passed and the girl never appeared. After waiting until well after dusk, they'd picked their way back to where they'd hidden the car and headed for the dilapidated old camp. After scouting around the camp, they kicked in the door of a cabin set far back in the woods and thanked God the electricity hadn't been turned off. They heated a can of beans on a hot plate they had brought with them. It had done little to improve their foul moods.

"We should just kill one of them," Frank repeated.

"That ain't gonna get us nowhere," Webb argued.

"You don't know what the hell you're talkin' about," Frank spat, fixing a hard stare on the younger man. Webb could see how dangerous Frank Rice could be. "Killin' somebody's the best way to get the rats runnin'. You should know that."

"I don't know it. Explain it to me."

"It's simple!" Frank dropped his tin plate on the table with a dull thud and got up to pace the room. He pulled a pack of cigarettes from his shirt pocket and lit one. He puffed heavily as he talked. "Let's say we go over and shoot that older sister; what do you think is gonna happen?"

"If Wright don't get us, the cops will." Webb frowned.

"You're still thinkin' too narrow! We kill the goose that's protectin' the golden egg, then Harold's gonna come runnin'! He ain't gonna give a good goddamn about his sister, but if that snake thinks his money is about to be found, he'll be there."

"And then we nab him . . ."

"Exactly!" Frank crowed.

"But what if he don't come?" Webb argued. He wasn't above roughing someone up, but spilling blood made him nervous. Spilling a woman's blood was even worse, especially since he had his doubts that she knew anything about Harold. "What if we kill her and Harold don't show up? Then what?"

"Are you crappin' out on me? It won't be the first killin' for me," Frank boasted.

"That isn't the way I do things."

"Listen to me! For the sake of arguin'," the older man said as he sat on the edge of the table, "let's say that Harold's an even bigger son of a bitch than I think he is. We kill the older sister, the younger one's gonna know we ain't playin' and is gonna sing like a bird! Lookin' at her sister's cold body will loosen her tongue!"

"What about Wright? He ain't gonna be sittin' around with his finger up his butt while we kill the sister."

"One bullet will take care of him."

The coldness with which Frank spoke disturbed Webb. He'd had enough of this place, enough of Frank, and enough of threats and violence to last a lifetime. Still, the boss wanted results, and he expected the two of them to get it.

"We should call the boss," Webb argued. "He'll know what to do."

Frank scowled. "With all the goings-on about us kidnappin' that kid, the whole area will be lookin' for anyone that's out of place. We show up to use a telephone, the sheriff will be on us like flies on a rotting corpse."

"I still don't like it."

"You don't have to like it," Frank growled.

Webb knew that Frank was determined to kill one of the Conrad girls. He'd convinced himself that it was the right thing to do, and no amount of arguing was going to change his mind. All Webb could do was go along and try to stop it.

"What are you doing out on the porch at this hour?"

Nona jumped at the sound of the voice. Simon stood at the bottom of the steps. It was late, nearly two o'clock in the morning, and she hadn't expected anyone else to be up and about.

"What are you doing?"

"Jack and I are taking turns patrolling the grounds."

"I have so much on my mind, I couldn't fall asleep."

"Are you going to let me come up there and join you, or are you saving that seat for someone else?"

She patted the place beside her. Simon sat down. In the darkness, she could see little more than his profile, but having him near was comforting. For several minutes they sat in silence, staring out at the shining lake. A handful of stars twinkled in the night sky, most of them drowned out by the luminescence of the nearly full moon. Somewhere in the distance, a coyote howled.

"I remember a time when Maggie was about nine years old," Nona started, giving voice to the thoughts that had kept her awake. "We lived in Little Rock, in a run-down tenement near the river. I was working for practically nothing as a waitress. Long hours and little pay. We just had enough to make ends meet."

Simon silently nodded his understanding.

"One day I was ten minutes late for work. It was the heart of the winter, and I hadn't given myself enough time to get there. The owner was a wretched old man who tried to pinch all the girls' butts. When he tried for mine, I slapped him right across his wrinkled old face."

"Sounds like you." Simon chuckled.

"When I showed up late, he wouldn't even listen to my excuses and fired me. Just like that, I didn't have a job. I was mortified! By the time I got home I was a wreck. I sat down at our little table and started worrying that we'd have to move and that we wouldn't have enough money for food." With each word, Nona's voice became more choked with emotion. A tear made its way down her cheek. "Maggie listened for a while and then left the room. The next thing I knew, she was standing in front of me with a candy bar she'd gotten for Christmas. She must have been saving it, but there she was, holding it out for me. She looked at me and said, 'Don't cry, Nona. I'll take care of you.' "

"She loves you," Simon said softly.

"That's what makes this so hard," Nona explained as she wiped the tears from her eyes. "I'm all she has. She's all I have."

Simon reached out and took one of her hands and enveloped it in his own. His skin was rough but warm and inviting. He pulled her closer and wrapped his arm around her. She leaned against him, resting her head on his shoulder.

"Simon, thank you for being here." She sniffled.

"Put the notion out of your head that we won't find her," Simon scolded. "You're one of the strongest women I've ever met. You're going through a difficult time now, but you won't give up hope. We could hear from the kidnappers any day. Hell, you've stood up to my guff from the moment you first laid eyes on me. If that isn't courage, I don't know what is."

"You're right," Nona admitted.

"Of course I'm right," he said as he turned her head to look down into her wet eyes. His gaze was piercing, even in the sparse light of the porch. "If you don't believe me, just ask."

A longing filled Nona as she held his gaze. She hadn't felt this way since they'd sat in the truck together. Even though that had only been a few short days earlier, it felt as if months had passed. She ached to touch him and have him hold her.

"You'll not ever be alone if you want me," he whispered, repeating the words he'd said before. His warm breath fell across her face. The anticipation of the kiss grew so great that Nona felt it as a weight on her chest. When finally their lips met, the joining was sweet and tender. Her hand squeezed his tightly, never wanting to let go. She leaned on him, her head snuggled against his chest, listening to the rapid beating of his heart.

"Oh, Simon," she sighed. "I'm so glad you're here."

"So am I, my sweet," he whispered as he ran his hand up and down her back. "We'll not give up hope. We'll find her."

Simon's words echoed in Nona's head as she was lulled to sleep by the rhythm of his heart and the touch of his hand.

Chapter 18

Maggie sat patiently in front of the cracked mirror, her hands clasped together in her lap, as Dusty's mother combed out the tangles in her hair. Maggie could see that she had begun to look more presentable.

Morning sun flooded the small room with light, and the sounds of chirping birds came in through the open window. Mr. and Mrs. Hathaway's bedroom was tiny, but there was enough room for a bookcase and a chest of drawers. Judging by the number of books displayed, this was a reading family, Maggie decided.

"Would you like me to put your hair in a French braid?" Denise smiled into the mirror. "I've missed having a girl around to do things with. I used to do this for my little sister. Dusty's a fine boy, but I don't think he'd take too well to his mama braiding his hair!"

"Probably not," Maggie agreed.

Maggie had awakened early, hoping to get back to Nona and Mabel, but the Hathaways had insisted that she wait until Dusty and Avery could look around in the woods. Only when they returned would they leave for the camp. Time dragged. When Denise offered to comb through her hair, Maggie had agreed immediately. Anything to hurry the clock!

"Is your sister as pretty as you are?" Mrs. Hathaway asked.

"Oh, she's much prettier than I am! She's got this bright red hair that always seems to attract attention," Maggie explained.

"What about you? I bet you have your share of boyfriends."

"Oh, no! Not me!" The truth was that she'd never been much interested in boys until just lately. They had gone from being creepy little sneaks, through being gangly with squeaky voices, to becoming rather attractive teenagers. She felt awkward and unsure of what to say or do when she talked to them.

"That'll change soon. You're going to be pretty as a picture in a year or two . . . not that you aren't already. It's one of the strangest things. One day you think there isn't anyone in the whole world who knows who you are, and then guys start knocking on your door!"

"I don't know about that," Maggie murmured.

"Don't worry! That's what happened to me when I was your age."

"Really?"

"Yes, really! When I met Avery, I was teaching school in San Francisco. I knew instantly that he was the man for me. They say you don't fall in love at first sight, but I would argue that. Avery made my knees wobble and my heart sound like a locomotive going uphill. It took me a while to figure out that I had fallen in love with him. Later on we made plans to come here, and I have never regretted leaving the city. We've been here sixteen years. Dusty was born here."

"Well, he certainly seems to know every inch of these woods."

The slam of a door and the pounding of footsteps interrupted their talk. Avery stuck his head into the room, his face wet with sweat.

"What's up, sweetheart?" Mrs. Hathaway tried to make her voice light, but she sounded concerned.

"A couple of men are coming this way," he said between gasps. "It could be the guys looking for Maggie."

Before Maggie could even open her mouth, Denise was up out of her chair and pulling her into Dusty's room.

"You can hide in here," she said.

"Thank you," Maggie whispered. She was so scared she was breathless. The room seemed even smaller than it had the day before. It was hard for her to imagine she could hide in such a tiny space.

"Get in the chest." Denise pointed at a battered, steel-gray chest lying at the foot of the bed.

"But I won't fit—," Maggie began.

"Hush now!" Denise cut her off. "We don't have time to argue."

The woman quickly lifted the lid and pulled out two quilts. She motioned for Maggie to climb in.

Maggie hesitated, unsure of what she should do.

"Quickly!" Avery warned from the doorway. "They'll be here any minute!"

"Trust me, darling," Denise said softly, placing a hand on Maggie's shoulder.

Returning her gaze, Maggie knew she was trying to help. Gathering all of her courage, Maggie stepped into the chest, lay down on her side, and did her best to fit.

"Keep quiet," Denise warned as she covered her with one of the quilts.

The lid was lowered and Maggie was thrown into a near-panic. All was silent but the loud hammering of her heart. She held her breath, hoping that the men would not come into the house. Seconds passed before she heard one knocking on the door.

"And we commend the eternal soul of Ernest Leasure to You, O Lord! Receive him and take him into the kingdom of heaven."

LeAnn looked down into the hole in the ground in which Ernie's body lay. The casket was little more than a pine box. A mound of red earth was piled next to the hole, a pair of shovels stuck in the pile, their handles glinting in the morning sun. A couple of men stood at the cemetery gates, smoking cigarettes and waiting for their time to work. Soon the service was over. Ernie was in the ground.

"Ashes to ashes, dust to dust," Pastor Kent said softly.

A Baptist minister with a small congregation in Home, Willis Kent was an overweight young man with thinning blond hair. His face was soft, his skin pale. LeAnn had never met the man before that morning, but he'd acted as if she'd been part of his congregation all of her life, and she'd warmed to him instantly. She'd allowed him to assume the best about the man Ernie had been. Now that he was gone forever, it seemed the very least she could do.

Jack stood silently beside her, his hat clutched loosely in front of him. He'd helped her make all of the funeral arrangements, calling into town and contacting the right people. He'd gone with her when it was time to pick a casket and to set up Ernie's interment in the Home Memorial Cemetery. She'd hated having to burden him by asking for his assistance, but he'd insisted that it was no trouble. Through all of her hardship, he'd been there to walk, to talk, and to listen. *What would I have done without Jack?*

"Amen," Pastor Kent finished, closing his Bible.

"Amen," Jack said softly.

Slightly embarrassed that she'd been thinking about another man at her own husband's funeral, LeAnn quickly added, "Amen."

After accepting further condolences from the pastor, LeAnn stood and stared down at Ernie's coffin. She'd expected to be sadder. She'd expected to cry, to be flooded with memories of all the good times that they'd spent together, but in the end she'd felt little. The truth was that Ernie Leasure had been a terrible husband and not much better as a person. He'd always be a part of her life, the child she would give birth to would make sure of that; but she wouldn't carry him in her heart. Her feelings would be buried, too.

Turning to Jack, she said, "I'm ready to go."

"Now, don't be in a hurry on my account," he protested. "You take all the time you need. If you'd like, I'll go back to the truck and wait for you, give you a little privacy."

"There's nothing left for me to say, Jack. I've been grieving for years."

He nodded solemnly and pressed his hat back on his head. He offered her his arm, not wanting her to slip in the still-damp grass, and they walked back to his battered pickup truck.

"Thanks again for coming."

"I told you before, LeAnn," he explained. "I'm here for you whenever you need me. This is no trouble at all. It's the least I could do. I'm only sorry more folks couldn't come."

"It can't be helped with Maggie still missing."

For two days and two nights everyone had been waiting for news of her. No word had come. There had been enough hardship in LeAnn's life; she didn't wish any for Nona and Mabel.

"I'm sure they'd all be here if they could."

LeAnn suddenly stopped walking and turned to face Jack as he halted beside her. Looking up into his face made her heart flutter in a way it never had before. His eyes were the bluest she'd ever seen. It had been the same from the first time she had gazed at him. This quivery feeling was something she'd never experienced.

"I'm just glad that you're with me," she said softly.

Jack reached out and took her hand in his own. His skin was rough; it was a working man's hand, and she could feel its strength. They looked at one another for what seemed forever but she never wanted to speak, to break the moment; on the contrary, she wanted it to go on forever.

"I don't want to be anywhere else," he finally said.

They walked the rest of the way back to the truck hand in hand.

Avery Hathaway cautiously moved to the door. A man he didn't recognize stood on the porch staring at him through the thin screen. His frame was large. He wore a wrinkled shirt and his belly hung over the belt in his pants. He wasn't the sort that'd usually be traipsing around in the woods. Sweat ran in rivers down the sides of his face. He lifted his hat and wiped his forehead with the sleeve of his shirt. His dark hair was wet with sweat, his clothes equally soaked. Avery glanced quickly at the man's waist before looking away. A pistol hung from a holster at his hip. Another man, little more than a skinny kid, stayed in the yard.

"Something I can help you with?" Avery asked innocently.

"I hope so," the man answered. "I'm looking for a young lady that's been missing for a couple of days from Tall Pine Camp. Her name is Maggie Conrad. She's fourteen years old, tall, with light brown hair. We're asking around to see if anyone has seen her."

"Sorry, I can't help you."

The man only nodded in reply. He craned his neck to look over Avery's shoulder, examining the inside of the small house. The heel of the man's hand came to rest on his gun and his fingers drummed along the hilt. Avery cursed himself for putting his shotgun in the kitchen; having it closer would have made him feel more secure. He heard a rustle behind him as his wife moved to stand next to him.

"Ma'am," the man said politely with a nod of his head.

"Why are you looking for her? Is she family?" Mrs. Hathaway asked bluntly.

"Afraid not, ma'am," he said as he fingered the tin badge pinned to his shirt. "I'm a deputy with the county sheriff's office. We were called in to help look for the girl."

"What do you think happened?" Avery asked matter-of-factly.

"Could be a number of things, I suppose," the man said as he wiped his brow again. "She's from the city and not used to the country. She could have wandered into the woods and found herself turned around, not knowing how to get out. Course, it could have been something else. Somebody might have taken her against her will. You've lived here for quite a while. Do you have any suggestions as to where she might be?"

Avery regarded the man with suspicion. A tin star and the story of being a lawman searching for a missing girl were easy things to come by, the pistol at his side even easier. Maggie hadn't said much about the men who'd taken her, so for all Avery knew, the man before him was not what he pretended to be. It was clear he was fishing for information. Avery wasn't going to give him the satisfaction of taking the bait.

"No. Sorry I can't help you, Deputy."

The man nodded absently and turned to step off the porch.

Avery could feel the sweat forming on his brow. He half expected the man to turn, pull his gun, and force his way into the house, but instead he simply stood on the porch. Finally, he turned back to them and said, "Remember what I said. If you see the girl, hold her. We'll check back with you tomorrow."

Avery nodded.

Denise snatched her husband's hand and held it tightly as the man descended from the porch, conversed with the man in the yard, and headed back into the woods. In a matter of moments, both were lost from sight. Denise started to the bedroom to let Maggie out of the chest, but Avery held her in place.

"We need to make sure they're gone," he said softly. "They might have settled down out there to watch us."

"You're right," she agreed. "They could be watching with a pair of binoculars."

For the next fifteen minutes, the Hathaways went about their everyday chores. Denise went to the kitchen and peeled potatoes while Avery went to the shed and milked the goat.

After a while, Denise opened the chest lid. Maggie was damp with perspiration. "Stay here in Dusty's room. We're not sure they're gone."

"Was it one of them?" Maggie whispered as she climbed out of the small chest and stretched her aching legs and back.

"Avery didn't think so."

"One of the men who took me was bald with a black mustache."

"This man wasn't bald. He had a badge and a gun and said he was a deputy."

Chapter 19

"Y_OU_ MADE A MISTAKE!" Webb couldn't resist the dig.

"_I_ made a mistake!" Frank snarled.

"You're the one who wanted to take the girl."

"Shut your mouth! When something's got to be done, I do it."

"The end justifies the means, huh, Frank?"

"You're damn right, and you'd better not forget it. I haven't gotten to where I am by being gutless."

Webb was tired and hungry. He and Frank had spent the whole day moving from one spot to another, watching the camp with a pair of powerful binoculars. Groups of men, most of them in the company of a deputy sheriff, roamed the woods. Many of them carried guns. The dumb shits didn't have any idea how close they had come to him and Frank several times during the last few hours. The sound of voices and the crackle of their radios always preceded the deputy and his men, giving Frank and Webb time to leave one spot and settle in another.

The searchers' latest move had brought them to within

a couple hundred yards of the last cabin. A sheriff's car was parked in front. An overweight deputy, a cigarette in his mouth, leaned against the fender talking into his radio. Webb got the impression from his jovial tone that he was not conducting police business, but rather flirting with the dispatcher.

"Yeah," Frank said. "We sure screwed up."

Webb was surprised to hear Frank admit it, and didn't mention that there was no "we" about it. Frank and Frank alone had made the decision to take the girl. Webb had no choice but to agree with him.

"I don't think the kid knew anything about Harold. We scared the shit out of her though. If she had known anything, she'd have told us."

"Her sister could have told her something . . ." Webb's voice trailed, and he wondered why he was trying to appease Frank.

"We'll have to take the redhead now."

"With all the cops hanging around and Wright glued to her side?" Webb asked incredulously. Then: "We're not going to be able to waltz in there and snatch her."

"It only takes one bullet to stop Wright." Frank slid his hand down to the butt of his revolver. "We need that girl."

For the next twenty minutes the men sat silently and watched the movement in the camp. Webb knew that it needled Frank to have failed with the young one.

Frank was frustrated. Webb was like an old woman— too weak at heart to take action, but opinionated enough to rub it in about the girl.

Suddenly, the door to the cabin nearest them opened and a woman stepped out onto the porch. In that instant an idea came to Frank. "Wait a cotton-pickin' minute," he exclaimed.

"What is it?"

"Look there." Frank pointed at the cabin. A woman had come out onto the porch and stood with her hands spread over her ample stomach. A man joined her. He took her arm and helped her down the steps. They walked toward the center of the grounds.

"I don't get it," Webb confessed.

"That's Ernie's old lady. She'd be perfect."

"Perfect for what?"

"For grabbing, you dumb ass." A plan was quickly growing in Frank's mind. He was amazed that he hadn't thought of the possibility before they had taken the girl. This could be an answer to their problem with a lot less hassle.

Webb's brow furrowed. "What do we want with her?"

"She's been here with these broads for nearly a month. She's bound to have heard something. If old Ernie found out anything, he probably told her before he could get back to us."

"We'd be pushin' our luck with two kidnappings."

"Stop your bitchin'. Ain't nobody going to be watching that fat cow," Frank continued, ignoring the younger man's concerns. With every passing second, the plan seemed more logical. "That skinny fella she's with don't look like much. Besides, ain't no one else around. Everybody's out looking for the girl."

Frank paused when he heard the rustling of brush. He nudged Webb and they pressed back deeper into the woods. The last thing Frank wanted to do was run into a trigger-happy deputy who'd have no qualms about shooting them.

After a tense minute of their straining to hear another sound, there was a crackling of dried undergrowth. A hundred feet away, a man pushed his way through the brittle brush. He was dressed in work clothes, his sleeves rolled up to his elbows. With a groan, he stepped over a fallen tree trunk, opened his britches, and began to relieve himself.

Webb glared at Frank, hoping to root him into place. There were times to run, times to fight, and times to ride it out. This was definitely the latter.

Sweat ran down the sides of Webb's face while he waited for the man to stop peeing. As soon as he had finished, the man crashed back through the underbrush in the direction of the camp. When he reached the road in front of the cabins, he hailed the deputy leaning on the squad car.

"Move," Frank hissed.

Without further pause, he and Webb quickly left their hiding place and pushed deeper into the woods.

"Damn, that was close," Webb said breathlessly when they finally stopped and hunkered down behind a felled tree. Their clothes were wet with perspiration.

"How'd that guy get so close to us?" Frank's voice was accusing.

"Don't think it was my fault."

"You should have been watching our backs."

"What about you?" Webb spat. "You're awfully quick to blame someone else for your shortcomings." After spending a week in his company, he realized that when you got right down to it, Frank was not as smart as he thought he was. Webb's dislike for him had increased steadily. He wished that he were back in Chicago, belly-ing up to the bar and shooting the breeze with his bud-dies.

Webb turned his head to listen. He heard the sound of voices; one of them was a girl . . . maybe *the* girl. He saw Frank pull his revolver from the band of his trousers.

Maggie followed along behind Dusty as he made his way down the narrow path. The going was difficult; she had to be careful to stay away from the prickly barbs on the bushes that grew on either side. The sun was on its down-ward journey. The mid-afternoon shadows grew longer with each passing hour. Maggie had no idea how long they had been walking. Dusty had said they would reach the camp before dark. She wondered if he had miscalcu-lated.

After the man in the uniform had come to their door, Denise and Avery had been anxious for Dusty to return from surveying the woods. When he had, he told them he had seen no sign of anyone, and they all agreed that it was best to get Maggie back to the camp as soon as possible. After emotional hugs and promises to return later, Dusty and Maggie left for Tall Pine Camp.

Several hours later, Maggie was bone-weary. Her feet felt as if each weighed at least a hundred pounds. Her hair was wet and stuck to her neck. She asked in a low mur-mur, "How much farther?"

"I'm not real sure," Dusty said without looking back.

"I've only been there a few times. We fish on the other side of the lake. I'm guessing it's a mile or two yet."

They walked in near-silence. The crackling sounds of their footsteps mingled with the chatter of birds settling in the treetops. A slight breeze came up, bringing with it the scent of pines. Squirrels busied themselves in the underbrush in their constant search for food. Maggie wanted to talk to this strange boy, to ask him about his life, but she hesitated. She was shy about talking to boys, and he had told her to keep quiet. Dusty had risked a lot for her, and she would do whatever he told her to do. During the last couple of days, Maggie had known real fear for the first time in her life. Now she wondered if the men who had taken her had gone after Nona.

Behind every tree, bush, or boulder, she imagined one of them lurking. Several times her breath had caught in her throat as she thought she saw someone stepping out to stop them. Each time she had been mistaken. Still, the worry would not go away. Noticing that she had fallen a bit behind Dusty, she hurried to catch up with him.

"So, tell me about your life," the boy said suddenly in a low tone. "I bet it's a lot different from mine."

Not sure that she had heard him correctly, she closed the distance between them and asked softly, "What did you say?"

"Tell me about yourself. Where did you live before you came here?"

"We lived in an apartment in Little Rock."

"I've never been to Little Rock."

"Where do you go to school?" Maggie asked.

"I don't. My mom and dad teach me. They both have

teaching certificates. My dad was a college professor; my mother taught English literature. In the winter I have to study at least six hours a day. My mother sent away for the college SAT exam. I scored high enough for college admission when I was fourteen years old," he said proudly.

"You must be pretty smart." Maggie looked at him with admiration.

"I don't know about that." Then, "How old are you?"

"I'm fourteen."

"I'm two years older than you."

"Don't you miss being around other kids?"

"Sometimes. But there are quite a few kids in the area my age or younger. All the families get together on the Fourth of July and at Christmastime. My mother is going to start teaching all of the grades in September."

"What do you do for fun?"

"I read, listen to the radio, hunt, fish, and study."

Maggie grimaced. "I don't think studying would be much fun."

"I want to learn as much as I can. I'll need a scholarship to attend a good university."

"Then what will you do?"

"I want a job in the space program. My dad gave me a telescope last year, and it whetted my interest in outer space."

Listening to Dusty's words made the time go faster. She wanted him to keep talking.

"Dusty, I . . ." Maggie started to tell him how much she liked being with him, how different he was from any boy she had ever met.

Suddenly, Dusty threw his arm out to keep her behind him. "Shh . . . Be quiet."

Fear gripped her when she saw a figure step out of the bushes ahead of them and stand in the path. Her frightened heart began to pound. She reached out and placed her hand on Dusty's shoulder.

This is no shadow. This is real.

An old man with a shock of white hair and a thick beard blocked the path ahead. His eyes were yellow in the late afternoon light, and his clothes hung on his thin frame. He looked like a scarecrow or something you would see on Halloween in a scary house. He raised one gnarled finger.

"What the hell're you doing here?"

Chapter 20

Nona and Mabel came out onto the porch as the burnt orange sun began its descent over the windblown treetops. A dozen vehicles, several of them from the sheriff's department, sat at various angles along the road in front of the campground. Another day was ending without their finding Maggie.

"We can't give up hope," Mabel said as she put her arm around Nona. "We'll find her, I just know it."

Nona nodded silently. Mabel always looked on the bright side of things. But her eyes were red from crying and her hands fluttered nervously. None of them had slept more than a few hours at a time since Maggie's disappearance. Mabel put up a good front.

The feeling of helplessness was the most alarming to Nona. From the moment she had realized that Maggie was missing, Nona had had to stand to the side and let others take over the search. She realized that if she were to go out into the woods, odds were that she would become lost. Instead, she had stayed at the camp, beside the phone, and let others do the looking. Every hour was worse than the one before. *How much more can I take before I lose my mind?*

Nona looked up to see several groups of men break through the bushes at the far end of the campground. A few wore drab brown, the uniform of the sheriff's office, but most of them were volunteers from town. Rifles were slung over their shoulders and flashlights hung from their belts. Two of them were clad in the bright orange that hunters usually wore to identify themselves to other hunters. Nona's eyes searched for any sign that Maggie was with them or that they had found anything that belonged to her. Without a word, she hurried down the steps to meet them.

Nona passed several men who nodded a greeting. With every step, the frustration and helplessness that had defined her for the last two days steadily turned to anger. She'd held in so much for so long.

"Sheriff Carter!" she shouted.

A slightly overweight man with thinning hair, Sheriff Amos Carter stepped away from the other men and waited for Nona to reach him. In his mid-fifties, he wore a uniform that was stretched tightly over his sizable middle. Despite his wife's nagging, he hadn't yet come to grips with his weight problem, and his clothes were always a bit too small. With an oval face and drooping eyelids, he had a well-earned reputation as a patient man who waited to hear all sides before making a decision. He had always been calm and pleasant when speaking to Nona.

"Howdy, Miss Conrad," he said with a faint smile. He

passed his fingers through his thinning hair before he continued. "Sorry to have to tell you, but we found no sign of your sister. We're going to start again in . . ."

"Why are you quitting for the day?" Nona asked sharply, cutting the man off in mid-sentence. "There's still plenty of light left. We're wasting time when we should be out searching."

"I understand that you're upset, but—"

"I don't think you do understand, Sheriff," Nona cut in again. She didn't want him, or anyone else for that matter, telling her how she felt. The truth was, the storm of emotion that was boiling through her was indescribable. She could no longer control it. "My sister is out there somewhere, and you people are calling it a day?"

"Now, Miss Conrad." The sheriff took a step toward her, raising a calming hand. "You need to understand that the men are tired. They've been searching the woods for the past couple of days. They need to get home to see about their families, eat, and get some rest."

"They're not the only ones who're tired," she blurted, tears filling her eyes.

"I understand that, but I don't expect these men to roam around in the woods after dark. They are volunteers and are out there searching because they want to, not because it's their job."

"But it's your job. You and your men are paid to do this sort of thing."

"Even I have my limits, Miss Conrad." Sheriff Carter brought his arms up and crossed his chest. He'd spoken in an even tone, but there was irritation written on his face.

The anger that filled Nona was becoming so great that even the sheriff's calming tone made little difference. She knew what he was saying was the truth, but she stubbornly refused to admit it. All that mattered was finding Maggie and bringing her home.

"I don't care!" she shouted and was about to say more before she was cut off by a pair of strong hands that grabbed her shoulders from behind. She was so surprised, she let out a small yelp of alarm. Turning her head, she found herself staring into Simon's piercing eyes. *Where the devil did he come from?*

"Sorry for the interruption, Sheriff." He spoke to the lawman, but his eyes never left Nona's. "This has been a trying time for all of us, and sometimes we say things we later regret."

"Not a problem, Mr. Wright. I've been guilty of doing just that myself. We'll be back in the morning to look a mite closer at the west side of the grounds. In case anything happens, call me."

"Thank you, Sheriff."

Before Nona could protest, Simon pulled her firmly by the elbow and started to lead her back across the yard. His grip was tight enough that she couldn't break free. He moved quickly and she stumbled along beside him.

"What do you think you're doing?" she muttered angrily.

"I could ask you the same thing."

"What's that supposed to mean?"

"Keep quiet," Simon ordered and pulled her along. Rather than protest, Nona pressed her lips together and struggled to keep up with his fast pace.

Ahead of them, she saw that Mabel had left the porch and was talking to a couple of volunteers. She held a plate of cookies she had baked to help keep her mind off Maggie and what might be happening to her. When the two women's eyes met, Mabel looked grim, but she turned back and smiled at the men, who thanked her for the cookies.

Upon reaching Nona's cabin, Simon stomped up the steps, thudded across the porch, and whipped open the door. He pulled Nona across the threshold, followed her inside, and slammed the door behind him.

"What in the hell do you think you're doing?" he barked. "Those men out there have been trudging through the woods looking for Maggie. They're doing everything they can to help, and you start accusing them of not doing enough."

"What are you talking about?" Nona spat out. "I've had to sit here and wait for two days, unable to do a damn thing! You're the one who insisted we take this to the sheriff. Is it wrong of me to expect them to do their job?"

"They are doing their job. After what happened to LeAnn's husband, they realize the seriousness of this and are leaving no stone unturned. Sheriff Carter is a good man, a good cop. He's doing everything he can."

"If he's such a good cop, why can't he find one fourteen-year-old girl?"

"That's not fair."

"Fair?" Nona retorted incredulously. "You think it's unfair for me to expect them to do their job. You said yourself that they were experienced in that sort of thing."

"They don't have anything to go on," Simon argued.

"We have the descriptions of the two men that accosted her in the boat. Have they been looking for them?" Nona asked stubbornly.

He stepped closer to her, his hands taking hers in a soft embrace, his eyes staring down at hers. She thought of jerking away from him, but she couldn't bring herself to do so. He was silent for a moment before saying, "You think I don't know how you feel? I feel terrible after promising to protect you and Maggie. I made a promise and I couldn't keep it."

"I don't blame you, Simon," she said, meaning every word. When his arms closed around her, she wrapped hers around him. "I'm glad you're here and I'm sorry that I was so stubborn at first, but you didn't help matters any by not telling me who you were."

"I know that, little redhead. That temper of yours boiled over."

She moved her arms up and around his neck. Simon was looking down at her. She felt a curious kind of panic, as if her body, her mind, her soul were being merged with his. Her legs felt weak, her throat tight. Her eyes could focus on nothing but him. She was breathing fast and so was he. She was acutely aware of his towering strength.

"I've never felt like this about a woman. I think of you every minute of the day. I didn't know it would be like this . . . both wonderful and like a knife in my heart." The strangled voice sounded miles from her ears.

Abruptly his lips found hers. She opened her mouth to his as the intimacy of the kiss increased. A surge of sensual pleasure coursed through her. It was so strong, so unfamiliar, so wonderful that she felt it all the way to her toes.

"Sweetheart, this feels so . . . right." He whispered the words, then feathered light kisses along her brow, her temple, and her chin. When she thought she couldn't bear the yearning another instant, she turned her mouth to meet his in a kiss that engaged her soul. His lips became demanding and hers parted underneath them, submitting. She tightened her arms around his neck and pressed the length of her body to his.

"You're something special." The murmured words were barely coherent, thickly groaned in her ear as he kissed the bare, warm curve of her neck. Thrusting his fingers into the disarray of her red curls, he drew her flushed face to his shoulder.

"How do you know? You've only known me a short time."

"I've known you for longer than you know. You just didn't know me." He stroked a strand of hair behind her ear.

Nona thought back to their first meeting and how her opinion of him had changed since then. She had not wanted to admit that she was falling in love with him. She had been interested only in keeping him at arm's length, fearing he would discover her secret. The image of the package Harold had sent her, and which was now buried in the bottom of her suitcase, came into her mind. Like turning on a switch, one moment it hadn't been there, the next moment it was.

"What are you thinking?" Simon's brow was furrowed with concern.

Try as she might, Nona couldn't decide what to do. She had not opened the package, respecting Harold's wishes; but on the other hand, was she right in hiding something so important from Simon? Should she open the package now?

"Talk to me, Nona." Simon gently shook her shoulders.

Looking deep into his eyes, Nona faced another dilemma. How could she tell him about the package at this late date? If she did nothing, if she kept the secret of the hidden package, it might mean Maggie would never be found. If Simon were involved in trying to steal the money back, it would break her heart and Maggie would still be gone. All that mattered was Maggie. Nothing more, nothing less. If she lost Simon's respect, so be it.

"There's something I need to tell you," she whispered.

"All right."

"I should have told you before. I don't know why I didn't. I guess I was waiting for the right time."

"Okay," he said calmly. "Tell me."

The words didn't come easily, but she'd gone too far to turn back. Her voice was little more than a whisper when she said, "I received a package from Harold just before we came up here. I didn't open it, not then and not since, so I can't say for sure what's in it. After what you've said about him, after what he's done, it may be connected to his crime."

Simon merely stared at her for a minute or two. His jaw clenched and unclenched. "Why didn't you say something to me? Why didn't you tell me this after I told you what Harold had done?"

"I didn't know you well enough."

"You mean you didn't trust me."

It was so near the truth, she didn't answer. "You're not being fair," she said weakly.

"Have I given you a reason not to trust me? You should have told me."

The anger that had fueled her attack on the sheriff was spent. It was all she could do to look into Simon's eyes.

"Where's the package?" he asked.

"It's here. In my suitcase."

"Let me see it." When she hesitated, he insisted, "Let's get everything out in the open, Nona."

Nona led Simon into the bedroom she had shared with Maggie. From beneath the bed, she pulled out her worn suitcase and set it upon the mattress. She opened the lid and there, beneath a couple of sweaters, was the parcel Harold had sent her.

"Here's the letter that came with it." She pulled the letter from beneath the string tied around the package and handed it to Simon. He read it quickly, then again more slowly.

Dear Nona,

I know that we have not kept in close contact these past years and, for that, I am sorry. However, I have a favor to ask. Please keep this package until you hear from me. I beg of you . . . DO NOT OPEN IT UNDER ANY CIRCUMSTANCES!

Regardless of how you feel about me, I do care deeply for you and Maggie. You are the only person that I feel I can trust. I will explain everything soon. For the sake of our father, I'm asking you to do this

for me. I promise that I will have your money and
Maggie's from our father's estate soon.

Your brother,
Harold

"Open it," Nona said with a deep sigh. "Open it, and be done with it."

Simon pulled out a small pocketknife and opened the blade, slipping it through the paper around the parcel. After cutting a gash in the side, he pulled away the wrappings to reveal a shoe box. With fingers that shook, Nona reached for the lid. She was filled with dread. With all the determination she could muster, she lifted the lid. What she saw made her gasp. Filling the inside of the box were thick bundles of money, and on top of them lay another envelope.

Chapter 21

FEAR KEPT MAGGIE FROZEN in the middle of the path. The strange man's eyes didn't blink as they stared at them. He was unlike anyone she had ever seen before.

"Answer my question, boy," the stranger demanded.

Maggie looked at Dusty, fully expecting him to be as frightened as she was, but she was surprised at what she saw. Dusty was staring back at the man, a smile creeping up at the corners of his mouth until it became a large grin.

"Dusty?" she asked in confusion.

"Don't worry." Confidently, he began walking toward the stranger, without the least hint of fear. Maggie's mind raced with all of the horrible scenarios that could happen to him. *The man could have a knife or a gun!* Before she could shout out to Dusty, he turned back and said, "I've known this guy for years. He's a little different, but then again, aren't we all?"

"Wha—" was all Maggie could manage in reply.

"What the hell are you doing here, boy?" the man repeated. "This isn't your neck of the woods. You taking your little friend for a walk and got yourself conveniently lost?" he added as he threw his head back and cackled, his white beard bouncing up and down on his chest.

"Taking your evening stroll, Randall?" Dusty asked as he went to the strange man and held out his hand.

"What are you doing here?" Randall asked again as he shook Dusty's hand. Now he didn't seem quite so frightening.

"That's something we don't have enough time to tell." Dusty smiled. "To make a long story short, I'm taking her to Tall Pine Camp."

"What's your name, little lady?" Randall asked.

"Maggie."

"I'm Randall Weatherspoon. Sorry if I put a fright into you."

When he came a few steps closer, Maggie had a closer look at him. His clothes were ragged, but clean. When he smiled, his teeth were straight and even. The fear she had felt at first slowly went away.

"That's all right." She smiled. "I'm just jumpy."

"Jumpy? You're as safe with this boy as if you were in church."

"She's had a scare," Dusty answered. "A couple of guys brought her out here and tied her to a tree."

"Why'd they do that?"

"They wanted some information."

"I've wondered why so many men have been roaming around the woods the last couple of days."

"What do you mean?" Maggie asked.

Ignoring her, Randall scratched his hairy chin. "The

fellas I've been watching looked like city fellas. One is bald as an egg."

"You've seen them?" Dusty and Maggie asked in unison.

"These two fellas were as nervous as a mouse in a room full of cats," Randall joked. "I suppose looking for you would account for that."

"When was the last time you saw them?" Dusty asked anxiously.

"Earlier this afternoon. They were headed in the same direction that you're going." Randall added, "I haven't seen them again for the last hour or two. They may be waiting up ahead for you."

"We need to change our direction." Dusty frowned as he looked at Maggie. "It'll cost us a couple of hours of walking, but I don't think we've got much choice."

"Another couple of hours?" Maggie despaired. She'd already been away from Nona for two days. Her sister would be worried sick.

"The boy's right," Randall agreed. "You keep going the direction you're headed, you could run right into them. They look like thugs to me."

"How do you know that, Randall?"

"I know a thug when I see one."

"They didn't catch you watching them?" Maggie asked.

At this, the grin under Randall's beard flowered into a full smile. "Little lady, there isn't any way I'll be seen in these woods unless I want to be seen. I came here to get away from people, and I've learned to be very good at it."

"We better get going if we want to make it to the camp before dark," Dusty interjected. "Thanks for the warning, Randall. We'll keep our eyes peeled."

They'd taken only a couple of steps down the path when Maggie looked back over her shoulder to where the old man had stood. She'd wanted to express her own thanks or, at the very least, to give a small wave good-bye. But Randall was nowhere to be seen, having disappeared back into the trees in the same ghostlike way he'd appeared.

"Randall's kind of strange," Maggie ventured.

Shortly after leaving the old man, Dusty had led Maggie off the scant trail they'd been following and pushed into a denser brush. For nearly twenty minutes, they'd trekked through thorny brambles that laced the space between the tall pines. Thorns had caught on her clothes and tangled in her hair, but she'd pushed on. The trek seemed never to end, but just as she was about to complain, they'd stepped onto another thin path. Dusty had smiled and winked before once again pushing on.

Now, as they walked back to the camp and Nona, the realization that she was running out of time with this amazing new boy hit Maggie hard. It was awkward to just walk along beside him without saying anything. She wanted to talk, to just hear his voice ramble on about this or that. When she finally worked up enough courage to speak, she asked about the grizzled stranger.

"Yeah, he's one of a kind," Dusty agreed with her. "He was out here before I was born, living off the land, like some kind of hermit. My dad says he's an educated man. He comes to visit my folks every month or two."

The idea that someone would make his home in the woods sounded crazy! Although she had enjoyed the stories of Robinson Crusoe and Swiss Family Robinson, she could not understand how Mr. Weatherspoon could do without a grocery store nearby or a movie theater.

"Why would anyone choose to live out here?" Maggie asked, but instantly wished she could take it back. Dusty and his parents had chosen this life, but she saw them as entirely different from Mr. Weatherspoon. "I'm sorry, Dusty," she added quickly. "I didn't mean anything by that."

"No offense taken." He laughed. "Randall's story is a little different from my folks'. He's told me a few things about his life before he came to the woods. As surprising as this might seem, Randall was once an accountant for some big firm in Chicago. He used to spend his days charting the movement of millions of dollars."

"You're kidding!" Maggie exclaimed.

"Nope. He might look like a hermit, but he's one sharp cookie. Had a big office in a skyscraper and made lots of money. One day, he got sick of all the runaround and stress and decided that he'd had enough. Walked out the door, quit his job, left his wife, and headed for the hills."

"He left his wife?" Maggie repeated, uncertain that she'd heard Dusty correctly. "What kind of person would do that?"

"I think it's more complicated than that."

"How? I'd hate anyone who did that to me."

Dusty was silent for a moment as they walked along

the path, the only sound the rustling of the fallen leaves. Finally, he said, "You know, I may not be the smartest guy in the world, but there's one thing I learned from my parents that I'll never forget. It makes a lot of sense when you apply it to Randall."

"What's that?"

"It isn't material things that make you happy. The first thing is finding someone to love and who loves you and taking the time to enjoy life for what it is rather than what others expect it to be. Randall was smart enough to figure that out and decided to make a change. It's hard for a person to admit he's truly unhappy, harder yet for him to find the courage to do something about it."

"But he made someone else miserable by leaving," Maggie argued.

"Sometimes you have to be selfish, especially where your own happiness is concerned. I can't blame him for that. Besides, who's to say she wouldn't have been more miserable if he'd stayed?"

They walked along in silence, Maggie trying to take in all that Dusty had said. He didn't talk the way other boys she'd known talked. He was thoughtful and introspective, and what he said made her think in ways she never had before. "I've never met anyone quite like you," she said aloud.

"I suppose not." He grinned and took her hand. They walked down the rough path toward the camp on the lake.

Webb didn't like what was happening, not one bit.

He sat at the table while Frank paced back and forth, a whiskey bottle in one hand and a knife in the other. They had returned to their run-down cabin from watching Tall

Pine Camp. Webb had fixed them a bite to eat. Instead of eating, Frank had decided to drink his supper.

"The only thing that's goin' to make those bitches tell us anything is if we put a sharp knife to their throats." Frank's eyes caressed the six-inch blade.

Webb remained silent. In the time he had known Frank, he'd learned that it often wasn't necessary to reply to his comments, especially when he had been drinking.

"The more I think about it," Frank continued, "we should go after that woman of Ernie's. I'd bet the farm he told her somethin' or she's heard one of the Conrads talkin' about Harold."

"But what if she doesn't know anythin'?" Webb interjected. "I'm not for kidnappin' a pregnant woman, Frank. What if she pops the kid?"

"Goddammit! She knows somethin'."

"She won't know where the money is."

"How do you know that, smart-ass? What if Ernie found the money and left it with the broad to hold for him?"

"If we can't find it, how do you think that idiot could find it?"

"She knows," Frank shouted.

"Just like you knew the girl knew something," Webb muttered under his breath.

"What was that?" Frank growled, stepping toward him brandishing the knife, the smell of alcohol on his breath. "What the hell did you say?"

"Nothin', Frank." The last thing he wanted to do was to get into a pissing contest with this drunken fool. He needed to have his wits about him if he was going to have any chance of keeping his head on his shoulders.

"Nothin'? Damn right it was nothin'! We've done things your way," Frank said as he took a big swallow of whiskey, "and we ain't got shit to show for it."

There was no point in arguing with Frank when he was in this condition. No amount of explaining was going to get through to him. Instead, Webb decided to bring up another subject. "What about Wright? We had an element of surprise the last time; it'll be different this time. They'll be stickin' to those women."

"Let 'em be ready," Frank scoffed. "We can still take the pregnant cow."

"That tall cowboy stays pretty close to her," Webb protested. It was Frank's kind of thinking that was going to get one or both of them killed. "We don't know who he is. He could be a fed or one of Wright's men. We'll have to be extra careful."

"Will you stop your bellyachin'? You think sittin' here with our thumbs up our asses is goin' to get anythin' done? The boss wants answers. We've got to find that stash!"

"I think we should call him before we do anythin' else."

"Ain't no time. Besides, he'll agree with me."

Webb wasn't so sure of that, but it wasn't smart to disagree with Frank right now. He had been pushing for him to call Chicago for a couple of days now, and Frank kept rejecting the idea. This was going to end badly; Webb was sure of it.

"It's about time we got a move on," Frank said as he looked out the window. It would be dark soon. He had decided to hit the campground shortly after everyone had retired for the night. He needed time to scout things out.

Webb got up and began to gather the things he'd need. Suddenly, a hand grabbed him from behind and slammed him hard against the wall. The force was so strong it blew the air from his lungs.

"What the hell?" he gasped.

Frank stood in front of him, his forearm pinning him to the wall. The blade in his hand pressed firmly against the flesh of Webb's throat. Looking into bloodshot eyes, Webb saw nothing but anger. Frank smiled, showing his dark, uneven teeth, his stinking breath blowing into Webb's face.

"Let me make one thing perfectly clear," Frank growled in a voice thick with menace and booze. "Don't even think of crossin' me. 'Cause it'll be the last thing you do."

Words froze in Webb's throat. He didn't even dare to nod his head because the knife was pressed so tightly to his throat. He'd known that Frank was a cold-blooded killer, but he hadn't known he was so crazy he'd turn against him.

"I'm tired of doin' things your way. I'm tired of you askin' me so many goddamn questions. We should have gone in there, shootin' the place up like I wanted to in the first place."

"Sure, Frank," Webb managed to wheeze out.

"Why in the hell do you give a damn about that kid anyway? You got a hard-on for kids?" Frank asked. "Tell you what . . . if I get my hands on her again, I'll let you watch what I do to her."

A flash of anger erupted in Webb, and he prayed his eyes didn't betray him. Frank was crazy enough to cut his throat and leave him where he fell. "Whatever you say, Frank."

"Damn right it is," Frank said and stepped back, taking the blade from Webb's throat and releasing his arm from his chest.

Webb's breathing slowly returned to normal. He kept his eyes on Frank, half expecting him to make another move against him.

"Get your things," Frank snarled. "I'll be waitin' outside."

Webb's eyes bored into Frank's back as he stepped out of the cabin and slammed the door behind him. A parade of thoughts marched through his head as he tried to figure out what to do.

"Damn," he said aloud.

Reaching beneath his bunk he pulled out his duffel bag. He'd come too far to turn back now. He had a job to do, and by God, he was going to do it. *But I'm doin' it on my terms!*

His fingers touched the cold steel of the revolver and he pulled it out of the bag. He'd brought the extra .38 in case of an emergency. If this didn't qualify, he didn't know what would! He wasn't sure if Frank knew about this gun, so he quickly stuck it in the waistband of his pants, pulling his shirt out to cover the bulge.

Things were getting out of control, of that much he was certain. The thought came to him that before this was over, he might have to kill the son of a bitch or the son of a bitch would kill him.

He picked up his duffel bag and left the cabin.

Chapter 22

OH, MY GOD!"

Nona couldn't believe her eyes. There, in the middle of the bed, were bundles of hundred-dollar bills bound in bank strips. She couldn't even imagine how much money was there; she had never seen so much in her entire life. Her mind reeling, she tried to comprehend it all.

Simon was silent as his hands sifted through the pile of money. His face was without expression, but his brow was furrowed.

"It's this damn money, isn't it? This is why they've taken Maggie!" she blurted. "If I'd known this was what they wanted, I would have given it to them."

Nona had known that her half brother was corrupt, but she had no idea that he was stupid enough to have stolen this money. Didn't he know that she and Maggie would be suspected as his accomplices? If he did, he evidently didn't care. She should have opened the package when she'd first received it and then turned the money over to the police. If she had, this mess would be over.

"Wait a second," Simon said, pulling her from her thoughts. "What's that?"

Nona's glance followed his to the floor and a note taped to the inside of the box. Written on it, in bold script, was her name.

"Another note," she said.

She reached for the note cautiously, as if she were a snake handler and the paper was poisonous to the touch. She pulled the paper from the tape, but before she could start to unfold it, a strange feeling came over her. Looking up, she found Simon staring at her intently. His eyes moved quickly over her face as if searching for something.

"What's wrong?" he asked softly.

"I guess I'm afraid of what it will say," she admitted. "Every bit of news I've had from Harold for the last few years has been bad. Every phone call, every letter, every time I've talked to him face-to-face has turned out to be bad for me and Maggie. This won't be any different."

Gently, Simon put his hand on her arm. The touch was comforting, and she thanked God that he was with her to share the problem her half brother had thrust upon her.

"This time it's different. I'm here with you." Simon bent his head toward her. His breath was warm on her face.

She looked into his eyes. "Thank you for being here."

"Go ahead and read the letter."

She opened the note and began to read.

My Dear Nona,

If you are reading this letter, then you believe something has happened to me and you felt the need

to open the package. I'm certain that you were surprised to see what was inside. Well, maybe not too
surprised! I know that you believe me to be a snake
in the grass and you're not far from the truth. I've
done some pretty despicable things in my life and I've
not been a good brother to you and our younger sister, and you may think I'm asking a lot of you to keep
this money for me. When the time is right I will
share it with you and Maggie. Be careful that you
don't tell anyone about it. Some people might think
it's stolen, but I assure you that with clever invest-
ments from our father's estate, I earned it for us. If
anyone asks you about me, tell them you haven't
heard from me in years. Another thing, if you try to
bank this money you'll have to explain where you got
it and both of us will be in trouble. I'll be in touch
with you in a few months and give you further in-
structions. Please believe me when I say I've done
this for you and Maggie as much as for myself

> Your brother,
> Harold

She had been surprised at the contents of the first letter, and she was even more surprised at this one. Harold
had been right; she thought him to be one of the most
contemptible people alive. Now he was trying to make
good for the wrongs he had done to her and Maggie . . .
maybe.

Without asking, Simon took the note from her hand
and quickly read it. When he finished, he folded the paper
and placed it back inside the shoe box.

"What could he have possibly been thinking?" Nona asked, her mind in turmoil.

"With Harold, you can't be sure."

"He is asking a lot to involve me in his scheme."

"Harold was looking out for himself and, by offering to share it with you, thought he was being generous."

"This is stolen money! I couldn't possibly keep it, even if he says he earned it with the money Father left us. I don't believe that. I think I'd be just as guilty as he is if I kept this money."

"Yes, you would, and I think Harold realized this when he sent you the money."

"Then why did he send it? Did he think I'd just hold it for him? Why didn't he put it in a bank someplace?"

"He's using you, Nona."

"I don't know what happened to change Harold. We were both taught by our father to be honest and respect the property of others."

"It's not all here," Simon said, breaking into her thoughts.

"What do you mean?"

"The money." Simon scratched his chin. "This is a fair chunk of cash, but it's not even close to what was stolen."

"He stole more than this?" Just being close to this much money made the hairs stand up on the back of Nona's neck. She couldn't imagine that Harold had taken more than this.

"Lots more."

"Then where's the rest of it?"

"Lining his pockets. He's using it to live the high life." Simon shrugged. "It seems to me that his generosity only went so far. I bet we'd find him sitting on the beach some-where sipping margaritas while you and Maggie deal with his crime."

Another flash of anger traveled across Nona's face. Harold had broken the law and left the mess in her lap.

"This money belongs to the bank."

"And that's exactly where it's going," Nona exclaimed firmly. "I'll take this money to the police. The sooner it's out of my hands, the better I'll like it."

"I don't think it's that easy."

"Why not?"

Simon took her hands and slowly explained. "I'm afraid that if Maggie was taken because of the money and it was known that you had turned it in, there would be no reason for them to keep her alive."

The power of Simon's words was as real as if he had struck her in the face. Nona's hand flew from his grip to her mouth. "Oh, my God! You're right, Simon! You're right!"

"Right now, they need her alive. If the money is still unaccounted for, the kidnappers will need her for lever-age. They'll try to force you to tell them where the money is."

"But they haven't contacted me, and besides, she doesn't know anything."

"We know that, but they don't."

"I'll kill them. I swear, I'll kill them if they hurt her," Nona said fiercely.

"That's why we have to be especially careful. We can't let anyone know about this. Not Mabel, not Jack, not the police. This has to stay between us until we get Maggie back."

"So what do we do?"

Simon began gathering the money up and packing it back inside the shoe box. "I'll keep it."

Nona thought briefly of her suspicion of him when they'd first come to the camp. He knew a lot about Harold, things that even she didn't know. It was a surprise to find out that he and Harold were related. Who was this man who was so willing to share her troubles? Nona knew she had feelings for him, was possibly in love with him, but she honestly didn't know much about him. As bizarre as it sounded, could Simon be involved in the bank robbery? Had he been after the money all along?

"We'll need to . . ." Simon stopped in mid-sentence, then turned to look at her. Straightening up, he studied her closely, his jaw rigid, his gaze steady. She was mesmerized by his eyes. They stood looking at each other as if they were two statues, frozen in time.

"You still don't trust me," he said quietly.

"Simon . . ." She was hushed by one of his fingers pressing gently on her lips.

"Nona," he said softly, "from the moment I saw you at my grandfather's apartment building, I wanted to know you and take care of you and Maggie because I knew what Harold was capable of doing. Yes, when I got you to come here, I knew Harold had robbed the bank. No, I didn't know he had squandered all of your inheritance."

Nona opened her mouth to speak, but Simon said softly, "Let me finish." His eyes held hers. "I've come to care for you and hope that you return my feelings. If anything should happen to you, I'd never forgive myself for bringing you here. As soon as we get Maggie back, I'll drop a few hints that you have given me a package to hold, so if they come after someone, it will be me."

"Drop a few hints? To whom?"

"Everybody. Jack, the Hogans, Russ, and the sheriff's men. Jack will spread the word." He finished and took his finger from her lips and kissed her softly.

Tears welled in her eyes. "I wish we had never come here."

The emotions that had frayed her nerves for the last two days suddenly overwhelmed her. She fell forward into Simon's embrace. Sobs shook her. She buried her face in the curve of his neck, letting go all that she had been holding back.

"Don't cry, honey," he whispered, and peppered her forehead with small kisses. "When this is over, we have some serious talking to do. I'll warn you right now, it'll be hard for me to let you go back to Little Rock."

"I probably won't go back to Little Rock when we leave here. I want to take Maggie to a smaller town."

"Don't think about that now. It's going to be okay, honey. You'll see."

Through the haze of tears that clouded her eyes, Nona said a silent prayer that he was right.

As LeAnn put the last of the dishes in the cabinet, she looked out over the lake at the glorious sunset; deep mauve and orange streaks raced up from the horizon. What few clouds were still in the sky looked like bruises against the vivid background. She couldn't hold back a smile.

"You look happy."

LeAnn turned at the sound of Jack's voice to find him standing behind her. Simon had insisted that Jack stay with her when she went to her cabin.

"I don't think I should be," LeAnn answered. "To tell you the truth, it seems selfish to be happy after all that's happened."

"Why do you think it's selfish?"

LeAnn shrugged. "There's been so much bad news lately. Ernie has been dead only a week. Even though we had problems, he was still my husband. On top of that, Maggie's still missing. It doesn't seem appropriate to smile."

"It seems like the perfect time to me," Jack said softly, his words chosen carefully, his eyes on her profile. She was pretty. Her wheat-colored hair lay in waves against her cheeks. He sniffed. "Your hair smells good."

LeAnn's heart thumped when she felt his nose in her hair and then his warm breath on her neck. She lifted her shoulder up to her ear. "That tickles," she said.

"That doesn't tickle," he answered. "I'll show you what tickle is." His fingers went down from her arm to her ribs.

"Stop that." She giggled.

Jack's lips touched her cheek. "You like this better?"

"Are you flirting with me?"

"Are you surprised at that?"

"Of course I am. Have you looked at me lately?"

"Sure. About every five minutes."

"Then you must know that my complexion is bad, I have no waistline, and my ankles are swollen."

"I don't see all that. All I noticed was that some time ago you must have swallowed a watermelon seed."

"Oh, you're so funny."

"Well, I've got you smiling, haven't I?"

Jack had helped her clean the cabin, refusing to allow her to lift even a chair. He had swept the floor and helped her with the dishes, something that Ernie hadn't done once during their brief marriage. Ernie had expected her to wait on him hand and foot when he was home. She wondered how it would have been with the baby. He would have been jealous of the time she spent with it. She felt a brief moment of sorrow for the man he could have been, for the boy she had known in school. She mentally shook herself. It wasn't good to live in the past. It was her baby's future and her own that were important now.

"Penny for your thoughts," Jack interrupted.

"I don't think they're worth that much." LeAnn's face was a deep shade of red. Not for anything did she want him to know about her problems with Ernie. That was over and done.

"The way you're blushing, I'd say they're worth a couple of dollars."

"Yes, but . . ." LeAnn's words were cut off by a solid kick from inside her belly. It wasn't the first time the baby had moved, but it was still enough to catch her off guard.

"What happened? Your face changed colors suddenly. You're pale now."

"The baby is moving around."

"You're not going into labor, are you?" he asked ner-

vously. The look on his face was a mixture of excitement
and fear.

"No, silly! The baby just kicked me really hard, that's
all." She laughed. The feeling was so wonderful that she
felt a powerful urge to share it with him. Taking his arm,
she rested his hand on her stomach and held it in place.
"Wait just a second, she'll do it again."

"She? How do you know it will be a girl?"

"Woman's intuition. When I think about the baby, I
just assume it's a girl. I just . . ." Another kick interrupted
her and she exclaimed, "Did you feel that? Did you,
Jack?" She looked into his face. His mouth was set in a
wide grin, a look of wonderment on his face.

"That was amazing!"

They stood in the kitchen, smiling at each other, waiting for another series of movements from the baby. She
was happy to be sharing this moment with him. She
knew, for certain, that her feelings for Jack were growing.
No man had ever paid her the kind of attention that he
gave her. She tried not to think that the reason he was
with her was because Simon had ordered him to stay with
her. Whatever the future held, she would have this moment to remember.

After a couple of minutes, LeAnn became aware of
barking dogs. She looked up at Jack and saw that he was
listening as well.

"What's got into Sam Houston and Cochise?"

"I better see."

Jack stepped to the door and looked out into the ever-
increasing darkness. LeAnn followed him and peered
over his shoulder. The sun was behind the hilltops. A few

lamps had come on around the camp. There was just enough light to see the dogs running back and forth along the edge of the woods, barking.

"Something's got them worked up." Jack stepped out onto the porch and searched the edge of the woods. "There's something out there they don't like."

"They didn't bark at the sheriff's men today."

"Cochise didn't feel threatened because it was daylight and Simon was with them." Jack moved so that his body was positioned in front of hers. "Go back in the house, LeAnn."

A low growl came from Cochise, frantic sharp barks from Sam Houston. LeAnn's imagination worked overtime. Whoever was out there might be the person who had killed Ernie and might have come back to kill her and her baby. She put both hands on Jack's arm and squeezed tightly.

"What is it?"

"Stay back. Stay behind me," he warned.

Suddenly, Sam Houston backed away from the bushes, his teeth bared, growling angrily, hair standing up on his back. LeAnn gasped as a dark figure stepped out of the shadows. A second, smaller figure followed the first.

She glanced at Jack and was surprised to see a gun in his hand.

Chapter 23

SIMON PUT THE LAST OF THE BUNDLES back into the shoe box and replaced the lid. It was a relief to Nona to share the responsibility with him. If Maggie had been kidnapped because of the money, whoever had taken her would probably be returning to the camp to look for it.

"Do you think they know we've got it?" She voiced her fears.

"Why do you think they're here? Of course they know. But I'm better equipped to take care of myself than you are . . ." He started to tell her that he was experienced in this sort of thing, but suddenly stopped, his lips clamping together tightly. He couldn't tell her that he was almost certain that Ernie had been involved and that was why he was killed.

"What were you going to say?" she asked.

"I was wondering why you didn't tell me about the money after we talked in the car and I told you I was Harold's cousin," he answered before walking to the window.

This was the same evasiveness that Nona had resented in him when they'd first met. It seemed he always answered her questions with a question of his own. She had become tired of the game.

"I didn't know you then and I don't know you now."

"What in the hell do you want me to do, Nona? Do you want me to take care of the money or not?"

"You make me so damn mad. I'm an adult. You don't have to shield me from anything, if that's your intention. Tell me what's on your mind."

"Right now, what's on my mind is that you're pretty when you're mad."

"You were not going to say that."

"Is it that red hair that makes you get mad so quick?"

"Why do people always think it's my red hair that makes me express my opinions?" she yelled.

"You don't have to yell. I'm not deaf," he teased with a flash of his trademark grin that she knew was meant to disarm her. "I figured if I told you what I was thinking, you'd end up smacking me upside the head. I thought I'd save myself the pain."

"Dammit, Simon!" Nona's temper erupted.

"Honey, did you know your eyes sparkle when you're angry? Our life together will never be dull." He was silent after that, staring at her with eyes that were both mischievous and thoughtful.

"Our lives together? Heaven forbid!" How could he be so irritating one moment and so sweet the next? Although she was thrilled to the tips of her toes at the thought of spending her life with him, logic forced her to ask,

"What's your connection in all this, Simon? You are more involved than you've let on."

"Dammit, Nona, I'll tell you as soon as we get Maggie back," he said huskily. "I'm doing everything I can to protect you and Maggie."

"You didn't do a very good job of taking care of Maggie," she blurted. Immediately she was sorry when she saw the teasing light go out of his eyes; his lips tightened and he turned away from her. "I'm sorry, I shouldn't have said that. I'm angry and frustrated."

"Most of the time people say what they really mean when they're angry." Simon glanced back at her.

"You just tell me enough to arouse my curiosity." One lone tear broke free of her lashes and began to slide down the side of her cheek. She didn't notice.

"Honey, sweetheart . . . I don't want you to worry." There was no doubting the sincerity in his voice. He moved closer to her, reaching out to take her hands.

"You know how to smooth things over, don't you?" She jerked her hands from his. "I guess you've had a lot of experience dealing with women."

"I've had my share of lady friends," he said quietly.

"Friends?" she said and tossed her head.

"I'm thirty-six years old."

"What's that got to do with it?"

"I don't know what in the hell we're even arguing about." His hand reached for her and he looked at her with a pained expression.

"Well if you don't know what we're arguing about, then there's no point in even discussing it with you." She jerked her hand from his and headed for the door.

"Nona! Wait!" *You stubborn little fool. Don't you know how important you've become to me?*

Nona paused in the doorway when she heard the sound of a shot and a scream.

Nona didn't hesitate for an instant. As she ran, she realized that Sam Houston's bark had turned into a whine.

"Stop right there!" LeAnn had followed Jack to the porch. He moved in front of her with a pistol in his hand. His voice was loud in the quiet night.

The two figures at the edge of the woods stood still. In the twilight, LeAnn couldn't see much, except that there were two of them. Sam Houston and Cochise continued to run back and forth in front of the figures, barking furiously.

"Get your hands up and move towards me!" Jack yelled.

Silence was the only answer to Jack's order. It was as if the figures were frozen in place.

LeAnn peered into the darkness. "Who are they, Jack?" she whispered.

"I don't know, honey," he said.

One of the figures suddenly jerked the other back into the thick bushes. They had taken only a few steps when Jack lifted the gun and shot into the air.

"Don't move!"

LeAnn jerked Jack's arm at the sound of the shot and let out a sharp shriek of surprise. She had opened her mouth to say more when a shout came out of the darkness.

"LeAnn? It's me, Maggie."

"Maggie?" LeAnn started forward. Jack pulled her back.

"Wait, LeAnn. We've got to be sure."

"It's her. I know it's her." Then: "Maggie, you've come back!"

Maggie's return had not gone as she'd expected it would. Darkness was about to set in when they reached Tall Pine Camp.

"I can't believe it," she exclaimed. "I'm finally home!"

With those words, she pulled away from Dusty and started for the camp. Before she took more than a few steps, Dusty grabbed her by the arm and stopped her.

He brought a finger to her lips to hush her. "We need to be extra careful now," he cautioned in a whisper. "If someone is looking for you, this is where they'll be waiting."

For the next few minutes, they picked their way along the tree line, Dusty increasingly alert. It was frustrating for Maggie not to break free of his hand and dash across the grounds, but she knew he was right. When Dusty was satisfied no one was around, they stepped out of the woods.

"Follow me." She smiled as she tugged gently on Dusty's hand.

Before they got very far, Cochise and Sam Houston were in front of them. Momentarily startled by the hair standing up on Sam's back, Maggie said, "Stop it, Sam! You dumb dog, don't you know it's me, Maggie?"

"It's not you," Dusty softly explained beside her. "It's me. He's never seen me before and doesn't know my scent. He's protecting you."

"Come on, they know me. They won't bite."

Ahead of them, a couple hundred feet away, was LeAnn's cabin. As soft light spilled from the open door of the cabin, Maggie saw LeAnn and a man. Was it Jack?

"This way," she said. As she led Dusty along the narrow road, Sam Houston ran back and forth barking. Before she could say anything, before she could even raise an arm in greeting, a man's shout split the night. The actual words escaped her, but the tone was harsh and threatening. She and Dusty stopped in their tracks.

"We're out of here," Dusty whispered, then took her hand and attempted to pull her back into the woods. She jerked away, then she heard the sound of a shot, followed closely by a woman's frightened scream.

"LeAnn?" Maggie shouted. "It's me, Maggie!"

Seconds later, LeAnn yelled, "Maggie?"

The next couple of minutes were a blur: After a moment's hesitation, LeAnn ran from the porch and hurried toward her. Maggie rushed to meet her and hugged her tightly. Both were crying. Jack joined them. Dusty remained alert. Sam Houston continued his bark, but now it signified welcome.

Tears clogged Maggie's throat. Back with people who cared for her, she could no longer hold back the sobs.

"Are you all right, Maggie?" LeAnn asked. "Nona has been worried to death. We all have."

Maggie smiled broadly and, through the bleary haze of tears, saw Nona running toward her.

"Nona, Nona!" Maggie shouted and rushed from LeAnn's embrace toward the arms of her sister.

"Maggie? Oh, thank God." Nona's legs couldn't carry her fast enough toward her little sister.

"Wait, Nona!" Simon finally caught up with her and grabbed her arm.

"Maggie, Maggie," Nona yelled, jerking her arm free.

As the space between them diminished, Maggie could see her sister's worried face. It was so dearly familiar. The two hugged each other and held on tightly. Tears flowed freely, but laughter bubbled up.

The young girl sobbed. "I'm so glad to be home."

"Oh, you darling, sweet girl. I've been so worried. Are you all right? Did they hurt you?" Nona framed her sister's face with her palms and smoothed her tangled hair back from her cheeks.

"Yes, I'm all right."

Chapter 24

MAGGIE AND DUSTY SAT AT THE TABLE with Nona and Simon, answering their questions and describing the kidnappers.

"Their names are Frank and Webb. Frank is the mean one," Maggie explained.

Dusty verified Maggie's descriptions. Simon realized Dusty was a smart young man. He had outwitted two very unscrupulous thugs.

"I'd like to meet your mother and father and thank them for looking after Maggie," Nona said.

"They don't expect any thanks. My folks are like that. If someone needs help, they help."

Maggie tried to remember every word Frank and Webb had said. When she told Simon and Nona what Frank planned to do to her, even the dirty words he used, she glanced at her sister's teary face.

"Oh, honey." Nona grabbed Maggie's hand. "I'll thank God every day for letting Dusty find you."

Later, Jack and LeAnn came and sat at the kitchen

table with Simon and Nona. Mabel scurried from the counter to the table, serving a hastily prepared meal for Maggie and Dusty. It wasn't much, a couple of ham sandwiches and a bag of potato chips, but the two youngsters ate as if a feast had been placed before them.

"And then Dusty brought me back here," Maggie said, and, her eyes lifting from Dusty's face, she stole a knowing glance at her sister. She had given her most of the story, but the one part she'd neglected to mention was the reason the men had taken her. That must remain unspoken between them at this time. "I'm back now," Maggie said with a sigh of relief.

"All I have to say is that I'm thankful the whole mess is over." Mabel brought another plate loaded with sandwiches to the table. "The rest of you might as well eat, too."

"There are all kinds of strange people in these woods," Dusty explained between mouthfuls of chips. "Myself and my family excluded. Some of them don't have the best intentions."

"Am I glad it was Dusty who came along!" Maggie exclaimed.

"We're all glad he found you." Simon smiled at Maggie.

Maggie shivered. "It was so cold out there!"

A feeling of deep relief grew inside Nona. Maggie had been through a horrible ordeal that could have easily left her scarred for life. Instead, she seemed the same stable girl she'd been the day she disappeared. The men who'd taken Maggie were still out there, however. The danger was not over.

As LeAnn listened to Maggie's story, she wondered if

the kidnappers had been responsible for Ernie's death. She was grateful that Jack had been with her and not Ernie, when Maggie and Dusty came out of the woods. Ernie was so impulsive that he might have shot one of them first and asked questions later.

"You about scared me to death, Jack," LeAnn explained, "when you pulled that gun and fired it."

"I'm sorry. I didn't have time to tell you I had one."

Jack glanced at Simon, waiting for him to explain his reason for being here, but instead, Simon got up from his chair and said he was going to call the sheriff.

Nona, conscious that Simon had not once looked at her, finished her sandwich and shook her head when Mabel offered more. "Maggie, the sheriff will probably want to ask you a few questions."

"I'll tell them everything I can remember." Suddenly a tremendous flash of lightning lit up the night. It was as if someone had thrown a switch. Seconds later, a grumbling peal of thunder rolled across the valley, shaking the glass in the windows and the cups on the table.

"That sounds like my cue to leave." Dusty got up from his chair and moved toward the door. "My folks will worry if I don't get back soon, wet or otherwise."

"But the rain is coming down in buckets. You're not going out in that, are you?" Maggie protested.

"It's only rain."

"It's a thunderstorm," Mabel said. "Your parents wouldn't expect you to go back through the woods during a thunderstorm, would they?"

"They'd be more worried if they knew you were out there where lightning could strike you. Stay until morning, son," Jack said. "Either Simon or I will drive you home. There's some kind of a trail up to your place, isn't there?"

"It's just a dirt path. It may wash out in the rain."

"You better listen to Mabel, Dusty," Maggie cautioned. "She won't take any lip from you, so you'd better just button yours. Besides, this way you'll get to have one of Mabel's world-famous breakfasts."

Dusty looked as if he wanted to protest further, but after looking at Maggie for a moment, he grinned. "Okay, I can't turn down a world-famous breakfast."

"Yea!" Maggie exclaimed gleefully.

It was plain to Nona that Maggie liked the boy as well as the idea of his spending more time with them. Maggie was growing up right in front of her eyes; she was turning into a typical teenager. As the others discussed the many merits of Mabel's breakfasts, Simon came to the door and motioned for Nona to come outside.

The wind had picked up, its sharp whistle signaling the weather's surliness. The sky was ink-black, broken only by flashes of lightning. The look on Simon's face matched the storm.

"What's wrong?" Nona asked coolly.

"I just got off the phone with the sheriff's dispatcher. Turns out that Sheriff Carter and a couple of his deputies are out on calls. This weather's causing downed power lines and trees over the road to the south of here. The dispatcher said she'd let him know about Maggie, but she didn't think he'd be able to make it out here until morning."

"Did you say anything to the police about the money?"

Nona asked as she looked into the sky. Another fork of lightning lit up the area, and a few scant seconds later thunder crashed.

"I haven't said a word to anyone."

"Damn this storm. That means we'll have to hold the money until the sheriff can get here." Nona frowned. Now that she knew what was in the parcel, she felt the sooner it was returned, the better. Even one more night seemed too long. If the men who wanted it were desperate enough to kidnap Maggie, they would do almost anything for it. From the look on Simon's face, she knew he was thinking the same thing.

"Don't worry. I won't run off with it before the sheriff gets here," he said sarcastically.

"Another couple of days, then?"

"Another couple of days . . . ," Simon echoed, then turned on his heel and left her standing on the porch.

Nona lay in her bed, tired all the way to her bones. Thoughts of Simon and their unresolved clash of wills swept through her mind. Her relief was great that Maggie was back. She went to look in on her. From the doorway she could see that her sister was asleep. The girl's head was tilted toward the light, and she looked so young and innocent. Dusty slept just as soundly on the cot in Mabel's room.

Everyone had listened to Maggie's story and filled up on Mabel's improvised dinner. After the rain diminished, Jack took LeAnn back to her cabin, suggesting that she would be more comfortable in her own bed. All were alert to the possibility that Frank and Webb could return.

"Can't sleep?" Mabel asked from a chair in the corner when Nona walked into the room. She'd insisted that she would stay awake and help keep watch. Nona had argued, but Mabel had had a tone in her voice that wouldn't be contradicted.

"I'm too keyed up. Frankly, too mixed up about Simon."

"You're in love with him, aren't you?"

"I don't know, Mabel. So much has happened. He acts as if he really cares for me and doesn't want anything to happen to me or Maggie. But maybe it's just that he's afraid the camp will get the reputation of being an unsafe place for families to vacation."

"You don't believe that. What a far-fetched notion!"

"He hasn't said anything about love."

"I can see that I need to give you a lesson on how to manage a man." Mabel got up from her chair and looked out the window toward Simon's cabin. "It seems that Simon can't sleep either. His light is on."

"I don't want to *manage* a man." Nona's voice held a disapproving tone.

"You seemed to manage Lester all right. If you had crooked your finger, he'd have lain right down and let you walk on him."

"I never had a serious thought about Lester, and you know it," Nona said irritably.

"Simon is a man who would want to know where he stood with a woman and would not be content to be left dangling."

"He's not dangling. He's not voiced any serious intentions. He's either trying to kiss me or giving me orders."

"And you're always putting him down, Nona. You know you're crazy about him. And it's obvious that he's nuts about you."

"When did you turn into Ann Landers?"

"I'm talking from experience. Pride has its place, but pride can stand in the way of your happiness. I know. I loved a boy a long time ago. We had a little spat and I told him never to speak to me again. He didn't, and I was too proud to make the first move and apologize. He started going out with my best friend, and before I knew it, they were married. I think of him sometimes and wonder if my life would have been different if I had swallowed my pride and apologized."

"Are you telling me to go out in the rain in my night-gown and apologize to that . . . Mr. Know-It-All?"

Mabel laughed. "I never thought of him as a know-it-all. If I was thirty years younger, I'd give you a run for your money, honey. Just because you're the only woman around, besides LeAnn, that is, and it seems that Jack has staked his claim there, doesn't mean that Simon will wait for you very long."

"Mabel, you don't know what you're talking about. He isn't waiting for me. Well, maybe he is. He may be waiting to get rid of us. We've sure caused him a lot of trouble. So far this summer, I doubt if the camp has made enough money to pay the electric bill."

"I don't think he's worried about that." Mabel settled back in her chair. "If you want my advice, go to him," the older woman said matter-of-factly.

"What?" Nona exclaimed.

"Oh, honey," Mabel said softly. "I know he can be

bullheaded at times, but he took on the job of looking after us, and we should be thankful."

"I'm thankful, Mabel. He's just so damn bossy."

"Men are that way about the women they love. It's plain to me that you care for him and that he has fallen for you. It's practically written on his face."

"But, I . . . ," Nona stammered, but she knew in her heart that Mabel was right. There was so much that had yet to be said between her and Simon, so many feelings that had bubbled to the surface but failed to break free. It was driving her crazy. "But what would I say?"

"Go. I've been watching during the flashes of lightning and there's no one out there. I don't think they'll stand in the rain waiting for one of us to come out," Mabel prodded with a soft laugh.

Before she could change her mind, Nona was out the door and standing on the porch. Mabel came out behind her. "Go on," she said.

Nona looked across the small gap between the two cabins and then jumped off the porch. The weather had worsened. Lightning forked across the sky to the south, and the rumbles of thunder were louder and closer together. Gusts of wind pushed the smell of rain before the storm, and the tops of the trees bent awkwardly. Pushing her flyaway hair from her eyes, Nona stepped up onto Simon's porch. The door banged open, telling her he had been watching from the window. Simon stood in the doorway, a startled look on his face.

"What's wrong?" he asked anxiously and came out onto the porch.

"Nothing. Simon, I don't . . . I mean, I . . . ," Nona

stammered, the words falling as randomly as they would if they were raindrops in the storm. Her heart hammered wildly and her legs felt weak.

"What's wrong?" he asked again.

"Nothing's wrong, but . . . ," she began, but once again found herself speechless.

"But . . . ?" Simon reached out, firmly took hold of her, and pulled her into the cabin.

Mabel watched until Nona was inside, then with a satisfied laugh went back to her chair.

Nona wrapped her arms around Simon's waist and buried her face in his shoulder. It was wonderful to be in his embrace. She melted against him, reveling in his strength.

"I'm sorry, Simon."

"I'm sorry, too, sweetheart. Don't cry. We've got Maggie back," he whispered tenderly as he pulled her close. "The rest will sort itself out."

They stood close together. Tenderly, his mouth found hers, nibbling, licking, caressing her until they both felt as if they were slipping into an oblivion from which they didn't want to escape. Without a word, he scooped her off her feet and carried her into the bedroom.

"Oh, Simon," Nona sighed. "There's so much I want to say."

"There will be time for that later, sweetheart. This time is for us."

He placed her on the rumpled covers of the bed and lay down beside her. They kissed each other hungrily. Her arms encircled him, her hands slid up under his shirt and ran across the smooth skin of his back. He sat up, removed his shirt, and gathered her close to him. His chest was warm and she felt the heavy beat of his heart. *He felt so good.* His scent was all male, fresh and clean. This was what she had always dreamed about.

"I've wanted to hold you like this, kiss you like this," he whispered into her ear. "I want to feel you naked in my arms."

Confidently, his hands found the buttons of her nightgown and pulled it over her head. Scant seconds later, his calloused fingertips were cupping her breasts. His rough fingers danced delicately over the soft skin, teasing at one nipple until she felt as if she would explode. Between breaths, she tugged at his belt, wanting desperately to touch him in the same way that he was touching her.

When the belt was free, Nona gently held Simon's erection. She rubbed her fingers over the taut skin as he moaned in her ear. At the same time, his fingers pushed down between her legs, probing into the hot wetness.

When his beloved weight pressed her gently but securely into the bed, she could feel the pounding of his heart against her breast. With a groan of pure bliss, Simon pushed, hard and with urgency, into Nona's softness. She gasped into his ear as he swiftly embedded himself in her depths. Pleasure soared through every nerve of her body as they moved as one. She was aware of nothing but the broad shoulders she clung to, heard nothing but the low murmur of sweet words he whispered in her ear before his mouth covered hers. Then she was beyond seeing or hearing as she slipped in to uncharted, but beautiful, oblivion. They gave in to the feelings that had flickered to life soon after they'd met. With every passing moment, they floated farther away into a world that consisted only of their hands, their lips, and the heat of their bodies.

Minutes passed before Simon, still deep inside of her, lifted himself up on his elbows and gazed into her face. He brushed back her hair with gentle fingers.

"Well, what do you think, little redbird?"

"Oh, Lord," Nona exclaimed. "I . . ."

"It was wonderful," Simon whispered. "I've spent so much time thinking about you, wanting to hold you, wanting to be with you like this, that I was nearly out of my mind. You've put a spell on me, sweetheart."

Nona sucked in her breath. She couldn't take her eyes from his face. "Don't stop. Don't stop loving me."

Occasional flashes of lightning filled the room, silhouetting bodies pressed together in a fierce passion that had overtaken them both. When Simon moved within her again, she welcomed him. Without hesitation their bodies joined in mutual, frantic need.

"Simon!" she cried out.

As the movement and their caresses increased in urgency, the heat between them became fierce. With his hands gripping her bottom, Simon pulled Nona tighter with every thrust, as if he were afraid she would somehow slip away from him and disappear into the night.

"I'll never let you go," he moaned. "Never. You're mine now."

"And you're mine. Don't stop," Nona said as she raised her hips off the bed to meet him.

Locked tightly, they clung to each other and surrendered to the powerful forces they had unleashed. As the pleasure rose to dizzying heights, Nona lost her awareness of everything but the man who was pushing her to such bliss. Finally, the concert they'd been performing together reached its end, climaxing in a frenzy that drowned out the storm pounding the earth outside the cabin.

Hands gently touched her moist body. Her limbs quivered but began to settle into a quieter place. When she turned to look at him, he was already drinking her in with his eyes, a contented smile curling at the corners of his mouth.

"I'm in love with you, Nona Conrad," he said softly.

Tears of joy filled her eyes.

"There's something I have to tell you," Simon said.

Nona looked into Simon's eyes and was surprised to see his gaze draw away from her own. They'd been lying in bed, talking happily, when he'd suddenly grown colder, more distant. Something was weighing on him, pressing down on his shoulders until he spoke its name, releasing him from the burden of containing it. When he finally sighed and spoke, the words sent a shiver across her bare skin. "I haven't told you the whole story about who I am and where I come from. There's more you need to know."

Much in the way that their lovemaking had made her dizzy, Nona now reeled from what Simon had just suggested. All of the doubts that had played themselves out in her mind now suddenly came to the fore again. Was he after Harold's stolen money? Was he involved with Maggie's kidnapping? "What . . . what are you talking about?" she managed.

"Whoa, whoa, whoa," he said, holding his palms out to her. "Don't worry. I haven't been using you or lying to you."

"Then what are you saying?"

"What I'm telling you is that I'm not just involved in this situation because my grandfather owns the bank that was robbed." He paused for a moment, taking stock of the situation, and then added, "I'm also working for an agency that's trying to get back the money Harold stole."

"An agency? You mean like the FBI?"

"No, no. Nothing like that," he said firmly. "It's more like a detective agency. I was hired by the insurance firm that represents the bank. I brought you here originally because I suspected Harold had given you the money."

Nona's cheeks flushed a deep crimson. "Why didn't you tell me this before now?"

"Because I had to make sure you had it. There was no point in telling you anything more if you didn't have it." He put one hand on hers, gave it a quick squeeze, and added, "Besides, I also had to be sure you weren't in on it with him. For all I knew, the two of you were a modern-day version of Bonnie and Clyde."

Nona knew he meant for her to laugh at his joke, but instead it made her angry. *How dare he insinuate that I could have been involved with a snake like Harold?* She knew she was more upset than she should be, but she couldn't help herself. Without a word, she got up from the bed and hastily gathered her nightgown from the floor.

"What are you doing?" he asked.

"I'm getting out of here." In the scant light provided by the lightning, Nona hurriedly drew her nightgown over her head. The sooner she was out of the cabin, the better.

"Don't tell me you're angry about this."

"You're one heck of a detective, Mr. Wright," she answered coldly. "You felt hurt that I didn't trust *you,* when all the time you didn't trust *me*!"

"That's not fair. I've not lied to you."

"What's not fair is your not telling me the whole truth when we found the money!" she barked. "You may not have been lying to me, not really. But you sure weren't telling me the truth, either!" Turning on her heel, Nona left the room and headed for the door.

"Nona, wait!" he shouted from behind her.

Outside, she was struck by the growing ferocity of the storm. Beads of rain, whipped into a frenzy by the gusting wind, stung her face. It had turned colder, and she shivered, but she didn't care. She was leaving. Lightning flashed, and thunder crashed right behind it. She hurried toward her own cabin, but before she could take more than a few steps, a pair of arms grabbed her from behind.

She turned her head quickly, ready to force Simon to let her go, to tell him they needed some space between them for a while. But it wasn't Simon who clamped a hand down on her mouth.

This man had a mustache.

Chapter 25

Nona, wait!"

When Nona left the bed, Simon sprang up and grabbed for his pants. After the door slammed shut, he cursed long and loud. He jerked on his jeans, tugged his shirt over his head, and reached for his boots. His heart was hammering with anger at himself for not making Nona understand his position.

Simon couldn't help but think about all the trouble Harold had caused. He swore that if he ever got his hands on him, he would beat the bustard to within an inch of his life.

Hadn't I just told her that I love her? Hadn't I just made love to her?

"Son of a bitch!" he shouted as he stubbed a toe on the trunk at the foot of his bed.

True, he hadn't been completely honest from the beginning, but he had done what he thought was right. When he'd first told her about Harold taking the money, there had been no point in telling her he was a detective, or that Jack was working alongside him on the case. If he had told her, she would have been all the more suspicious of his motives. He had not revealed his total involvement, but that didn't change the fact that the feelings he'd developed for her were real.

Simon sprang out onto the porch. The storm was upon them in full force. Wind-whipped rain pelted his face, and he tried to shield his eyes with his hand. Looking toward Nona's cabin, he could see no sign of her. Surely she hadn't gone inside already.

Lightning flashed, lighting up the area. His heart sank clear to his toes when he saw Nona, at the side of the cabin, in the grasp of a man. She was struggling against his superior strength.

"Nona!" he shouted into the wind. Then: "Let go of her, you son of a bitch!"

He leaped off the porch and had taken no more than a few steps when he was struck on the back of the head. His legs crumpled under him. Before everything went black, his last thought was *Oh, God, Nona. Nona.*

Webb stood over the fallen man, the pistol heavy in his hand. He and Frank had watched the redheaded woman come out of her cabin and go into Wright's. They had waited for her to come out, even though she had stayed half the night. He was certain that she and Wright had something going. *Lucky bastard!* He knew Frank would not stop at knocking the man out, but no one would die if Webb could manage it. Webb shoved the gun back into his belt.

Leaving Wright lying on the wet ground, he ran over

to where Frank was still struggling with the woman. The little redhead was putting up quite a fight. It was taking all of Frank's strength to hold her, and, damn him, he was enjoying himself.

"We need to get out of here," Webb insisted when he reached them.

"We need to knock this bitch upside the head," Frank sneered, holding his hand over her mouth. "It'd sure make gettin' her out of here a hell of a lot easier. Damn whore! If she bites me, I'll kill her. Tap her on the head like you did Wright."

"I ain't hurtin' her if I don't have to."

"Don't start that shit now!" Frank snarled. "Grab hold of her arm so we can get movin'. Unless you killed Wright, he'll be after us."

Webb reached down and seized Nona by the arm, trying to protect himself from her vicious kicks. A bright flash of lightning was followed by a loud boom of thunder rumbling down the valley. Instinctively, he flinched. This wasn't the kind of storm that could be easily ignored.

"Damn, that was close!" Frank jerked on Nona's arm, ignoring her puny attempts to kick him. "If I had time, bitch, I'd take the starch out of you."

They moved slowly. Nona's kicking, combined with the wet grass, made every step hazardous. Several times Webb's feet slipped out from under him, sending him down to one knee with a stab of pain. Through it all, he refused to let go of Nona's arm.

"Come on, goddammit," Frank snarled. "You little bitch. You've been givin' it to Wright. Now you're goin' to give it to me."

"We didn't come here to rape women, Frank," Webb argued.

"Tend to your own business."

"This is my business. I'm tryin' to keep you from getting sidetracked."

They made their way across the grounds toward the tree line. With every flash of lightning, with every rumble of thunder, with every second, Webb waited for a shot in the back. That cowboy wasn't a pushover, and he hadn't hit Wright hard enough to knock him out for long.

"Nona!" A girl's voice carried over the sound of the storm.

They stopped and turned back. Through the streaming rain, Webb saw the young girl standing on the porch in her nightgown. She stood staring out into the night with her hands in front of her. She had seen them take her sister and would surely spread an alarm.

"Well, don't that beat all!" Frank shouted, the wind diminishing the strength of his words. "I suppose it figures that little bitch'd come runnin' home to her big sister! But hell, I ain't gonna complain."

"Keep goin', Frank," Webb cautioned, trying to hurry him along, fearful of what he might have in mind.

Frank shouted a vicious curse into the wind. With one hand still clutching Nona tightly, he reached into his waistband and pulled his revolver. He leveled it at the girl on the porch.

"Run, Maggie! Run!" Nona shouted frantically when she saw the gun.

"Here's my chance to get rid of her. Then this one will talk."

Time seemed to stand still for Nona and Webb. The wind whipped the rain around them. Flashes of lightning lit up the grounds, preceding claps of thunder. The tree branches above them swayed in the strong wind.

Through everything he had ever done, Webb had tried to avoid hurting a woman or a child. Now, as Frank prepared to shoot Maggie, something in him stirred . . . something that moved him to action.

"No, Frank! No!" Webb shouted. Just as Frank's finger began to tighten on the trigger, Webb lunged with all the speed he could muster. His hand struck Frank's elbow, pushing the gun hand high just as he pulled the trigger. The sound of the weapon firing was like a clap of thunder.

The force of his lunge at Frank brought Webb crashing to the ground on his hands and knees. The wet grass and mud rushed up to meet him. He swiveled his head quickly, hoping beyond hope that he had been in time. Maggie stood unharmed on the porch, the shot having missed her.

"You stupid son of a bitch!" Frank roared.

"I told you not to hurt her!"

Frank strode over to where Webb knelt and, cocking the pistol, pointed the gun at his head. The rain poured down on his bald head and face. He was furious.

"I told you not to get in my way!" Frank's angry voice rose above the din of the storm. "I warned you what would happen if you put your neck on the line for that twat!"

Webb closed his eyes and waited for what was about to come. Frank was crazy; he was beyond listening. But, instead of hearing the gunshot that would end his life, he heard another voice, far fainter but nonetheless urgent.

"Maggie! Get Jack!" Simon struggled to get his wobbly legs beneath him. One hand went to the back of his throbbing head and came away wet and sticky with his own blood.

"Goddammit, Webb! Can't you do anything right?" Frank cursed. "I ought to blow your damn head off!"

"Run, Maggie!" Simon shouted.

As if someone had snapped his fingers before her eyes to wake her from a trance, Maggie sprang to life. Without any hesitation, she leaped off the porch and began sprinting into the night, her bare feet throwing splashes of water from the growing puddles. In a matter of seconds, she was completely swallowed from sight by the storm.

A movement from behind caused both men to look back. Nona was scrambling away. In all of the confusion, Frank had loosened his grip.

"Jesus Christ!" Frank swore. He paused for a second, glaring down at Webb with hate-filled eyes, his mouth opening and closing as if he wanted to say more. Then, without a word, he took off at a dead run after Nona.

Struggling to his feet, Webb began to follow.

Nona ran headlong into the snarling teeth of the wind. Her hair was plastered across her face by the chilly rain, and her legs were weak with fear, but still she willed herself to keep going. These were the men who had abducted Maggie. The bald one had tried to shoot her! Now they had no intention of giving up. They had come back for her.

"Where the hell are you goin'?" a voice shouted from behind.

Shutting the words out, Nona pushed on. Ahead of her, a pair of unoccupied cabins loomed. She sped toward one as fast as her legs could take her. If she could get inside and barricade the door, it might hold her attackers off until help could arrive.

She remembered Simon saying Mrs. Hogan had not been well for a few days and her husband had taken her to see the doctor. When she reached the steps leading up to the door of the Hogan cabin, Nona felt her feet slipping out from beneath her. A large puddle of rainwater and mud had formed there, and she hadn't seen it until it was too late. Suddenly, she crashed to the ground, her right knee slamming hard into the first step.

Stinging pain shot up her leg and through her body.

Rolling over onto her stomach, she peered back into the night behind her. A well-timed flash of lightning showed that her pursuers were swiftly narrowing the gap between them. She had to move . . . and fast! Scrambling to her feet, Nona took one tentative step; her leg hurt terribly, but she was reasonably sure it was not broken. Hobbling up to the porch, she crossed to the door.

"There she is," a man shouted.

Nona fell against the door, her hand searching for the knob. When she found it, the knob rattled in her hand. *Please, God, don't let it be locked.* Then, with a loud click, the door swung inward. Nona shot through, slammed it shut behind her, and threw the dead bolt.

"Thank God," she said aloud and leaned against the wall, her heart pounding.

The inside of the cabin was pitch-black. Most of the windows had been boarded up in preparation for remodeling. Only one window near the kitchen area had been spared, but little light came from the stormy outdoors. A musty odor assaulted Nona's senses as she stumbled forward into the unknown.

"Simon! Oh, my darling Simon! Where are you?" she gasped. *Have they killed you? I haven't told you how much I love you. If they kill me, please take care of Maggie.*

Over the rolling thunder, Nona heard the sound of footsteps thudding across the porch, followed by the rattling of the doorknob. When the man found the door locked, he began kicking at it.

"Open this goddamn door!" he shouted, his voice full of rage.

Creeping to the back of the cabin, Nona moved cautiously into the kitchen and leaned against the counter. Her leg throbbed in agony. When it came time to run, would she be able to move fast enough?

The pounding against the door resumed with an even greater ferocity. Frank was putting all of his weight into the effort. If he placed a hard kick on the knob, the lock would give way and he'd be inside. She would have only seconds before he was on top of her. She was just beginning to formulate a plan of escape when suddenly the pounding stopped.

"Go check the back!" one man yelled from the porch.

"What do you—?" another voice answered.

"Go around the side! No! Over there, you stupid son of a bitch!"

"Oh, no!" Nona muttered to herself. She'd been so intent on getting in the front door, she'd forgotten to lock the back one. Fear gnawed at her gut, and she knew she had to leave immediately.

The window above the sink was small, but with effort she'd be able to squirm through. When she flipped the lock and threw the window open, she was struck by a blast of cold, wind-driven rain. Wincing with pain, she climbed up onto the counter. She heard the door bang against the wall and a shout from the man who was now inside the cabin. Half expecting to be grabbed from behind, Nona let go and fell out onto the rain-soaked ground.

"She's outside!" a voice shouted from the kitchen window.

Not bothering to look around, Nona got up and ran as fast as her injured leg would allow. Her only chance was to plunge into the woods and find somewhere to hide. As she ran, branches and leaves struck her, slowing her pace.

With each step, she expected to be caught. She strained to hear any sound of their pursuit, but couldn't discern anything above the din of the storm. Wind whipped the tree branches into a frenzy; thunder crashed. The pounding of her heart was nearly overpowering.

Coming to a small clearing, Nona saw something that gave her hope. Up ahead was a jumble of toppled trees. They looked like they'd fallen years before; rotted husks and broken branches littered the ground. If she could get behind one and wait for the men to go past, she could . . .

Without warning, a heavy weight crashed into her back and drove her down onto the wet ground. The air

was compressed from her lungs. She screamed in pain
when the man fell on her injured leg. Unable to struggle
against her captor, Nona was roughly flipped over and
pinned to the ground. Her attacker stared down into her
eyes, his breath ragged and fetid.

"You're gonna pay for that, you bitch. When I'm finished with you, you'll wish you were dead."

Chapter 26

Maggie sped through the storm toward LeAnn's cabin. Around her, bright flashes of lightning were immediately followed by thunderous crashes that sounded like gunshots. With every one, she flinched. She was breathless with dreadful anticipation of a bullet that never came. Her soaking-wet nightgown was stuck to her skin.

The distance between their cabin and LeAnn's seemed endless. Maggie forgot her stiffness from the long walk back to the camp with Dusty as fear put wings to her feet. She had wakened from a fitful dream to the feeling that something was wrong and had slowly moved through the front of the cabin as Mabel slept soundly in her chair. Looking out the door, she'd seen two men trying to drag Nona toward the woods. She'd sprung out onto the porch and shouted her sister's name. Immediately, she'd heard a gunshot, then realized that the bullet had been meant for her! It seemed too strange to be real.

When she reached LeAnn's cabin, the lights were off.

With a final burst of speed, Maggie shot up the steps, leaped across the porch, and yanked open the door.

"Jack!" she shouted. "Come quick!"

"What's wrong?" Jack asked as he sprang up from the cot where he had been dozing.

"It's . . . it's . . ." Maggie tried to explain, but her breath was coming in ragged gasps.

"Take it easy, Maggie." Jack reached for the gun that lay on the floor. He slid it into the waistband of his pants. "Calm down and tell me what's happened."

Taking a deep breath, Maggie managed to say, "Two men dragged Nona into the woods! When I shouted for her, one of them shot at me! Simon yelled for me to get you. Hurry!"

"Where's Simon now?" Jack asked, his voice steady.

"Back there, by our cabin." She pushed her wet hair out of her eyes.

"Has he gone after them?"

"I think he was hurt. I didn't wait to see."

Jack strode quickly toward the front door.

"What about LeAnn?" Maggie asked.

"I need you to stay with her."

"No! I'm coming with you."

"Jack!" Suddenly, a cry came from the back of the house. Jack and Maggie stopped in their tracks. A few seconds later, another cry rang out. "Jack! Help me!"

Battered and exhausted, Nona was dragged deeper into the rain-soaked woods, between the two men, one arm gripped tightly by each of them. She knew they were a good distance from the camp. Her leg ached and her chest throbbed from where the man had landed on her.

Still, Nona clung to hope. Her ears strained for any sound that Simon was coming for her. She wanted him to come, but also feared it. The only sound she heard was that of the two men bickering.

"You are one stupid son of a bitch!" Frank growled.

"I told you I wouldn't let you hurt her."

"And I told you that if you got in my way, I was gonna make you pay for it. You're lucky this bitch ran, or I woulda gunned you down like a damn squealer. That little tramp will shoot off her mouth. Before you know it, the whole goddamn sheriff's department is gonna be down here lookin' for us."

"They didn't find us before."

"Ain't no guarantee they won't this time!" Frank snapped. "You let that girl get to you and kept me from doin' what needed to be done."

"There was no reason to kill her."

"That's what you think. If you were so hot for her, why didn't you go ahead and screw her when we had her?"

"Because she's just a kid," Webb retorted.

"I hear they're the best."

"I've done some rotten things, but I've never ruined a young girl."

"Young? She's all of thirteen or fourteen. In some places, girls that age have already had a couple of kids."

"Not my kids, Frank."

Frank sneered. "So you've got scruples, but I get the job done, and I've got a good bank account to show for it."

Webb nodded toward Nona and said, "Let's just get

what we need from her and be done with it. The sooner we're out of here, the better."

While the two men snarled at each other, Nona kept her mouth shut and tried to keep her wits about her. Sooner or later, they would ask about the money Harold had taken. If they tried to make her talk, if they tortured her, would she still be able to keep the secret?

"Do you and Wright have something going? Has he been in your pants?" The words pulled Nona away from her frantic thoughts. She turned to look into Frank's face and felt a wave of revulsion.

"You're an animal."

"That's the nicest thing you've said to me yet. I like you already, sweetheart. You're gonna be a hell of a lot more fun than your sister."

"You took Maggie, you low-life scum."

"Yeah. What are you goin' to do about it?"

"Knock it off, Frank. We don't have time for this," Webb cautioned.

"Come on. Just 'cause you've got eyes for the kid sister don't mean you get dibs on both of 'em! You're younger than me, so it makes sense you'd want the other one, but this little darlin' is all mine!"

"Just keep movin'. We need to get out of here."

Nona was silent. She knew Frank was trying to get a rise out of her by talking about Maggie. Rain thudded against the ground in ever-larger drops, ripping through leaves on the branches and drowning out nearly all other sounds. The wind cut through the trees, impeding their progress as they struggled toward some unknown destination.

"What did your sister say about us?" Frank prodded her, his rough voice rising over the storm.

Unable to resist, Nona answered, "Actually, she said you were stupid and ugly, and if she got the chance, she'd kill you. So far, I feel the same way."

Frank laughed. "Sounds about right. I had me a real good time with her once I got rid of Webb. Her tits aren't much bigger than fried eggs." He laughed again. "What I did to 'em would make that red hair stand on end. Guess what else I did to her?"

Nona stopped. The idea that this man had touched Maggie in a sexual way, violating her when there was nothing the girl could have done to stop him, caused rage to consume her. Maggie hadn't said that she'd been molested.

"What the hell are you talking about?"

"She didn't tell you that?" Frank continued. "I guess I'm not surprised. I can't say she liked it all that much; I was pretty rough with her. You see, I'd been drinkin' and it bein' her first time, she wasn't very cooperative. But if I could have kept her for a day or two, I would have taught her to like it."

"Shut your mouth, Frank!" Webb shouted. "She doesn't know you're lyin'." He loosened his hold on Nona's arm.

"Lyin', my ass," Frank said. He leaned closer to Nona, his hand still tight on her wrist. "Kinda hard to think that your sister's a woman on account of me, ain't it?"

Nona's fist flew out and struck Frank hard across the mouth. She'd hit him so hard that her hand hurt. She was so angry she would have killed him where he stood if she'd been able.

As lightning flashed, Nona saw blood at the corner of Frank's mouth. He daubed at his lips and worked his tongue across the inside of his cheek. "You ain't got no idea who it is you're dealin' with, bitch. You play rough with Frank Rice, you'll find yourself dead."

Without another word, Frank sprang with the raw ferocity of a wild animal. Wrapping a rough hand around Nona's throat, he slammed her into a large tree. She hit it with such an alarming force, the back of her head bouncing against the trunk, that the air was driven from her lungs and she saw stars.

"Frank! Stop it—" Webb said more, but thunder drowned out the rest of his words. Frank increased the pressure on Nona's neck. He was out of control and beyond reasoning.

"How about this, bitch? Wanna hit me again?"

Nona's vision blurred and the man's face began to fade. His grip was like a vise! She was unable to get air into her lungs, and her feeling of panic was soon overwhelmed by her struggle to breathe. Her nails dug deeply into Frank's flesh as she tried frantically to pry his hand from her neck. *Am I going to die here? Will I ever see Simon or Maggie again?*

"Si-Si-Sim—," she sputtered.

"You think you're so goddamn smart!" Frank bellowed as he leaned his weight into her. "Did you think I was just gonna stand here and let you hit me and get away with it? You're nothin' but a goddamn slut!"

Nona's hands slid from Frank's and fell uselessly to

her sides. The blackness was everywhere and she felt heavy; she wanted to close her eyes and go to sleep. Her tongue lolled around in her mouth, but even over the incessant ringing in her ears, she heard the crack of a gunshot. Her last thought before darkness swallowed her was that Simon had told her he loved her.

"You rotten son of a bitch! Ain't you full of surprises!"

Somewhere in the back of his mind, Webb supposed he'd always known it would come to this. As he stood in the pounding rain, the pistol in his hand, his mind raced for a way to make Frank listen to reason. He was a madman. How can you reason with a madman? He couldn't stand by and let him commit a cold-blooded murder.

The way Frank had attacked the woman had been vicious. Webb had yelled at him, but he hadn't stopped. In the end he'd pulled his gun free and fired it above their heads. Frank reacted to that; it was the only language he understood.

"What in the hell do you think you're doing?" Frank snarled.

"I'm tryin' to stop you from killin' that woman."

Taking a deep breath, trying to keep his hand from shaking, Webb leveled the gun at Frank's head. He knew that Frank wouldn't hesitate to shoot him if he got the chance. "I don't want to shoot you, Frank. I want to do what we came here to do . . . find that damn money. Ain't no reason to kill anyone."

"You saw that bitch hit me!"

"Only after you taunted her about touchin' her sister."

"How do you know I didn't feel that brat up?"

Indecision raged in Webb's mind. If someone had been following them, odds were high that they'd heard the gunshot, even over the roar of the storm. If they were near, they could be on top of them in moments. If he was going to deal with Frank, he needed to do it quickly.

"So what are you gonna do, kid?" Frank prodded him. Even with a gun pointed at his head, he was argumentative. "You gonna shoot me in cold blood? You got the balls to do it?"

"You don't want to find out."

"I've got friends, kid. You'd never make it back to the windy city."

"I don't think the boss would like what you've been doin' here. He doesn't want to draw the attention of the FBI. I told you kidnappin' was a federal offense. He ordered us to find the money, nothin' more and nothin' less. You ain't got no one to blame but yourself if the feds come down on us."

"I'm sick of your bitchin'. I should've shot you when I had the chance," Frank grumbled. Before Webb could answer, Frank suddenly dived to his left and yanked his gun from his waistband. Startled, Webb pulled the trigger and fired. The bullet slammed into the tree behind Frank. He fired again, but Frank had rolled away.

"Shit!" Webb swore.

Before Webb could take aim and fire again, Frank suddenly righted his roll and fired at him. Searing-hot pain roared through Webb's right shoulder as the bullet ripped through skin and crashed into hard bone. The force of the blow spun him around; the pistol flew from his hand and landed somewhere behind him among the wet leaves. He fell onto his back, the pain nearly rendering him unconscious. As one hand went to his wound, the other clawed at the ground around him, hoping by some miracle to find his gun.

"Oh, God! Oh, Jesus!" he prayed through stiff lips.

The rain fell on his face and he blinked rapidly. Frank appeared above him, his gun pointed down at him. Webb knew that Frank was going to kill him.

"Betcha didn't think it'd go quite like this, did ya?" Frank placed his foot on Webb's shoulder and pressed down with all of his weight. Webb howled in agony, his hand feebly trying to push Frank's foot away. He felt nothing but an all-consuming pain.

"You . . . you . . . you bastard," Webb managed to spit out.

"You don't know the half of it." Frank smirked. "I warned you, kid. You can't say I didn't. Crossin' me is the dumbest thing you coulda done. Now it's time for you to get what's comin' to you."

Before Webb could move, Frank fired the gun into his chest. For the briefest of moments, Webb couldn't feel anything and wondered if the man had missed. Then, growing in intensity until it felt as if he'd been probed with a hot poker, pain washed over him and he knew he was going to die.

"Hurts like a bitch, don't it?" Frank asked as he leaned down into Webb's face. "But it ain't gonna kill you just yet. You'll lay here and bleed to death, which is more than you deserve."

Frank laughed and walked away, leaving Webb to die in the rain.

Chapter 27

Simon! Simon, what happened?!"

The words slowly penetrated down into the murky darkness that had once again swallowed up his thoughts. The pain was intense; it was as if a thousand church bells had decided to peal at the same time inside his head. His arms felt disjointed, wobbly, swimming around on their own. For the moment, standing was out of the question. He knelt in the pounding rain. The rain mixed with blood and ran down the sides of his face.

"Answer me! Where are Nona and Maggie?"

Nona! Memories of seeing Nona being dragged into the night flooded back into Simon's mind. The bastards had come back to finish their job . . . to get their dirty hands on Harold's stolen money! He had to get to his feet. He had to get to Nona.

"Simon! Talk to me!"

Turning his head slowly, Simon tried to focus his eyes on whoever stood next to him. Through his glassy sight and the rain, he finally made out Mabel's lined and worried face.

"It's Nona . . . The bastards took Nona," he stammered, his tongue feeling as thick as a cinder block in his mouth. Even when he spoke, the dull ringing in his ears wouldn't stop. He had a concussion; he hoped it was a slight one. "They grabbed Nona when she left my cabin and coldcocked me when I came out after her. I saw her break loose and run."

"I'd fallen asleep in my chair when a gunshot startled me awake. When I ran out here, I found you like this. Oh, Lord! I shouldn't have been sleeping."

"It's all right, Mabel," Simon interjected. His head throbbed like a jackhammer. "What matters is finding Nona."

"What about Maggie? Where is she?"

"I sent her to get Jack. I'll need his help to go after them," Simon explained as he tried to rise from his knees. When he reached his feet, the whole world swam in front of his eyes and he swayed from side to side, nearly falling back to the ground. Mabel put one steadying hand on his shoulder. "I can't let them get away."

"You shouldn't be going after them at all." Mabel frowned. "You're hurt, Simon. Hurt badly. In the shape you're in, if you somehow did manage to catch up to them, you'd be in no condition to protect yourself or Nona. You'd end up getting both of you killed."

"Don't worry about me. I'll manage. These men will kill Nona if she doesn't tell them what they want to know."

"What are you talking about?" Mabel repeated. "What could Nona possibly know that they would want?"

Ignoring Mabel's questions, Simon turned and staggered back into his cabin. He couldn't tell her now. It would take too long.

With every step, he felt a bit better. His head was still foggy, but his vision was improving and the ringing in his ears had begun to fade to a dull roar. Mabel was right about one thing: If he were to catch up to the men, he'd need to have his full faculties to help Nona. Anything less and they'd both be dead. He needed to be prepared.

Yanking open the top drawer of his dresser, he pulled out a pair of pistols. After checking both to make sure they were loaded, he slipped one into the waistband of his pants. Mabel entered with Dusty beside her, soaking wet and slightly winded from running. His hair was plastered to his head.

"What happened?" Dusty asked.

Simon handed the boy his rifle. "I need you to keep an eye on things while I'm gone. If there are more of them, and there could be, they'll be coming for Maggie. Stay near her, and whatever you do, don't let her out of your sight. I guess you've used one of these before?"

"Yes, exactly like this one," Dusty explained. "Hunting's a way of life in these parts. I'm no stranger when it comes to guns."

"Good." Simon nodded. Turning to Mabel, he added, "Try to reach the sheriff's office and tell them what's happened. I hope the lines haven't gone down in the storm."

Back outside, they discovered that the weather had worsened. The wind, in particular, had grown rough with gusts nearly strong enough to knock a man off his feet. In this weather, the criminals couldn't have traveled far, not when they had to haul Nona along, but finding them was going to be difficult. They had headed north; he'd start that way.

"I'm worried about your head . . . ," Mabel said.

"I'll be all right. When Maggie returns with Jack, tell him which direction I'm going and that I'm just a few minutes ahead of him. He'll know what to do. Stay together and keep your eyes open." With that, Simon took off into the night on unsteady legs.

"Jack! Help!"

Before the chilling words could even sink in, Jack had rushed across the room and jerked open the door to LeAnn's bedroom. LeAnn was sitting up in the small bed, the covers pulled up around her neck. Confused and concerned, Jack went to her.

"What is it?" Jack managed to blurt out. "What's wrong?"

"I'm sorry if I scared you, but I didn't want you to leave." Her cheeks flushed a deep shade of red, and sweat stood out on her forehead. Her breathing was ragged, nearly panicked. Where her hand gripped the blanket, her knuckles were bone-white. "It's just that . . . ," she started to say, but a look of intense pain crossed her face, and she sucked in her breath through clenched teeth.

"She's having the baby." Maggie, beside Jack, spoke matter-of-factly.

" 'Fraid so." LeAnn winced and smiled at the same time.

"Now?" Jack asked incredulously. "I thought you weren't due until September!"

"Well, it's not like you can plan these things!" Maggie said confidently.

"It's definitely now," LeAnn admitted. "I wasn't feeling all that well earlier. I had pains in my back and hoped it was just nerves or something I ate. But while I was lying here, listening to the storm, it got worse. Then my water broke and I knew for sure."

Jack knew he had a hard choice to make, but when the time came to make up his mind, he found the choice wasn't hard at all. "Maggie," he said calmly. "Go get Mabel. Tell her LeAnn is having the baby. She'll know what to bring."

"What? But what about . . ."

"Now."

"But Simon told me to come and get you! Nona needs you . . ."

"That's why you have to go and get Mabel," Jack said. He looked and spoke calmly. "Go as quickly as you can. I'll stay here until you two get back, and then I'll go find Simon."

Excited, Maggie hurried to the door. Before she stepped outside of the room, she turned back and asked, "Will you be all right here? Do you know anything about babies?"

"I've birthed foals and calves back on my ranch," Jack said, trying to smile. "Not quite the same thing, but it's a start. Go get Mabel."

"Right," Maggie said and was gone.

Jack sat down in the rickety chair at the side of

LeAnn's bed. He could see that she was hurting and trying not to let him know. But the pain in her eyes gave her away. He took one of her hands in his and held it tightly.

"What was Maggie saying about Simon and Nona? Is everything all right?"

"Don't worry about a thing." Jack's smile came easily. "Simon needs me to help him with something. A boat loose from the dock, I suppose, but it can wait until Mabel gets here." He felt slightly uncomfortable about lying, but the last thing he wanted to do was upset LeAnn. She had enough to think about without worrying about Nona. This baby was coming early, and that could mean complications.

"Well, as long as it's not too important."

"LeAnn . . . there's no place I'd rather be right now than here with you."

How could this have happened to me? I never intended to fall in love with her, or with anyone. A pregnant woman whose husband hasn't been dead a week or two has completely captured my heart. I wish to God this baby was mine. If we could have been married before it was born, it would have been mine legally. I'm not sure how she feels about me, but she is comfortable with me and doesn't seem to be as scared when she is with me. I wish we had had more time together before her baby was born, but that's not to be.

"I have to admit . . . ," LeAnn started, drawing his eyes down to her, but another wave of pain washed over her, and in another minute she couldn't speak. Quick bursts of air hissed through her teeth as she squeezed Jack's hand with surprising strength. Finally, the pain subsided enough for her to relax slightly.

"A bad one?" Jack asked.

"Uh-huh. I'm glad you're here with me." She smiled sheepishly. "Although it embarrasses me for you to see me like this."

Jack raised her hand to his mouth and kissed it. "You needn't be embarrassed. It's the most natural thing in the world for a woman to give birth."

"But . . . I'm not your wife. But . . ."

He interrupted. "Don't talk like that," he said sternly. "I had hoped that we could get better acquainted and have an understanding between us before the baby came. I told you that I'd stay by you no matter what the circumstances, and I'm sure not going to change my tune now." As he settled in to wait for Maggie to return with Mabel, he silently prayed that Simon could manage without him for just a little while.

Simon moved as quickly as he could across the campground. The pouring rain had turned the earth to a muddy soup beneath him, and twice he fell to the ground. Filthy and soaking wet, he searched for any sign of the men and Nona. They'd moved off toward the tree line and away from the roads that serviced the camp. He was reasonably sure that they hadn't gotten into a vehicle and driven away. He saw no tracks in the mud. Somewhere, in the raging storm and the dark woods, Nona needed him desperately.

Moving along the tree line and peering intently at the ground, Simon soon found footprints in the fresh mud.

He couldn't be sure how many there were, but certainly more than one set. With his gun held out in front of him, he pushed between a pair of tall bushes and was soon enveloped by the woods.

As he pressed forward cautiously, Simon calculated all the odds that were stacked against him. The bastards had succeeded in keeping Maggie hidden in the woods for days, undetectable to the dozens of men who had been out looking for her. If not for Dusty, she might never have escaped. What hope did he have of finding Nona now, especially after the blow to his head?

"Dammit," he muttered.

Passing under a low-hanging branch that swayed menacingly in the heavy wind, he entered a small clearing littered with fallen trees. There, in the mud, were the clear signs of a struggle. It looked to Simon as if someone had been thrown to the ground. Had Nona struggled against them? Had they hurt her for her defiance? Preferring not to dwell on such a possibility, Simon pushed farther into the forest.

Time moved slowly. As the lightning and thunder played in tandem, Simon moved down a thin path between the imposing trees. It was hard to see all the way to the ground, but he was fairly certain that he was following the right set of tracks.

"Oh, God!" a voice coughed out.

Simon froze in place, his heart pounding. He strained to hear a sound other than the rain and whistling wind, something so he could be certain he hadn't imagined it. Unsure of himself, he could only wait.

"Somebody . . . help me . . ."

This time, Simon heard the voice clearly. It had come from a spot ahead of him and to the left, off the narrow path and into the brush. Gripping the pistol tightly, he stepped into the soaking greenery and moved toward the cry.

Off the path, his visibility was even worse. Even with the frequent flashes of lightning, little of the light penetrated the tree cover. For a moment, he worried that he would stumble over the person who had moaned, so he slowed even more. Finally, as he rounded the trunk of a large tree and came into a clearing, he saw a shape lying sprawled in the grass. As he waited, the shape coughed and lifted a hand.

"Help me," a man's voice said weakly.

Cautiously, his eyes open for any signs of a trap, Simon made his way over to where the man lay on his back, his hands on his stomach. Even in the near-darkness, he could see the bright stain that had spread across the belly of the man's shirt. The coppery smell of blood was strong.

"What happened?" Simon asked. "Where's Nona?"

After another fit of coughing, the man said, "Is that you, Wright?"

Shocked, Simon answered, "Yes. Where's Nona?"

The man didn't answer for a long while. His body twitched with pain, his hands laced over his blood-covered midsection. Simon had the sudden fear that the man would die before he could tell him what had happened, before he could tell him where they'd taken Nona. He needed answers.

"How do you know who I am?" Simon said.

"We've been . . . been watching the camp for weeks. All . . . I . . . wanted was the money . . . I didn't want anybody to get hurt. He just wouldn't . . . wouldn't listen. He'll hurt . . . hurt her bad."

"Who are you talking about? Who's going to hurt her?"

"Frank . . . Frank will hurt her. He . . . shot me when I tried . . . tried to stop him from choking her. I couldn't . . . couldn't hit him . . . I couldn't . . . make him quit. He's . . . crazy."

A sickening feeling spread throughout Simon's gut. Frank had shot this man and left him to die. Frank was now alone with Nona somewhere in these woods. He had to find them soon. "Where did they go?"

"You'll never . . . never find them in . . . this storm."

"Goddammit! I said, where did they go?" Simon demanded. Time was running out with every passing second. His blood turned cold with dread. "Come on, man, tell me which way they went!"

Even as Simon raged at him, the man remained still. Was he keeping silent out of choice or was he too weak to answer? Finally, he slowly raised a shaky arm and pointed back toward the path that Simon had been traveling.

"He took her . . . that way . . . ," the man managed to say. "We had a cabin . . . about five miles . . . to the north. It . . . it looks abandoned . . . from the outside. He'll take her there . . . to make her talk . . . hurt her if she . . . don't."

Without another word, Simon began to move back toward the path. He knew that there was nothing he could do for the man; his wounds were too severe and he'd soon bleed to death. Nona was his only concern.

"I'm . . . I'm sorry," the man croaked out before Simon was out of earshot.

"Not as sorry as that son of a bitch is going to be."

Chapter 28

As the pounding rain continued to fall, Nona rubbed her wet arms for heat. Although the action didn't warm her, something about it was comforting. Comfort was what she needed; the last hour had been one long nightmare. After being roughly slapped awake, she'd been horrified to learn that Frank had shot the other man and had left him behind to die. She'd wanted to do something for him, but Frank would have none of it, and with a snarl and a shove, he'd pushed her farther into the woods.

Silently, she cursed herself for the weakness she felt overwhelming her. She hadn't wanted to cry, but her tears mixed with the rain as it washed down her cheeks. *This man is a heartless killer!* He'd kidnapped Maggie and shot a man in cold blood without the slightest hint of remorse. Nona could only imagine what he had in store for her if she failed to give him what he wanted.

But what can I do? she thought frantically.

Even if she were to run, to try to break free, where would she go? Frank and the other man had spent days, maybe weeks, scouting out the area around the lodge grounds. He was familiar with the terrain. He would find her. Then there was the matter of her damaged leg. She was sure she hadn't broken anything, but her knee hurt as if it had been hit with a sledgehammer. She wouldn't get very far on it. If, by some miracle, she were to find a road, what were the odds that someone else would be on it as well? Slim to none, she guessed.

"Just get that idea outta your pretty little red head," Frank warned.

"Get what out?"

"Any thoughts about runnin' off. I ain't in any mood to go chasin' after you in this shit," he said as he waved the pistol at the storm above. "I'd rather just shoot you and take another crack at your sister."

Nona swallowed the bile that was building in her throat. Every time Frank opened his mouth, he revolted her. The things he said, especially about Maggie, made her skin crawl. *Why won't he just shut up?! I can't stand to* . . . Suddenly, a thought occurred to her. If she could keep him talking, it might make it easier for someone to find them. If Simon were looking for her, he'd hear the bastard's voice. It wasn't much, but she had to try.

"Maggie said you wanted money," she prodded.

"You know it ain't just any old money." Frank laughed. "This ain't about pocket change or Grandma's family jewelry! You ask me, I think there ain't no doubt you know what this whole mess is about. I'm bettin' you're a touch smarter than that sister of yours."

"If I did know," Nona continued, happy that he hadn't

told her to keep her mouth shut, "don't you think I'd just tell you and be done with it?"

"Maybe . . . maybe not. Depends on what Harold promised you outta the deal. I reckon if I was in your shoes and somebody promised me a cut of several million bucks, I'd keep my trap shut, even if there was a gun bein' waved in my face. That's why I gotta be sure you ain't lyin'."

Nona's face blanched at the mention of how much Harold had stolen. When Simon had told her that not all of the stolen money was in the parcel, she hadn't bothered to ask him how much Harold had actually taken. No wonder these men were after it!

"I haven't talked with Harold in a long time," Nona said defensively. "And I don't plan on doing it any time soon. But why would I? . . . He's a good-for-nothing liar who's made Maggie and me miserable."

"I don't doubt that for a second." Frank chuckled. "He's a worthless son of a bitch, Harold is. But then again, why'd he bother sendin' you a parcel right before you left to come up here?"

Shocked, Nona came to a stop on the path. Dread filled her. Turning to Frank, she asked, "You think he sent me the money?"

With a speed that Nona hadn't expected, Frank's arm shot out, grabbed a fistful of her nightgown, and yanked her closer to him. A flash of lightning lit up his face, and if she had been able to, she would certainly have recoiled from his fearsome eyes and malignant smile.

"That's what I'm talkin' about," he snarled. A rumble of thunder followed behind his words. "Caught in your own bullshit! You ain't nothin' but a lyin' bitch, just like that brother of yours! Harold sent you that damn money, and I want to know where you're hidin' it!"

"I don't know—," Nona began, but Frank cut her off.

"I'm through playin' with you!" he shouted, enraged by her continued denials.

He flung her to the ground as if she were nothing more than a rag doll, and the fabric of her nightgown tore open across her chest. She landed hard on her back. Another flash of lightning forked across the sky high above; and, from where Nona lay, Frank looked both gigantic and grotesque, as unreal as what was happening. "I know how to make you tell me where it is!"

Reflexively, Nona tried to move backward, her hands scuttling across the wet ground, but she couldn't get any traction in the mud. There would be no escape now. Even if she were to spill her guts, to tell Frank about what she'd found in the parcel, she knew he was going to hurt her . . . badly. She wanted to open her mouth, to scream out into the storm for help, but fear had stolen her voice.

"You asked for this, bitch!"

Frank bent down to grab her, but, suddenly, as his hand was mere inches from her, someone slammed hard into his side, driving him into the bushes beside her. Nona struggled up to her knees as quickly as she could, but the darkness of the forest had already swallowed the fighters. Sounds of a struggle reached her over the rain: grunts and groans, as well as the thud of a punch. *What's happening? Has Frank's partner somehow managed to follow us?* The urge to run gripped Nona, but something held her in place. Finally, as another flash of lightning lit up the night, she saw who had come. *Simon!*

Jack stood up and put his hand on the butt of his gun at the sound of feet thundering across the porch. Even over the roar of the storm, the noise had reached him. It had been ten minutes since Maggie had left to fetch Mabel, and he had spent the time wiping LeAnn's forehead with a wet washcloth and holding her hand during contractions. Even though the women were due to show up, Jack was prepared for anything.

"LeAnn?" Mabel's voice called from the front door. "Jack?"

"In the bedroom," Jack answered.

Mabel rushed through the doorway and set the first-aid box on the table. She gave Jack no more than a glance before heading straight for the bed. Maggie and Dusty trailed in behind her, each one of them soaking wet from the storm. The boy nodded to Jack, then moved to the door and stood watch.

"I'm here, honey," Mabel said softly. "Everything's going to be fine."

"I'm sorry for the trouble," LeAnn answered.

"Don't say anything of the sort. Women have been having babies since the beginning of time, and each one of them would tell you that when a baby decides it's time . . . it's time. You don't get much of a say in it."

"That's what I told Jack," Maggie chimed in.

Suddenly, a powerful contraction washed over LeAnn. "Oh . . . ," she moaned, her head rolling on the pillow.

Her neck was taut, and her face was white and slick with perspiration.

"Just ride through this," Mabel soothingly reassured her. "Pant, honey." She demonstrated by breathing in and out rapidly. "I've been in on a dozen deliveries," she lied, trying to reassure LeAnn. "Panting seems to help." To Maggie, she said, "Get a pitcher of water from the kitchen, put it in a pan on the stove. We'll need warm water sooner or later. Just try to breathe in and out, LeAnn. It'll be over before you know it. Go to the bathroom, Maggie, and bring me all of the towels you can find."

Maggie rushed off to follow Mabel's orders as the older woman stood, drew off her dripping-wet overshirt, rolled up her sleeves to above her elbows, and unfastened the top two buttons at the neck of her blouse. Pulling a few strands of henna-colored hair out of her eyes, she turned to Jack and said, "Simon needs your help."

"Is everything going to be all right here? This baby's early."

"I'll take care of this. Go."

Jack walked over to the bed and placed his hand lightly on LeAnn's damp forehead. Running his fingers over the loose strands of her hair, he said, "I have to leave, but Mabel will be with you until I get back. Before you know it, you'll have a brand-new baby."

"Don't worry about me." LeAnn's voice was weak, but she gave him a strong smile.

To Mabel's surprise, Jack leaned down and kissed LeAnn's forehead, then headed for the door, where he clapped a hand on Dusty's shoulder. The boy looked grave but determined. "You'll need to keep alert. Watch over all of them while I'm gone."

Dusty nodded and lifted the rifle Simon had given him.

"If someone tries to get in, don't wait to ask questions. If you hesitate, there won't be time for anything else," Jack said as he gave one last look over his shoulder at LeAnn before stepping out into the driving rain.

"How long have you been in labor?" Mabel asked.

"I don't . . . don't know for . . . certain," LeAnn managed as another wave of pain struck. Her hands clenched the bedsheet in tight fistfuls. "I wasn't feeling well . . . earlier tonight . . . but . . . ," she managed as another roll of thunder drowned out her words.

"That's all right." Mabel hushed her. "Don't worry, honey."

"Jack thought we should go to the doctor, but I told him we wouldn't make it in time, especially in this storm. I didn't want to have this baby in the car on a dark road."

When Maggie came back with a few skimpy towels, Mabel went to the door and asked Dusty to move to the window; what was about to happen was nothing for the boy to see. Returning to the bed, she pulled the sheets out of the foot of the bed and peered beneath them. Lifting LeAnn's legs and bending them at the knee, she positioned herself to see how things were coming. Blood and water had stained the bedcover, but nothing seemed amiss. She removed the wet bedding and placed a layer of towels beneath the pregnant woman's lower body. Mabel knew that they had done all they could for now. Even if this child was coming prematurely, they'd be ready for it.

"Have you ever done this before?" Maggie asked.

"Not alone. A dozen times with others," Mabel lied. "I sat by my mother's side when she had my little sister. I couldn't have been much older than you, Maggie. It was something that I'll never forget."

For the next hour, LeAnn dozed fitfully. Even asleep, her breath came in pants. Mabel and Maggie kept themselves busy, as lightning and thunder raged outside the small cabin; Maggie watched over the sleeping woman, and Mabel gathered the other things they would eventually need, like string to tie the umbilical cord and a sharp, clean knife to cut it, as well as baby clothes for the child. She lit a kerosene lamp in case the electricity went off.

Suddenly, LeAnn jerked awake from her light sleep, a wild look in her eyes. Her breath came fitfully and her face was a mask of pain. This contraction was powerful; LeAnn's body shook as she tried to control it. When she spoke, her voice was little more than a whisper.

"I think . . . it's coming . . ."

"Hold on, LeAnn. It's time." To Maggie, Mabel added, "Go get the pot of warm water. Put it over there on the dresser beside the dishpan. We'll need it soon." Without answering, Maggie left the room.

Throwing off the light bedcover, Mabel once again positioned LeAnn's legs, placing her feet flat on the bed. She put the palm of her hand on the hardened mound of the belly and waited for another contraction to arrive. Maggie burst back into the room with the pot of water and so hurriedly set it on the dresser that some of the liquid sloshed over the side.

"Oh . . . Mabel! It . . . it hurts!"

"You're doing fine, honey. Everything is as it should be. Hold on to the head of the bed."

"But . . . but I just . . ." Pain seized LeAnn again and she became lost to the world, her cries filling the small room. After several minutes, her voice fell in intensity and sounded weak. "I can't . . . stand much . . . more."

"It'll be over soon. The head is showing. Take deep breaths and push as hard as you can."

LeAnn reared back and grabbed at her abdomen as the pain took her again. She let out a loud cry and quivered in agony, then grabbed the head of the bed and began to push with all of the strength she could muster.

"That's it! That's it, LeAnn!" Mabel shouted. With Maggie watching over her shoulder, the older woman gently reached out as the child's head appeared. Slowly, she pulled the tiny baby from its mother's body. With crimson-stained fingers, she laid the child onto a blanket, tied the string around the umbilical cord, and cleanly cut it with the knife. As Mabel wiped the baby's nose and mouth with a cloth, the newborn's tiny voice began to fill the room.

"Is that . . . Is that my baby?" LeAnn asked weakly.

"It is!" Maggie exclaimed as tears began to course down her cheeks. "It's a girl, and she's beautiful!"

As Maggie took the small bundle and handed it to LeAnn, Mabel massaged the exhausted woman's stomach. After a short time, the afterbirth came out easily. Mabel rolled up the used towels and packed fresh ones between LeAnn's thighs.

"My baby!" LeAnn said in amazement. "My baby girl!"

The child seemed healthy: plump red cheeks and the right number of tiny fingers and toes. A small tuft of dark hair was plastered to the baby's head. She cried out, her arms and legs waving.

"What are you going to name her?" Maggie asked.

"Sophie. After my grandmother."

"Well, little Sophie," Mabel said. "You picked one heck of a time to make your appearance. I doubt that any of us will ever forget this night."

Chapter 29

DESPERATELY PUSHING, CLAWING, AND TEARING, Simon tried to position himself so he could get a hold on the man. Strength matched strength as they grappled in the tall, wet grass. His muscles throbbed from the exertion. He'd wanted to remain calm and not allow his anger to rule his head, but what he had discovered minutes before had caused him to erupt in pure rage.

After leaving the wounded kidnapper behind, he'd pushed relentlessly down the path that the man had indicated. Through the whipping wind and rain, he'd picked his way forward as quickly as he dared, the enveloping darkness and the pain in his head making his progress even more difficult.

Finally, after what had seemed like hours, he'd heard the faint sound of voices coming to him over the pounding of the rain. He'd stopped and strained his ears to localize them. Finally, he could distinguish the argument between a man and a woman.

Simon had run through a stand of thick brush beneath

a tall elm, its branches swaying menacingly in the gale-like winds, and he had halted in his tracks at the sight that met his eyes. Time had seemed to stand still, the images moving like frames in an old movie; the man holding Nona on the ground, her nightgown tearing open, and him reaching for her.

The thought passed through Simon's mind to shoot the man where he stood, but something took hold of the anger burning in his belly and he stayed his hand, fearing the man would shoot Nona. Instead, Simon found himself rushing through the rain, a growl building in his gut and, with all his strength, hurtling himself into the man on top of his woman.

"Get off her!" he shouted.

The next couple of minutes erupted in a barrage of punches to the stomach, elbows to the face, and knees to the upper thighs and groin. Both men had been overwhelmed by their animal instincts as their teeth gnashed together and their eyes burned with bloodlust. Frank, his barely contained fury now let loose as if it were flood-waters burst free from a dam, landed a solid blow to Simon's chest. Then with the smallest of spaces between them, he managed to separate himself and roll to his feet. Simon then did the same.

When, reflexively, both men went to their waistbands to draw out their guns, both of them came up empty-handed. The force of their collision had sent the pistols flying.

"Damn you, Wright!" Frank snarled. A small stream of blood leaked from the corner of his mouth and ran down over the stubble of his chin. "I guess I'm gonna have to kill you another way!"

"You're welcome to try, you son of a bitch!"

"I aim to!" With that, Frank reached down to his boot and, from a large scabbard tied to his calf, pulled out a knife. The blade was long, about six inches, and it gleamed menacingly in the flashing glare of a streak of lightning. Holding it out in front of him, Frank slashed through the air. "I'm gonna gut you like a pig!"

The two men began slowly to circle each other. Every step or two, Frank lashed out with the knife, trying to thrust it into Simon's body, but the other man quickly pulled back, leaving the knife to strike nothing but air.

"How long can you keep this up?" Frank laughed.

"Longer than you," Simon countered.

"We'll see about that." Like a cat, the thug shot forward and caught Simon's forearm with the tip of the sharp knife. Blood instantly flowed from the cut and ran in rivulets down his arm to drip on the ground below. The wound stung, but Simon paid it no heed. "Ain't quite as fast as you thought you were, huh, Wright?"

Simon tried his best to ignore the man's taunts by keeping his attention on the blade and himself between the madman and Nona. He listened for the slightest sound from her, but he noticed nothing. Had she dragged herself off into the bushes or was she seriously hurt? If so, he'd make this bastard pay with his life.

After another halting feint, Frank suddenly darted forward with determination, the knife held upright in his hand. Simon stepped forward himself and, with a powerful stroke of his left arm, drove wide the wrist holding the weapon, while simultaneously hitting the man hard in the ribs with his other fist. Air wheezed out of Frank's lungs as he stumbled away.

"Not bad," Frank gasped. "But it ain't gonna be good enough."

Once again, the two men began to circle. Simon knew that he must disarm the thug if he was going to have any hope of surviving and saving Nona. It would only be a matter of time before the knife found its mark.

As if to show how valid Simon's worries were, Frank threw out his knife hand while Simon was flat-footed. Although he jerked his head away at the last instant, the steel still found the soft flesh of Simon's cheek, just below his eye. If it had been but half an inch higher, he could have been blinded. The cut ached with the ferocity of a hundred bee stings. Simon blinked rapidly, trying to clear his thoughts.

"Matter of time," Frank muttered.

In that instant, Simon knew the man was right; he had to end it quickly. He'd have to be decisive or he'd be dead . . . and Nona would be left to the madman. Saying a silent prayer, Simon waited for his moment and, when it appeared, he struck.

Taking a quick step toward Frank's right, Simon suddenly stopped and darted to the left. Frank saw the opening Simon's first step had given him, took the bait, and lunged forward; but, once there, he found no target. Now standing to the other man's left, Simon threw a thunderous punch to the jaw. The force of the blow sent rain spraying from the thug's wet head and he staggered, his legs trembling. With a slap to the man's hand, Simon sent the knife hurtling into the dark forest. Now they'd be evenly matched.

"It ain't gonna be that easy!" Frank screamed and rallied with a punch of his own, his bony knuckles colliding with Simon's face. Blood filled Simon's mouth, and his head, still unsteady from the earlier blow, swam dizzily.

For the next couple of minutes, the two men stood toe-to-toe and traded hard blows. A pounding shot to the ribs was followed by a stiff jab to the chin, which was in turn answered with a strike near the ear. Simon was so full of anger that he could hardly feel the punches that struck him; they only served to make him throw more of his own. Finally, Simon landed a blow flush with Frank's nose, breaking the hard cartilage beneath. As blood spurted out, the man crashed hard onto his back.

Briefly, Simon hoped that Frank would stay down. Lightning flashed and he saw how misguided those hopes were. In that quick moment, Frank's eyes had looked at him much like those of a cornered animal; he would either fight and live or die trying. Still, it was what Frank had clutched in his hand that truly frightened Simon . . . It was a gun.

Simon turned to jump out of the way, but he was far too slow to escape a bullet. The gun's recoil came at the same time as the peal of thunder roared, making it sound as if the shot had come from the heavens above. The bullet tore through the soft tissue of Simon's left shoulder with the force of a sledgehammer. The bullet threw him to the ground.

I've been shot! he thought with shock. He must have knocked the man right on top of his own gun! Where only moments before he'd felt he had his opponent beaten, he now faced his own death!

"Now, ain't that a bitch." Frank chuckled.

As Simon clutched at his pounding shoulder, he tried to gather his scattered thoughts and stiffen his weakened legs. Seconds later, he found Frank standing above him, the pistol pointed directly at his head. *Oh, God, Nona. I never got a chance to tell you that you are the love of my life and that I loved you the minute I saw that red hair shining in the sun.*

"Not too often killin' somebody is personal to me," the man explained as he cocked the pistol's hammer. "But I gotta admit, I'm gonna take pleasure in this."

Simon closed his eyes as the sound of the gun firing filled his ears.

When Frank had stood above Nona, the storm raging around them, she'd believed that she would die. All of the hope that she'd attempted to nurture during the long march through the waterlogged forest had simply vanished in an instant, as if it were no more than a puff of smoke. That was why, when Simon had come hurtling out of the darkness and into Frank, she'd been utterly dumbfounded by it, and fearful that it was an illusion.

Nona could only marvel at the fury of the attack. She knew that she should either run for help, scream out to Simon that she was safe, or wade into the fray and try to help him. But instead, she stood paralyzed as the fight broke out in front of her, nothing more than a spectator at the most gruesome of sports. Her spirits rose with every blow that Simon landed against Frank, and sank when the fists struck him, but still she did nothing more than watch.

Finally, when Simon had landed the blow to his opponent's nose, her spirits had soared! It was going to be over now! They were safe! She was just about to run to him and throw her arms around his waist when the shot rang out. Her hands went to her chest to see if it was she that had been shot, so real did it all seem, but none of her blood had been shed. When Simon fell to the ground, she'd known he hadn't been as lucky.

"Now, ain't that a bitch."

At the sound of Frank's voice, the rage deep inside Nona rose up. All of the anger that she'd felt when Maggie had been kidnapped. All of the indignity she'd had to swallow when she'd been forced to march through the woods at gunpoint. All of the frustration of dealing with Harold and his conniving schemes and plans. Frank had walked over to stand above Simon, a gun in his hand. She'd been conscious when he'd dealt with Webb, and she knew what was about to happen. Without a sound, she began to move.

"I'm gonna take pleasure in this."

Desperation fueled each of Nona's steps. Just as she was about to reach Frank, she leaped into the air and landed square on the man's back. As she struck him, the gun in his hand went off, the sound of the shot ringing off the trees that surrounded them. Now it was fear for Simon that fueled her; at that distance, how could Frank have missed his target? Fearing the worst, she fought with the ferocious intensity of a caged animal, clawing and scratching with all of her might.

"You stupid bitch!" Frank howled as her fingernails clawed across his cheek.

"I hate you!" she screamed back. "I'll kill you!"

Frank stepped around blindly, Nona's extra weight making it hard for him to keep his balance. She continued to punch him in the ears, rake across his skin, pull on his hair, anything and everything she could think of to cause him as much pain as he had caused her.

Finally, he managed to grab hold of one of her arms and roughly toss her off his back and onto the wet ground. Nona had no more than hit the earth than she was back on her feet and charging the still-dazed man. Her small frame collided with his and her hands beat against his chest and face.

"I'll kill you!" she shrieked again.

Deep within, Nona knew that she wasn't doing any damage, but she kept on fighting. She no longer feared his gun, knife, or the threats that he'd uttered. What did threats mean when she'd lost Simon?

Without warning, Frank's hand swung out and struck the side of her face, swatting her away as if she were nothing more than a fly annoying a much more dangerous predator. Crashing back to the ground, Nona sobbed as the pain and loss suddenly overwhelmed her.

"Bitch!" Frank bellowed. "You goddamn bitch! I'm gonna kill you!"

Illuminated by another flash of bright lightning, the thug suddenly loomed over her again, just as he had only minutes before, his hands held out in front of him, ready to attach themselves to her slender neck and choke the life out of her. Nona wanted to scream, to continue fighting, but hopelessness had overcome her, and she could no more lift a finger to stop him than she could move a mountain.

Another roar of thunder came from above and Nona reflexively shut her eyes. When, seconds later, she opened them, what she found momentarily confused her. Frank had fallen down onto his knees beside her, his eyes wide with an emotion that she couldn't quite place . . . perhaps it was shock mixed with a touch of fear. His hands had moved to his own chest. There, in the center of his shirt, a red stain had begun to spread.

"What the . . . what the hell?" he murmured.

Where Frank knelt, he was only a dozen inches away from Nona and she quickly tried to move away, slipping and sliding in the grass and mud in her desperation. Behind his suddenly glassy eyes, Frank noticed her movement and reached out to grab her leg. Another roaring blast split the night, and Frank was sent hurtling backward into the rainy muck. His face contorted into a chaotic mask and his muscles spasmed once . . . then twice . . . as he fell silent. After one hiss of air through his teeth, Frank was dead.

"But . . . but what . . . ?" Nona mumbled.

"Behind you, sweetheart."

Nona turned at the sound of the voice to see Simon leaning up on one elbow, a pistol held in his shaking hand. Even in his pain, he forced one of his trademark grins.

"Simon!"

Nona shot to her feet and ran the short distance between them, all of her own aches forgotten. Lifting his scruffy face as gingerly as she could, she began to plant soft kisses on his rough lips.

"I thought that he'd killed you! I thought I was too late!"

"He was doing his best," Simon admitted between kisses. "He would have succeeded if you hadn't jumped on his back. Not only did the shot miss me, but you knocked the gun out of his hand. By the time I crawled over to it, he'd just forced you to the ground. You saved my life, Nona."

"And you saved mine," she said as tears began to roll down her cheeks. Through it all, Simon had kept his word to her; he'd promised to take care of her and keep her safe, and that was exactly what he'd done, even if it had nearly killed him. Now, she'd do everything she could to stay with him. "I love you, Simon Wright! I love you!"

Under the still-thundering storm, drenched by the pounding rain, Nona and Simon held each other and knew that better days awaited them.

Chapter 30

THE RAIN BEGAN TO SLOW as Simon and Nona hobbled beneath the thick stand of trees. Jack, who'd found them mere seconds after the last shot had been fired, was a few steps behind. His work shirt was wadded up and pressed tightly to Simon's shoulder wound. It would do until they got back to the camp.

As they crossed the waterlogged grass, Nona hoped the worst was behind them. They'd passed Webb as he lay dead in the wet grass. Even though he'd played a role in the villainous plot, Nona was grateful to him for interfering when Frank tried to choke her to death.

Once they handed over the money to the proper authorities, it would all be over. Nona tried to support Simon. She could see that he was exhausted.

"Lean on me, Simon. We'll get you to the doctor."

"Mabel can patch me up."

"No. You're going to the doctor."

Soon, they passed through the tree line and found themselves back on the campground. Even though all of the cabins were just where they'd been hours earlier, they somehow looked different to Nona. Shaking her wet hair, she began to feel the joy of being home.

Jack led the way to LeAnn's cabin. Not only did he want to check on LeAnn, but Mabel had brought the first-aid box when she came to stay with her.

Dusty watched them approach. He was standing guard on the porch with Simon's rifle in his hand. When he realized who they were, he came to meet them.

"What happened?" the boy asked. "Is it over? Did you get them?"

"Get Mabel, Dusty. Tell her Simon has been hurt. I'll tell you all about it later."

"She's inside," the boy answered and held open the door.

They managed their way up the steps and into the cabin. Jack hurried into the far bedroom to see about LeAnn. Simon sat down at the table in the kitchen and slowly began to peel off his shirt. Nona sat beside him and Maggie hovered near.

"We'll get you to the doctor," Nona said again. "It's all over. I'm so glad."

"Not so fast, sweetheart." Simon had a worried look on his face.

With gentle fingers, Mabel touched the area where the bullet had entered; then she moved around to look at his back. "This isn't so bad."

"That's what you think!" Simon winced.

"The bullet passed all the way through the flesh of your shoulder. I don't think it struck the bone."

"That's all fine and dandy, but my shoulder still feels like it's being stabbed with a hot poker!"

"You'll live," Mabel said as she left the room.

Nona looked up from the bullet wound to see Simon staring at her intently. She knew that she would remember this day as long as she lived: being dragged into the woods, Simon getting shot, and the killing of two men. She would also remember something more pleasant . . . much sweeter, the way that her heart pounded as they'd made love and the strength of his voice as he'd told her he loved her.

"Simon, I . . ."

"Shhh," he said softly, putting one finger to her lips. "There's something I want to say to you before we go any further. Something I need you to know."

Nona nodded her head in agreement, even though her heart felt like lead in her chest. The last time that he'd had something that he needed to tell her, she'd reacted badly and run off into the night. With a small sense of dread, she waited for him to speak.

"I'm sorry, Nona," he said gently. "I'm sorry I didn't tell you the whole truth about me and what I was doing here sooner. It was never about trying to trick you or deceive you into telling me where the money was."

"I didn't think that."

"Yes, you did." Simon smiled slyly. "But that's all right. I'd have thought the same thing if I'd been in your shoes. But know one thing . . . The insurance company hired me to get Harold's stolen money back . . . They didn't hire me to make love to a beautiful redhead."

"Stop teasing," she chided him.

"I'm not teasing. I'm telling you the truth. Nona," he said as he took her hands in his own, "I've been crazy about you from the moment I laid eyes on you back at the apartment building in Little Rock. I want to be with you forever."

"Oh, Simon."

"Do you want to be with me?"

"You know I do, but where do we go from here?" This was the question that Nona had been dreading asking. Now that she knew what he did for a living, how could she expect him to stay with her? He had a life far away from this camp . . . far different from any she had ever known.

"Why do we have to go anywhere? I was thinking of settling down somewhere . . . someplace like a camp on a lake with a bunch of tall pines around it. Of course, I'd need help from a gorgeous redhead if I wanted to do it right."

"What?" Nona asked incredulously. "Are you serious?"

"Dead serious." He laughed some more. "As a matter of fact, I've been giving serious thought to quitting the detective work."

"But . . ."

"No buts, sweetheart. I want you to stay here with me. Do you want to spend your life with me?"

"There's Mabel and Maggie to consider."

"You and I both know that Mabel loves it here and wanted to stay before this whole mess started. As for Maggie, we can find her a place to go to school this fall. If you want it to work, we can find a way."

Nona nodded her agreement.

"I love you, darling," he whispered.

"And I love you."

"We'll have a good life together."

When Mabel returned, she found Simon kissing Nona.

"I knew it was just a matter of time before you two fell in love. The only thing was . . . I was afraid you'd kill each other first."

Simon stood on the porch of his cabin and looked out over the lake. Bright orange and red streaks ran into the crystal clear blue of the sky above, painting a breathtaking picture on nature's canvas. Millions of drops of rain dazzled in the light of the new day. Birds called to one another as life moved on after the terrible storm. The people of Tall Pine Camp had wakened to a brand-new day.

LeAnn was the beaming mother of a healthy and beautiful baby girl. With the exception of the weary hours when sleep finally took her, LeAnn had never stopped smiling. Jack gazed as proudly at the tiny squirming infant who lay in her mother's arms as if she were his own.

Dusty had left for his home at first light with a promise that he would soon return. Mabel sent an invitation for him and his parents to come for dinner on Sunday. Maggie was still sleeping when he left; and though she'd be disappointed when she woke up, she'd have something to look forward to.

Nona had finally listened to Simon and they'd returned to her cabin. She'd lain down on the bed and fallen instantly asleep. Simon had stayed with her throughout the night.

While his shoulder still throbbed if he moved too

much, the sharp pains had subsided to a dull ache. Nona insisted they would go to the doctor come morning.

The sheriff had been called and told what had happened during the storm. While the nasty weather had kept him and all of his deputies busy throughout the night, he'd promised to be at the grounds shortly after sunrise. Simon had gone to his cabin to get ready for him.

Simon was putting on a clean shirt when he sensed someone standing in the doorway behind him.

"Morning, Russ," he said without turning around. "I've been waiting for you."

"How'd you know it was me?" a gravelly voice asked.

Very slowly, Simon raised his hands to show that he was unarmed, then turned around to face Russ Story. The camp's handyman stood in the doorway, a pistol in his hand. In the faint light of the early day, Simon could see the man's set features.

"A lot of reasons."

"Enlighten me."

"The easy one is, that I saw you out of the corner of my eye when I left LeAnn's cabin last night," Simon said with a faint smile. "I knew you were trailing along behind me every step of the way. At first, I thought you might want to have a word with me about something down at the docks. But that's not quite what you had in mind, was it?"

"Not exactly."

"I didn't think so." Simon nodded. "Maybe it's that I know Russell B. Story has a record a mile long. Robbery, assault, larceny . . . You failed to mention your police record. I checked on you when you applied for a job and

I've had my eye on you from the moment you came here, waiting for you to make your move. I knew an old con like you wasn't here just to fish. When Ernie Leasure was killed, I knew right away you had done it."

"How did you figure that out?" the older man sneered. "You can't prove it."

"You're right I can't, but I know you did it. You identified Ernie even when his wife had a hard time recognizing him with his face beaten to a pulp. Why did you kill him?"

"I had my reasons."

"Mind sharing them with me?" Simon said sarcastically.

"I was just looking for a place to lay low for a while, then these two out-of-towners showed up. I recognized one of them. It only took a few phone calls to find out what they were up to. Leasure was working with them. I'd been watchin' and waitin' for Maggie to give me a hint of where the money was hidden, and I didn't want Leasure horning in."

"You think I've got it?"

"Of course you've got it. I ain't stupid." Russ chuckled. "Make no mistake about it, I'll kill you if you don't hand over the money. All I want is the money. I've seen you and the redhead makin' eyes at each other. You're her big hero now! Hell, for a second I thought you and I was playin' the same racket and you were trying to get in her pants in order to find out about it."

"Something changed your mind," Simon prodded.

"The little talk I had with Ernie. He told me about you being an insurance investigator." Russ scratched a hand across the salt-and-pepper stubble on his chin. "But that's all water under the bridge. You got Frank and Webb out of the way for me, so just hand over the money and I'll be out of your hair."

"You and I both know you'll shoot me just as soon as I give it to you."

"Yeah, you're probably right about that, but if you hand it over nice and easy, I'll just shoot you in the leg."

"And if I don't?"

The handyman gave a scratchy, throaty laugh. "Then I'll shoot you right between the eyes and go have a talk with the redhead. And if that doesn't do the trick, I'll work over her feisty little sister. With you out of the way, they'll be more likely to talk, especially if I show them what I did to you."

"I don't know if you'll have time for that," Simon said with a shrug of his shoulders. "After all, I just got off the phone with the sheriff. He and his deputies should be here soon."

"Then we don't have a minute to waste." The man took a step closer to Simon, the gun catching a ray of light through the open window. Russ's eyes glinted with malice. "Where is it?"

Simon made no movement and remained silent. He crossed his arms over his chest.

"You're a cool customer, Wright," Russ remarked.

"And you're a fool if you think you can get away with this."

"And who's going to stop me?"

A voice came from the doorway. "You made a pretty

good call when you said this wily old con would come out sooner or later."

A look of surprise came over Russ's face when he heard Jack's voice. His eyes darted from side to side as he tried to size up the situation. He kept the gun pointed steadily at Simon's chest.

"Put it down, Russ," Jack prodded. "There's no point in getting hurt."

"I ain't thinking about hurting the bastard. I'm thinking about killing him."

"It's you I was thinking about," Jack said softly. "I've got this gun pointed right at your spine."

For the briefest of moments, Simon actually thought that Russ would take his advice. Instead, he whirled around and tried to squeeze off a shot at Jack. However, before he could shoot, the cabin was filled with the thunderous blast from Jack's gun. The bullet caught Russ in his side, and his own gun flew out of his hand and clattered to the wooden floor. The handyman sank to his knees, his free hand trying to stanch the flow of blood from his side.

"Goddammit, you son of a bitch!"

"You're not quite as smart as you thought you were," Simon said.

"Why didn't he shoot you when he first came in?" Jack asked.

Shaking his head, Simon answered, "He's after the money like I told you he was. If he could have disarmed you, he would have killed both of us and maybe Nona and Maggie, too."

Russ lay groaning on the floor.

"Shut up your moaning. You got better than what you gave Ernie," Simon said.

"Maybe I'm not through yet, Simon. I could still mash his face in with the butt of this gun," Jack threatened softly in his Oklahoma drawl.

"He's an old man, Jack. Would you do that to an old man?" Simon looked contemptuously at the man on the floor.

"Damn right I would. I learned a long time ago that a rattlesnake is more poisonous the older he gets."

"I don't know about a rattler, but this old man is a vicious son of a bitch." Simon picked up Russ's gun and looked down at the wounded man. "Be glad it was Jack who shot you. He's a better shot than I am, and I would have aimed for your ugly head."

The screen door slammed, and Nona and Maggie burst into the room.

"What's happened?" Frantic, Nona ran to Simon. Her hands moved over his chest. "Are you hurt?" she asked, the sobs in her throat choking her.

"I'm all right. So is Jack. The only casualty is lying on the floor."

"Why'd you shoot Mr. Story?" Maggie demanded, hands on her hips, glaring at Simon.

"He didn't shoot him. I did," Jack said.

"Well, why'd *you* shoot him? He's bleeding." Maggie took steps to reach the man on the floor. "He needs help."

"Stay away from him, Maggie," Simon said curtly "You don't get near a rattlesnake until you're sure it's dead."

"Why did you shoot him?" Maggie said to Jack. "Look how he's bleeding."

"I shot him because he was going to shoot Simon. He can bleed a bucketful for all I care."

"Russ was going to shoot you? Why, Simon?" Nona stayed close to Simon and looked into his face anxiously.

"He was after the same thing Webb and Frank were after. When he first came here, I thought he was a harmless old con, but I kept my eye on him."

"I liked him," Maggie blurted. "Can't we help him?"

"The sheriff's on his way. He'll call an ambulance."

"I've got to go tell Mabel. She won't believe this one. She liked Russ, too." Maggie ran out the door.

Simon put his arm around Nona and led her from the room. From the porch they looked out onto the lake. It was calm. The trees and shrubs were shiny green after being washed by the rain. It was a beautiful day.

"I never dreamed that Mr. Story was partner to Frank and Webb."

"He wasn't their partner; he always worked alone. He found out why they were here and decided to get the money for himself."

"Oh, gosh, it scares me to think of all the times that Maggie spent with him down on the dock."

"Yeah, I started wondering about him when he went to the outhouse and left Maggie out on the lake in the boat."

"But he was always so nice to Maggie."

"Honey, he's a hard customer. He probably thought that Maggie didn't know about the money or you'd have kept a tighter rein on her. When he saw Frank and Webb were on the lake, he went to the outhouse to allow Frank to have the sister who probably didn't know anything."

"Is he really that vicious?"

"Yes. Money will do strange things to people. He probably saw this as his golden opportunity."

Simon moved behind her, put his arms around her, clasped his hands together, and pulled her tightly back against him. "It's over, honey."

"Not until we get rid of the money."

"We'll go into town today, and I'll ask the banker to put it in his vault until we find out who's going to be in charge of it. Let's forget about that and talk about us."

"What happens now?" Nona asked, then lifted her shoulder when Simon buried his face in the curve of her neck and bit her gently. "Simon! Stop that. Someone will see."

"They'd better get used to that if they're going to be hanging around here, because I plan to kiss my wife whenever and wherever I want to."

"Your wife? Are you planning on getting married?" Nona's heart raced so fast she could hardly breathe.

"I am if a certain redhead I know will have me."

"I guess then you'd better ask her." Her mind was whirling. He continued to nibble on her ear.

"How about you and me getting hitched, Red?"

"That's not a very romantic way to ask a girl to marry you."

"I'll get down on my knee if that's what it takes."

"Why do you want to marry me? We don't even like each other . . . sometimes."

"Number one: I'll have to marry you to keep you out

of trouble. Number two: I'm crazy about you. Number three: I'm crazy about you and I want to get you in my bed."

"You've had me there already." Nona could feel the pounding of Simon's heart against her back.

"That was just a sample of what's to come."

"I'll not marry any man who doesn't tell me he loves me."

"I said I was crazy about you." He kissed her on the neck. She lifted her shoulder to squeeze his face. "I love you, Nona. I love you, Nona. I love you, Nona. How's that?"

"You know I've got Maggie?"

"*We've* got Maggie."

"And Mabel . . ."

"We've got a family already."

"Oh, Simon. I'm so glad we came here. I love you, you know."

"It's about time you said it. Do you think our kids will have red hair?"

"Heaven forbid!"

"Kiss me, little redbird."

Epilogue

Three years later

NONA STARED OUT THE WINDOW of the lodge building.

The lightest dusting of snow covered the ground and blanketed the evergreens, giving everything a crisp, clean appearance. A gentle wind set the snow whirling here and there as if it were strokes from a painter's brush.

"It looks like we're going to have a white Christmas after all." Simon slipped behind her and put his arms around her waist. Her body instinctively nestled against him, his strength and warmth filling her with happiness and love.

The remodeling of the camp had been completed the year after Simon and Nona were married. It was modern and convenient, but still retained a rustic atmosphere. Mabel was in her glory working in the gleaming kitchen. Nona took care of bookings and the ordering of supplies. Simon said she was his right hand.

"It's beautiful, isn't it?"

"Not as beautiful as you," he said softly. "Thank you for my wonderful Christmas gift."

As she looked up into his deep yet tender gaze, she said, "I didn't do it all by myself."

"It was a chore I'll gladly repeat."

Nona thought about all that they had been through and how it had forever changed their lives. Even now, years later, she couldn't believe that they'd all survived. Well . . . not everyone.

Harold's body had been found in a cheap hotel room in Kansas City, his throat cut and his belongings ransacked. When she'd spoken with the police, Nona hadn't been surprised to learn that they hadn't apprehended his killer. She doubted that they ever would. The jewelry and remaining cash had never been recovered.

The money that Harold had sent to Nona had been turned over to the proper authorities. Simon's grandfather, the owner of the bank Harold had robbed, had wanted to give Nona a reward, but she'd refused it.

Russ Story recovered and would serve the rest of his life in prison for the murder of Ernie Leasure. He would never be able to indulge his love of fishing again.

"Do you think Jack, LeAnn, and little Sophie will be able to get here?"

"Of course. There isn't that much snow. The Hathaways should be here soon."

"How are things going in the kitchen?" Nona asked.

"Beats the heck out of me." Simon shrugged. "They've been in there for hours, laughing and carrying on, so I'd like to think that something is getting done. It better be, because I'm starving!"

They crossed the room, passing the large Christmas tree in the corner. It was decorated with handmade ornaments and strings of lights. At the base of the tree was a pile of brightly wrapped Christmas gifts. Sam Houston slept soundly in front of the fireplace, one leg kicking as he dreamed. Cochise was outside romping in the snow.

Pausing at the doorway to the kitchen, Nona and Simon watched as Maggie prepared a salad and Mabel pulled a pie from the oven and set it on the counter to cool. After all that had happened, life had turned out well for both of them.

Mabel had taken to her position at the lodge. She enjoyed the guests who came to hunt and fish. This past year, one of the guests had tried to lure her away and move to Tulsa. He had offered her a substantial amount of money to manage his restaurant. Another man had wanted to marry her.

After Simon finished remodeling all of the cabins, hunters had flocked to the grounds; the camp had been full for almost all of the hunting season. Mabel, with Mrs. Hogan's help, did all of the cooking. Nona had never seen her so happy. To do Russ's work, a handyman was hired and his wife did the cleaning.

Maggie was now a lovely young woman of seventeen. Denise Hathaway had tutored her along with Dusty, and she had passed her college entrance exam. Both Dusty and Maggie were enrolled at the University of Arkansas. Dusty was majoring in astronomy and Maggie in environmental studies. Nona was not as upset about Maggie's leaving for college as she would have been had Dusty not been going to the same school. Dusty and Maggie had been friends since they first met. Maggie's affection for the boy who found her in the woods after she was kidnapped had increased over the years. Dusty was now a handsome young man of nineteen years. He seemed to have his feet firmly on the ground and was still protective of Maggie. Nona and Simon would not be the least bit surprised if the two of them decided to spend their lives together.

It had been discovered that Randall Weatherspoon, the hermit who had lived in the woods for years, was a very wealthy man. He donated enough money to build a school for the local children. Nona helped Denise at the school occasionally. The enrollment increased each year as families moved from the city. The Weatherspoon School would have to be enlarged soon to accommodate the growing enrollment.

"Isn't it ready yet?" Simon asked. "Can't I at least have coffee and one of those hot rolls?"

"Oh, you," Mabel answered. "The way you act sometimes, you would think we mistreated you. I'm not going to let you nibble before dinner. Besides, Dusty and his parents aren't here yet."

"Do you think they'll make it in this weather?" Maggie asked anxiously.

"I'm sure they'll come," Nona told her. "Simon says there isn't all that much snow. It's just enough to make things look nice and clean."

"Don't worry about it, squirt." Simon winked.

Nona looked forward to their friends coming for Christmas. Jack and LeAnn had left for his ranch in Oklahoma a few days after they were married at the camp. Jack had insisted they stay long enough for LeAnn to recover from the birth of Sophie. The baby had not suffered any complications from being born a bit prematurely. She was a lively child, and Jack doted on her like a proud father.

"Are you excited about telling them our news tonight?" Simon whispered to her.

"Of course," she answered, careful that no one overheard her. "Aren't you?"

"Yes, I am." The lines at the corners of his eyes crinkled when he was teasing. "You'll make a wonderful mother. If we have a girl, I hope she has red hair."

"That's such a sweet thing to say. If it will make you happy, I hope he, or she, will have red hair, too."

Simon gave her a quick kiss. "Maggie will be thrilled to be an aunt."

There was a knock at the door. Mabel opened it to admit Dusty and his parents. They shook the snow off their coats and boots and, laughing, placed their Christmas gifts beneath the tree. Tonight Nona would tell everyone that she and Simon were going to have a baby and that Simon had decided to expand the camp with ten new cabins. Tall Pine Camp was truly a home for her and Maggie.

She sidled over to her husband and cuddled up to his back. She had never dreamed that the tall man who had annoyed her so the first few weeks they were here would turn out to be the love of her life.

Simon turned and wrapped his arms around his wife. "Are you all right?"

"I couldn't be better."

About the Author

Dorothy Garlock is one of America's—and the world's—favorite novelists. Her work consistently appears on national bestseller lists, including the *New York Times* extended list, and there are over fifteen million copies of her books in print translated into eighteen languages. She has won more than twenty writing awards, including five Silver Pen Awards from Affaire de Coeur and three Silver Certificate Awards, and in 1998 she was selected as a finalist for the National Writer's Club Best Long Historical Book Award.

After retiring as a news reporter and bookkeeper in 1978, she began her career as a novelist with the publication of *Love and Cherish*. She lives in Clear Lake, Iowa. You can visit her Web site at www.dorothygarlock.com.

More Americana from
"the Queen of American tales"
(Midwest Book Review)

Please turn this page
for a preview of
Dorothy Garlock's next novel

A Week From Sunday

Available in November 2007.

Chapter 1

Shreveport, Louisiana, 1935

"I'M TERRIBLY SORRY, my dear. Your father will be missed."

Adrianna Moore listened to the older woman's condolences with a slight nod of appreciation before moving on. The small parlor was filled with smartly-dressed men and women, all wearing black, who had come to pay their respects to the recently deceased. Some of the faces she recognized, mostly older gentlemen who had done business with her father over the years, but nearly all of the names escaped her. She knew she should say something, at the very least thank them for coming, but she couldn't manage to get the image of her father's coffin out of her head. It all seemed a horrible dream. Her sadness kept her mute amid the soft murmur of voices and the clink of coffee cups against their saucers.

The funeral itself had been a quiet affair. Thankfully, the Louisiana spring had cooperated; although drizzly rain had been falling for days, the morning had dawned with warm sunlight and only a light breeze rustling the treetops. High on the lone hill of the cemetery grounds, they'd laid her father to rest. Now, with that business concluded, she was required to play the role of hostess, a task that normally she'd be well equipped to handle. Today was anything but normal.

She moved from guest to guest, each stopping her for a few measured words of sympathy. She looked into forlorn faces, hands gently holding hers. Adrianna knew that they all meant well, but the things she was hearing only intensified her grief:

"Charles Moore was a lion of a man."

"Regardless of the crippling effects of his polio, he never let it get the best of him."

"I can't begin to tell you how much I learned from him about the banking business. It's a debt that I can never repay."

"He'll be watching down on you, Adrianna." A matron wiped tears from her fat cheeks.

Once, when an older gentleman with enormous jowls was telling her of a hunting trip he'd taken with her father before he had become stricken with polio, she found herself desperately fighting back tears. It wasn't the story that had upset her; she'd heard it a half dozen times before. What made her cry was the realization that her father had become a story, a legend in town. It had taken all the strength she could muster to get through the day, but somehow she'd managed to keep her composure through it all.

Finally, as the last rays of the spring sun disappeared over the horizon, all of the mourners had gone, leaving Adrianna alone in the large home she'd shared with her father for the last several years. Built from the earnings of

Moore Bank and Trust, the stately manor house had been constructed with the finest of materials. The interior was decorated richly but tastefully: a marble fireplace, an antique clock from Germany, as well as a crystal chandelier that hung over the dining room table.

This home was the only one she'd ever really known. Her mother had died when Adrianna was just fifteen years old. Her father had never remarried. Charles Moore had done everything for his only child. She'd wanted for nothing: piano lessons, private tutors, all the best that his banking fortune could buy. When his own illness had worsened, confining him to his bed or the wheelchair that he despised, she'd done her best to give him the same degree of comfort he'd always given her. But still his health slowly and steadily deteriorated.

Now he was gone and she was alone.

After the mourners left, she went through the downstairs rooms dimming the lights. Glancing up, she caught sight of her reflection in a mirror. At twenty-five years of age, Adrianna Moore had a head of dark brown curly hair that fell to her shoulders. Her soft, oval face was defined by high cheekbones and a warm complexion. Her father had always told her that her deep-set, emerald-green eyes were exactly like her mother's. He called her his "beautiful princess." At the moment, wearing a simple black dress, mourning the loss of her remaining family, she felt anything but beautiful; she was heartsick and exhausted.

"I daresay you get more stunning with each passing year."

Startled by the voice behind her, Adrianna whirled at the sound, her hand reflexively rising to her chest. With slow, measured steps, a man crossed the room toward her. In the scant light, she had to peer intently into the shadows to see her unexpected guest. Finally, there was the spark of recognition, a spark that sent a shiver down her spine.

"Oh! It's you, Mr. Pope. You startled me."

"How many times must I tell you, my dear, to call me Richard?"

He eased out of the gloom to stand before Adrianna. In his late forties, Richard Pope was a man who exuded an air of supreme confidence. Short, with a long face that was marked by full red lips, he had colorless eyes that, over a bulbous nose, looked straight into hers. His clothes were immaculate, his shoes polished to a perfect black. The sweet-smelling pomade he rubbed into his thinning salt-and-pepper hair made Adrianna's stomach churn.

"I didn't realize you were still here," she said, ignoring his comment.

"I was showing Judge Walters and his wife to the door and walked with them out on to the porch. I don't know if you recognized him . . . the wisp of a gentleman whose wife is as fat as he is thin," he explained. "He has always been very important to Moore Bank and Trust, and I wanted to give him my assurances that everything concerned with the company was in good hands. It's all about impressions, you know."

"Thank you for your help today, Mist— . . . Richard," she corrected herself. "What with the funeral arrangements, and all of the guests, I don't know if I could have managed without you." She hated to admit it, but he had been very helpful. With his legal guidance, her father's bank had continued to grow ever larger and more prosperous. Adrianna was certain that the only thing that mattered to Richard Pope was acquiring more and more money. As Charles Moore's health worsened, taking him away from the day-to-day operations of his bank, Richard's influence had grown. For the past several months, he had been essentially overseeing the business.

"It's the least that I could do. How are you managing through all of this?"

"All right, I suppose. I don't think that it has fully sunk in yet—that he's gone, I mean. He was always positive about things. Even after my mother passed away, I could never imagine the same happening to him."

"And yet it did," Richard said matter-of-factly. "He did die." Walking over to a small bureau, he proceeded to pour himself a generous glass of brandy from a beveled decanter. As he contemplated the amber liquid, a thin smile spread across his face. To Adrianna, he looked like a wolf preparing to sink his fangs into its defenseless prey.

"I'm sorry to have to leave you," she said hurriedly, wanting desperately to get away from the man, "but I am going to retire for the night. All of this has left me exhausted. Please let yourself out." Quickly, she turned on her heel and made for the staircase on the far side of the room. But before she could take even a couple of steps, his voice stopped her.

"Actually, my dear, there are things that you and I need to discuss. Business matters that cannot wait even for a night. I'm afraid that you'll just have to bear with me for a while longer."

Turning back, Adrianna felt a slight flare of defiance course through her body. She wanted to tell him that he would have to wait for her, but something in the way he was looking at her kept her from responding. From what her father had told her over the years, recounting his lawyer's smashing victories in court, Richard Pope was not the kind of man you wanted for an enemy.

"What sort of business matters?" she asked. "I'm afraid I don't know much about banking."

"Charles left a good man at the helm. It's not about the bank. Not really." Richard chuckled before swallowing the entire drink in one gulp. "It's actually about you, my dear. You and your future."

"What . . . what are you talking about?" Adrianna asked in confusion.

"I suppose that I shouldn't be shocked by your lack of understanding, sweet Adrianna. After all, you've been cuddled a bit too close to your father's weakened chest all of these years."

"I don't think I like your tone, Mr. Pope," she managed, hoping that her voice sounded stronger than she felt.

"There is no offense intended, I assure you," Richard said apologetically and went back to the bureau to pour himself another drink. "But let us call a spade a spade. You've always had household help. You've never worked outside this house a day in your life. You've never wanted for anything. Charles made sure that you were always provided for, and it wasn't until the very last that he saw the error of his ways."

A sickening feeling suddenly washed over Adrianna. Her knees were weak. *What in the blazes was this pompous ass talking about?* Keeping silent, she waited for him to continue.

"His greatest fear was that you would find yourself all alone, incapable of taking care of yourself," Richard explained. "As I was his closest confidant for all of these long years, it was only natural that he would turn to me to see after his most precious treasure. And that is why he decided to make me executor of his estate. I am completely in charge of you, your money, the bank, the house and everything in it. It's all under my supervision."

"What?" Like a thunderclap out of a clear sky, Richard's words struck Adrianna with dramatic force. Stumbling on shaky legs, trying desperately to stay upright, she managed to grab hold of a nearby chair and steady herself. Her eyes filled with tears, and her voice cracked as she said, "You must be joking!"

"Not in the slightest, my dear. The last legal document that your father ever signed was a change in his will . . . a change that made me executor."

"But not of me!"

"Yes, of you."

"I'm of age."

"Of course you are, but I'm in charge of your money."

As shocked as Adrianna had been by her father's passing, what Richard Pope was telling her shook her even more. *How could what he was saying be true? How could her father have done this to her?* Richard was lying. He had to be! With anger rising in her breast, she gave voice to her disbelief. "This can't be! My father wouldn't leave my future in the hands of someone else! He wouldn't!"

"And he didn't . . . not entirely."

"But you said that he left you in control."

Slowly, Richard crossed the room until he stood before her. She could smell the brandy on his breath. His smile nauseated her. Summoning what strength she had, she straightened her back and boldly returned his gaze.

"He hasn't left you without the means to provide for yourself. This was all part of his plan. All of this," he said, gesturing around the room, "the house, the bank, can still be yours. You can have everything to which you have grown accustomed."

"How?"

"By marrying me."

The words were no sooner out of Richard's mouth when Adrianna's hand shot up toward his face. She'd meant to slap him, the man's boldness on the day of her father's funeral providing the breaking point; but before she could make contact, the lawyer's hand grabbed her own in a tight, painful grip. With a strength she couldn't resist, he yanked her toward him until her body was pressed against his. Try as she might, she couldn't break free.

"Oh, sweet Adrianna," he said, licking his lips. "Haven't you noticed the way that I have looked at you all of these years? I have wanted you from the first moment I saw you. I knew that it would come to this . . . this union between you and me. Your father knew it, too."

"You're . . . you're hurting me," Adrianna pleaded.

"We will be married a week from Sunday. Because of your father's recent death, we'll have a quiet ceremony. I'll have the judge at my house when I come for you. We must keep up appearances, my dear. It wouldn't do to have people gossiping about my wife." His hands tightened on her arms.

"Let . . . let me go."

"I will never let you go!" His grasp tightened ever more. "You and I *will* be married!"

"Please . . ." Adrianna sobbed, the tears now flowing freely down her cheeks.

She would never know if it were her words or the sight of her tears that finally broke through Richard Pope's euphoria, but he suddenly released her and stepped away his hand darting to his pocket where he pulled out a hand-kerchief and wiped the tears from her cheeks. When he looked down at her, his eyes were flat but still menacing.

"I meant what I said to you, Adrianna," he warned, his voice deep and serious. "By making me the executor of his estate, your father gave his permission for me to pro-vide for you for the rest of your life. To that end, we will be married. The sooner the better."

Stifling a large sob that filled her throat, Adrianna looked at the man through wet eyes. Never in her life had she been so repulsed by another human being. No matter what, she would not give him the satisfaction of seeing her fear.

Richard once again grabbed Adrianna by the wrist. While his grip was not as tight as it had been before, it was still tight enough to cause her anxiety.

"Pack what you'll need. Everything else can be dealt with later. I will come for you a week from Sunday. Dress appropriately for your wedding." Gripping Adrianna's chin, he turned her head until she was looking directly into his face. "This is for the best, my dear. In time, I am certain that you will come to love me every bit as pas-sionately as I love you. As husband and wife, you and I will be the jewels of this town, just as your father in-tended."

After releasing her, Richard strode across the room and pulled open the door. "Remember . . . a week from Sunday," he said, and then he was gone.

After she heard the door close, Adrianna finally al-lowed herself to crumple into a chair, tears streaming down her face. Following so soon upon her father's death and funeral, this was more than she could endure.

Even if her father had worried about her well-being, he

would never have given control of his estate to a man like Richard Pope! The lawyer must have manipulated him into signing the papers when he wasn't of sound mind. In those last days, Charles Moore had been robbed of all he had built over his lifetime. Now that bastard Pope was trying to steal her!

But what could she do? She could try to challenge the will, to take the matter to a judge, but how was she supposed to compete with a lawyer like Richard? No, that would not work. But what other choice did she have? Pack up her things and wait for him by the door? He was planning to come for her a week from Sunday. That left her only eight days!

Chapter 2

Adrianna's hands gripped the steering wheel tightly as she peered through the rain-streaked windshield to the road beyond. Ominous gray clouds blotted the afternoon sky. The darkness they created was occasionally broken by flashes of lightning. But what scared Adrianna most was the driving rain and shifting winds that threw themselves against the sides of her car. Her arms ached from keeping the vehicle on the road. It seemed as if the heavens themselves were against her.

"I should have stopped in that last town," she muttered to herself.

The car's single windshield wiper coughed and burped as it did its best to clear off the water, but it was fighting a losing battle. Still, watching the blade move back and forth was lulling, like the metronome she'd used when taking her piano lessons as a child. But with every pass, as the wiper scraped against the glass, it spoke to her, reminding her of the words that had changed her life forever.

A week from Sunday . . . a week from Sunday . . . a week from Sunday . . .

"Today is that Sunday," she reminded herself grimly.

From the moment that the door had closed behind Richard Pope, Adrianna's mind had been set. She would leave and nothing would stop her! Still, the eight days that her father's lawyer had given her had gone quickly, and there had been much for her to do, all of which had to be managed with the utmost secrecy. With each step in the preparation of her departure, the knowledge that she would never return became clearer. As she'd gone around Shreveport to visit friends and loved ones, she'd done her best to say her goodbyes without emotion, fearful that any slip would betray her intentions. Once, when she'd been ready to leave a treasured friend, she'd felt tears begin to overwhelm her. Unable to stop, they had run hotly down her cheeks. To her relief, her friend had taken her show of sadness to be grief for her father and had embraced her tenderly. She never allowed anyone to know that she was planning to leave forever.

Of all that she'd needed to do, the most difficult task had been deciding where to go. As an only child, she had no brother or sister to run to, nor were there any cousins whom she knew well enough to impose upon. Her family was made up mostly of elderly aunts and uncles on her father's side who lived in or near Shreveport; running to them would offer her no sanctuary. In the end, she'd decided on one of her mother's relatives, Aunt Madeline who lived in Mississippi, as her only option. After the passing of her own mother, Madeline had come to stay with her and her father in Louisiana for a couple of months. Adrianna remembered her as a warm, friendly woman who was quick to offer comfort. *Surely, she'd be happy to see her niece!* Still, fearful of rejection, she'd decided not to call or write Madeline of her arrival. She'd have to hope for the best.

A week from Sunday . . . a week from Sunday . . .

Stifling a yawn, Adrianna kept her eyes focused straight ahead. She'd been on the road for hours after getting up before dawn in order to make her escape. Her father's car had received little use since its purchase; once Charles Moore's health had started to deteriorate he'd rarely gone out. Adrianna had learned to drive from necessity and had become confident in her ability. Leaving the house at first light, she'd overcome her selfish desire to look back, and pressed onward. The rain began an hour out of Shreveport, and had steadily grown worse. She was one of only a few drivers foolhardy enough to brave the bad weather, and she'd had the roads mostly to herself. The raging downpour was nerve-racking, but she had left Shreveport; she had done what she'd set out to do.

Although the thought of leaving her home had frayed her nerves, she had to admit to a twinge of excitement, too. She was moving on into the unknown. From this day forward, everything would be different. As loath as she was to admit it, Richard's claim that she had had an easy life handed to her by her father was partially true. Once she was settled she'd need to fend for herself: find a place to live, a job with which to support herself. In short, she'd need to start living.

From around a slight curve in the road, a town suddenly came into view. A small, weather-beaten sign announced it as Lee's Point. Adrianna had never heard of it. Through the rain, she could see a scattering of houses on the outskirts that grew denser as she neared the town's center. This was followed by a row of businesses lining the main street like towels hanging from a clothesline. No one was in sight, not surprising given the weather. Since she'd left Shreveport and moved into the countryside, she'd passed through many towns similar to this one, although they seemed to be spread farther and farther apart as the miles went by.

For the briefest of moments, she thought about stopping and riding out the storm. Surely the town would have a restaurant where she could have a hot meal. Besides, a bit of rest would do her good. But before her weary arms could pull the car into a parking spot, the image of Richard Pope's gloating face filled her thoughts, and she knew it would be foolish to stop, even if it were only for an hour or two. She'd stopped only once since leaving Shreveport, to get a sandwich and go to the restroom, and even then she'd hurried as quickly as she could. The fear of his finding her was too great to ignore. *If she were to be found . . .* As quickly as she'd come upon Lee's Point, the town was behind her and lost to view.

"Damn you, Richard Pope!" she swore.

Instinctively, Adrianna shivered at the memory of Richard grabbing her by the wrists and telling her that they would be married. She still couldn't shake her revulsion at the way he'd looked at her and the words he'd spoken; they'd been burned into her thoughts ever since. He'd been so confident, so sure that she'd come along willingly. *She was repulsed by the very thought of becoming his wife!* He had somehow managed to get control of her father's fortune, but he would never get control of her.

By now, back in Shreveport, he must have come to the house and discovered she was gone. She could only imagine how surprised and angry he would be. However, it was after he'd sufficiently calmed down that he would become truly dangerous. He was a calculating man, a trait that had made him both successful and wealthy as a lawyer, and he would come looking for her. The farther she went, therefore, the harder it would be for him to find her.

A sudden flash of lightning illuminated the sky above her. In the brief glare, she could see the trees bowing deeply in the face of the pounding rain and punishing wind. A broken branch skittered across the pavement in front of her car before disappearing into the gloom of the thick trees that lined the road. The storm was worsening. A pang of regret gnawed at Adrianna's stomach; maybe it would have been a good idea to have stopped at Lee's Point after all. But it was too late now to turn back.

It was also too late to pull the car over to the side of the highway. Since Shreveport, the conditions had worsened. While these county roads were paved, they were narrow and full of cracks and holes. The shoulders were a quagmire of mud. If she were to go off the hard surface the wheels would become stuck in the mud and she wouldn't be able to get out; she'd be at the mercy of a passing traveler's willingness to help, and she hadn't seen another vehicle for quite a while. No, it was better to keep going.

A quick glance in the rearview mirror showed the belongings that she'd tossed haphazardly into the back seat. She'd limited herself to the things she would need immediately, mostly clothing. She had also added a few family heirlooms that she couldn't bear to part with. Treasured most of all was a photograph of herself and her mother that had been taken shortly after her birth. For as long as she could remember, it had sat on her father's bedside table. The beautiful mother-of-pearl picture frame had greeted him every morning. The thought of Richard Pope having it made her heart heavy. She'd also scrounged up as much money as she could find. It hadn't been much, since most of her funds were tied directly to her father, but it would be enough to get her started.

Before she could break contact with the mirror, she took a long look into her own face. Her hair was a tangled mess. Blood-shot pupils stared back exhaustedly from under heavy lids. Deep, dark circles ringed her eyes, giving a clear indication of her stress and fatigue. *But what could she expect?* She hadn't managed to sleep for more than an hour or two at a time since Richard Pope had upended her life with his ridiculous demands. Her very bones ached with the weariness of her heart. As each of the eight days had passed, the uneasiness had increased. She wasn't sure how much more she could have taken.

The blare of a horn split through the noise of the storm, startling Adrianna's attention away from the mirror. Her eyes snapped back to the road. Through the rain-streaked windshield, she was horrified to see another vehicle coming directly at her! *While she'd been looking at her reflection, deep in thought, she'd drifted across the center of the road and into the path of another motorist!*

"Oh my God!" she cried out.

With all the strength her tired arms could muster, she yanked at the steering wheel, desperately trying to pull the car back to safety. Hand over hand, she turned and turned, but nothing happened. With horror, Adrianna realized that the wheels were sliding; with all of the water and mud on the road, the tires were skating across the concrete's surface. Even taking her foot off of the gas did nothing to stop her headlong plunge into a collision. All she could do was watch helplessly.

As the distance between the vehicles shortened, time seemed to slow to a standstill. It was as if she were in a movie, with every pass of the windshield wiper carrying the film forward another frame. Her arms were locked tightly at the elbows, her whole body tense and rigid, preparing for the impact she couldn't prevent.

Another fork of lightning pierced the sky, lighting up the dark afternoon gloom. In that brief flash, Adrianna received a clearer view of the other vehicle. It wasn't another car but a small truck, its back end covered with a soaked tarpaulin. Inside the truck's cab, two men stared back at her.

The very moment that the lightning's glare vanished, time leapt forward. With a sickening crunch, the side of Adrianna's car slammed into the pick-up truck's driver-side door. The screech of metal grinding against metal was deafening. The force of the blow shattered the car's windows, sending shards of glass raining down into the cab. As if she were a doll, Adrianna was thrown against the door, her head pounding hard into the frame before ricocheting off. The pain was enormous, her vision clouded and spun, but she refused to lose consciousness. Even now, her hands tried to move the wheel.

Her car bounced off the truck and flew back toward the center of the road. The force of the collision had been so great that it tipped the smaller vehicle up onto two wheels. All of the belongings she'd brought from Shreveport flew into the air and whirled about as if they were in the thrall of a tornado! Adrianna's heart was in her throat as she waited for the car to come back to the ground, but the force of the crash was too much. Slowly but surely, the car continued over until the passenger's side door slammed against the concrete. The vehicle's frame shook violently.

Still moving, the car slid forward on its side. Scared out of her wits, Adrianna somehow managed to hang on to the steering wheel, her body suspended above the wreckage below. Finally, after what seemed forever, the mangled vehicle came to a stop. Hot, searing pain filled Adrianna's arms, and she gave in to it and released her grip. With a thud, she fell among shards of glass and her belongings.

"Ohhh!" she sobbed as her head whirled with pain.

Rain fell through the broken windows, wetting her face and soaking her clothes. As she looked up through the drops, she could see out through the remnants of the front windshield. By some miracle, the windshield wiper continued to run, wiping at glass that was no longer there. In her frazzled mind, Adrianna could still hear the noise it was supposed to make. The words that had tormented her from the moment they'd been spoken were running through her mind as she finally gave in to the searing pain and fell into unconsciousness.

A week from Sunday . . . a week from Sunday . . . a week from Sunday.